THE REAPER'S CALL

THE REAPER'S CALL

R.L. PEREZ

WILLOW HAVEN PRESS

THE REAPER'S CALL

Published by Willow Haven Press 2021

United States of America

Cover Art by Blue Raven Book Covers

ISBN: 978-1-955035-10-1

www.rlperez.com

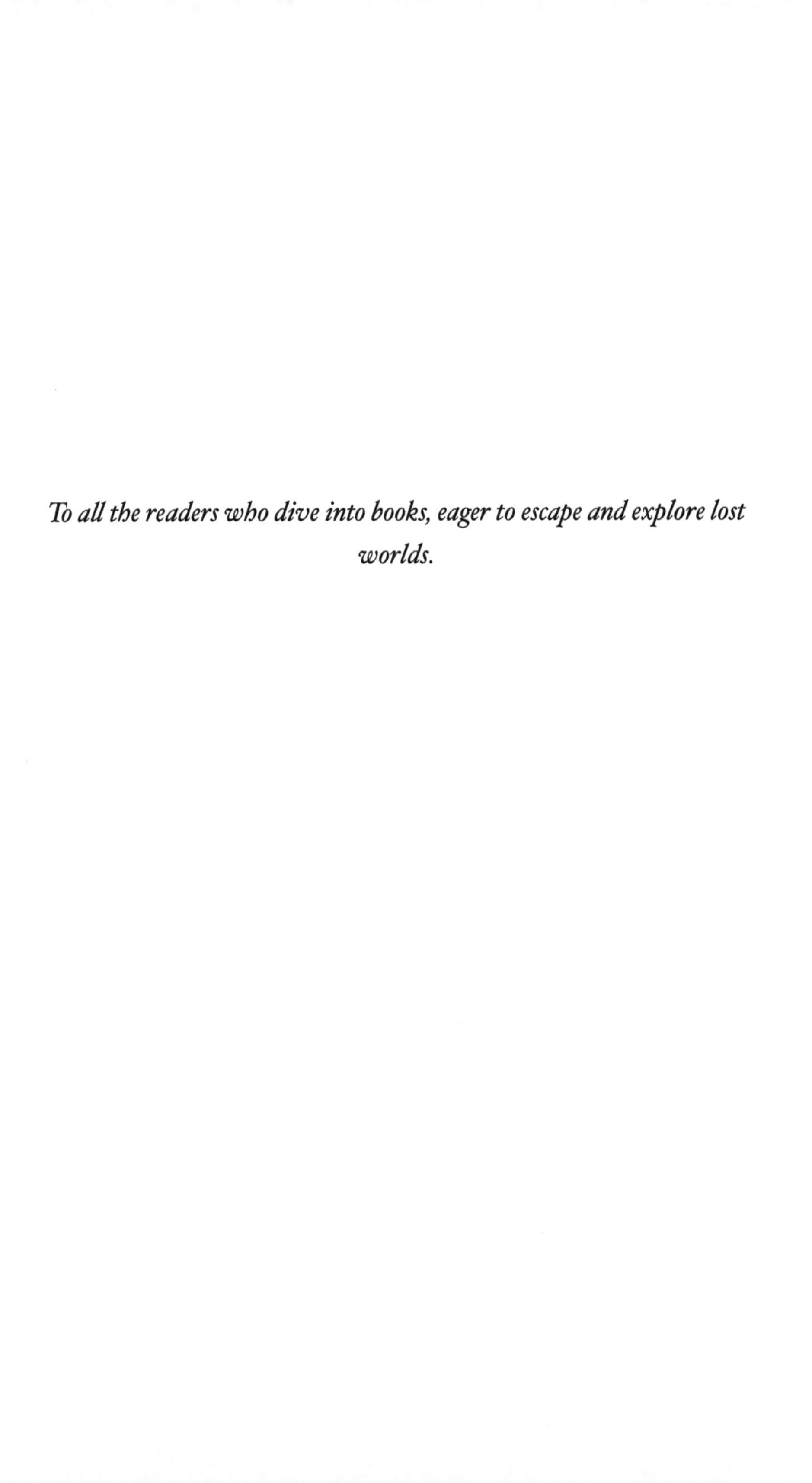

To all the readers who dive into books, eager to escape and explore lost worlds.

CHAPTER 1

CORA

THE ICY COLD BIT INTO MY FINGERS, EVEN AS I SHOVED them into the pockets of my hoodie. Strong wind stung my eyes, numbing my face.

We hadn't eaten in days. I had to venture out into the snowstorm to find us something or we would starve.

I'd cast a spell around my body to protect myself from the elements, but my magic wasn't as strong as it once was. It kept me grounded despite the billowing storm around me, but it didn't do much against the cold.

My fingers and toes felt like they were about to fall off.

The good news was most of the shops were closed, the owners tucked warm and safe in their homes. A perfect opportunity to steal some food.

My steps were a hasty shuffle against the ice-slicked sidewalk. At long last, I reached the small market—an easier target since they likely didn't have an alarm system. Not surprisingly, I was the only one outside, so I wouldn't have to hide my powers. A quick burst of purple magic, and the lock on the door shattered. I strode inside, relishing the shelter from the cold. Sure, there wasn't a heater running or anything. But at least it blocked the wind.

I rubbed my hands together and surveyed the area. Shelves of canned goods surrounded me. Perfect.

I grabbed a paper bag and started loading up on whatever would last. Instant meals, beans, rice, and canned produce. When my bag was full to the brim, I strode back outside to brave the storm.

By the time I returned to our hideout, my lungs burned and my bones rattled. My steps were disjointed, but luckily, Piper saw me right away and came to my aid. She scooped the bag out of my arms and shot me a grateful smile. "Good haul this time."

I barely managed a nod as I followed her into the abandoned warehouse. We'd been here a week. It was much nicer than the rusty old barn we'd been in last, but we needed to find a new place soon.

I collapsed on the pile of coats we used as pillows and shut my eyes for a moment to rest. The others rustled around, chuckling with delight at the food I'd grabbed.

"Nice work, Cora," Finn said with a whoop.

I said nothing. I was still waiting for the bitter cold to seep out of me. It felt like it had been infused into my bones.

Soft footsteps approached. A sharp vinegar scent stung my

nose. I didn't need to open my eyes to know Dex stood in front of me.

"Just give me a minute and I'll eat," I said sleepily. "Then you can feed from me."

Dex was a vampire. He couldn't eat normal food. To keep him strong, I'd offered myself as a Donor. Part of what kept my body so weak, no doubt. But as coven leader, I could hardly ask any of the others to do it.

It was my responsibility. It was my fault our coven had been reduced to ashes.

The four of us were the only ones left.

Dex sighed, and I opened my eyes to look up at him. His skin was more sallow than usual, and his expression was dejected.

"What?" I asked.

"How long will we keep going like this?" he asked, his voice a soft murmur.

"Just another day or two. When the storm settles, we'll find a new place."

"That's not what I mean." Dex hesitated. "I mean, how long will we keep running?"

I clenched my teeth. To be honest, I didn't know the answer to that. Until Quentin was dead? Until the Reapers finally responded to my distress call? Until Benny magically showed up?

Until Vince came looking for me?

But none of those things were certain. I couldn't rely on slim possibilities anymore.

"It's been a month," Dex went on. "We need to find a coven to join."

I shot him a sharp look. We'd discussed this when we first left Hinport. But Quentin had too many allies, and my magic was a dead giveaway. As soon as other demons saw my purple magic, they'd know I was different. And it wouldn't take long for Quentin to track me down.

"Give me a week," I muttered in a low voice. Resignation and grief filled my chest. But I had no other choice. "If no one's come to our aid in a week, I'll go on my own. You all can join the coven in New York. They'll keep you safe." I thought of my rallying speech right after the battle we'd lost. I'd sworn to my friends we would one day take our city back and have our revenge.

But we had no plan and no reinforcements. Right now, we were struggling to survive.

Dex shook his head and crouched on the floor beside me. "We don't want you to give yourself up, Cora."

"I'm the one with the target on my back," I hissed. "The war was my fault. Quentin wants *me*. Without me, you three have the best chance of survival. You can stop starving day after day, waiting for me to steal scraps of food like a hobo." Resentment stung my eyes, and I looked away from Dex. I'd thought my thieving days were over. Before I'd moved to Hinport, I'd been a starving orphan, fighting to survive by stealing off the street.

Now, I was right back where I started. But I'd fallen so

much harder. I'd been coven leader. A feared assassin. A strong witch. I'd found love. A home. A family.

That had all been ripped from me.

"We stood with you in the war," Dex said. "And we will continue to stand with you."

My throat felt hot. "Please let me do this for you," I whispered, still avoiding his gaze. I knew if I looked at him, I would cry. "It's the last thing I can do to keep my people safe. Please, Dex."

I felt him watching me, and I finally looked up. His red eyes gleamed with sorrow and understanding. He knew how much the death of my people weighed on me. How much that would torment me.

It was so much worse than turning myself over to Quentin. The raw guilt, the anguish of loss . . . It was all so heavy that sometimes I couldn't breathe.

"If it's truly what you want," he said softly, "then I will let you go. But . . . I can't speak for everyone." His eyes flicked to Piper, who stood only a few feet away. She watched us, her dark eyes narrowing with suspicion.

Something deflated in my chest. I had no doubt Finn would abandon me in a heartbeat to save his own neck. The only reason he hadn't already was because he was stronger with three allies on his side. But Piper? We were half-sisters. She felt as responsible for Quentin as I did.

She wouldn't let me go off on my own.

"One week," I repeated to Dex, who nodded before shuffling away. I felt Piper's eyes on me, so I reluctantly rose to my feet and sifted through the food bag, eager to avoid a confrontation with her.

I was only postponing the inevitable, though. After eating a can of ravioli and letting Dex drink from me, I sleepily curled up on the floor, using my coat as a pillow. When Piper approached, I suppressed a groan but straightened to face her. I still felt lightheaded from Dex's feeding. He never took very much from me, since I refused to drink vampire blood in exchange. Ordinarily, Donors drank afterward to restore their strength. The loss of blood and the numbing sensation of his venom made my head feel foggy.

"You're going to run, aren't you?" Piper asked, dropping to the floor beside me.

I sighed. "Run where?" But we both knew I understood her meaning.

"You can't, Cora."

"We can't go on like this forever." I couldn't keep the bite out of my voice.

"If you give yourself up to him, then what? You think he'll back off?" Piper shook her head, her expression souring. "He won't stop until he controls the entire magical world. We will never be safe with him alive."

"You lasted *your* whole life," I snapped, then immediately regretted my words.

Piper's head reared back. Her eyes stirred with darkness and torment. I inwardly cursed myself for dredging up those awful memories.

"I wouldn't have wished my life on anyone," she said in a

trembling voice. Her eyes burned with fury. "He manipulated me. Used me. Forced me to do . . . unspeakable things in order to survive." She shuddered.

"I'm sorry. I shouldn't have—"

"It's fine. I know what you meant. But Cora, that was different. He was just getting started. If he'd had the power back then that he has now, I would've been in worse trouble. I was lucky because growing up, he was just biding his time. Collecting more and more magic. Now that he's made his move, he won't stop until he's finished."

"What exactly does he want?" I asked in a hushed voice. "More power, obviously. But for what?"

Piper swallowed hard and dropped his gaze. "I think . . . he wants to enslave other casters."

Bile crept up my throat. "What?" I gasped in horror.

"I'm not completely sure, but . . . I remember he once experimented on a few witches using some mind-control elixir. It never worked. But those few failures really rattled him. I avoided him for days after, worried he would take it out on me."

My whole body went cold. Mind control? I remembered what Piper had told me before—that Quentin had targeted Second Tier Thinkers, or Telepaths. I'd assumed it was because they posed the only threat to his power. The only magic he couldn't replicate.

Perhaps it was more than just eliminating a threat, though. Perhaps he'd experimented on these Thinkers, trying to access a specific ability. When it hadn't worked, he'd cut his losses.

I glanced around the warehouse, looking from Finn, who snored loudly on the floor, to Dex, who rested his head against the wall across from us. What was happening in Hinport right now? Had Quentin already succeeded in enslaving the other demons? What if our tiny band of rebels was Hinport's only hope?

And we'd fled . . . leaving those demons at the mercy of Quentin.

I was no coward. And yet I'd bolted from a fight. I'd never done that before.

Agony flared in my head, and I closed my eyes, wishing things were different. That Vince was here. That I had more allies.

A burst of red light filled the warehouse, momentarily blinding me. In an instant, Piper and I were on our feet. Finn yelped and jerked awake, and Dex jumped up as well. My daggers were in my hands, my teeth clenched as I prepared myself for a fight. But as the red glow intensified, revealing a figure, my heart lurched in my throat.

Red magic was Reaper magic. Could it be . . .?

Before I could get my hopes up, the figure materialized. The first thing I noticed was that it was a woman. And my heart sank.

Then, as I made out her features, I staggered backward in shock.

Standing before me, her black wings stretched wide and her face hard with determination, was Vince's mother.

CHAPTER 2

VINCE

PAIN. ALL I KNEW WAS PAIN. MY HEAD HAD BEEN CLEAVED in two. My skin was on fire. A dozen hot needles dug into my flesh again and again.

I screamed, but the agony was so intense I couldn't hear my own voice. I saw nothing but darkness. Felt nothing but anguish.

Please, I begged. *Please.*

The wound in my head throbbed and pulsed like it had its own heartbeat. But somewhere inside me, a tiny presence stirred to life. I clung to it in desperation, searching for strength to overcome this, to heal myself from whatever was cutting into me over and over.

Please.

The presence shifted, and a beam of gold light ignited within me. I focused on it, gingerly reaching for it as if it were the embers of a dying fire and I was coaxing it back to life. The light grew, illuminating my surroundings. I was flat on my back. Grass tickled my arms. But the sky above me was still pitch black. I squinted, and the pain on my face intensified. A strangled cry tore from my throat, and this time I heard it. It echoed around me, blaring against my eardrums.

"Please," I moaned. "Please make it stop."

The light quivered inside me, flickering as if it was about to die out.

"No, no," I pleaded. "Don't go."

Something gentle caressed my mind, like fingertips brushing against my skin. It was soothing amidst the agony that consumed me. I sucked in sharp, ragged breaths, trying to calm my heart rate so I could *think*.

But this damn pain . . . It was everywhere.

Vince, the presence whispered.

Pain, pain, pain. I tried to shove it aside and *focus*.

You have a choice, the voice said. It sounded like Luke, but I somehow knew it wasn't him.

"What choice?" I rasped.

If you wish, this pain will leave you. But so will the light.

I went still. Though my head still felt like it was on fire, I remained frozen as I processed the voice's words.

Sudden understanding struck me. The light—the voice within me—was the timeline. The Call.

I remembered what Luke had said after we'd found out Hector was a Timekeeper: *Not everyone has the Call. Those who do go through a rigorous testing process before they become a Timekeeper.*

This was my test. If I could endure this pain, then I would pass.

But . . . how long would the pain last?

My body convulsed, no longer able to remain still with my head splitting open. I clenched my teeth, trying to bury my mind so deep within myself that I couldn't feel anything.

But all I felt was my face being carved in two. Like knives digging into me. Again. And Again.

I remembered the gold magic inside me, the timeline. How it had influenced me when I'd time traveled. How it had kept me safe and guided me to preserve the timeline.

If I failed this test, if I lost that presence, did that mean I wouldn't be able to time travel anymore? The thought made me feel strangely empty, though I didn't know why. It wasn't like I desperately *needed* to time travel. It just helped me feel safe. Like I could protect myself—or anyone I cared about—so long as I had that power.

Realization gleamed in my mind. Becoming a Timekeeper would empower me. It would help me stop Quentin from destroying the timeline—destroying the *world.*

It might help keep Cora and my parents alive.

I grasped at that thought. Cora's face swam in my mind, her eyes ablaze with determination and that fire I loved so much. I saw my parents smiling shyly at each other, finally reunited after ten years apart.

The gold power curled toward these images like a tendril

of smoke. I sucked in a breath as the faces of those I loved glowed and glistened. The ethereal light grew inside me until it pierced through the darkness. The sky slowly brightened, and the moisture on the grass tickled my skin. I inhaled again, relishing the fresh outdoor scent of daybreak.

And then, so gradually I wanted to scream, the pain in my head receded. A dull throbbing took over, pulsing with a sickening rhythm that made my stomach heave. But the fire, the slicing and cutting—it vanished.

My chest shook with my shaky breaths. Carefully, I sat up. My head spun, and nausea swirled in my stomach. Brief pain flared in my head, and I hissed before raising my hand to my forehead.

Then, I froze. My hand trembled. Panic tightened in my chest.

A gaping gash ran from my eye to my lip, stretching wide over my cheek. The edges of my skin puckered, and the wound felt moist. My fingers came back soaked in blood.

This time, I couldn't hold back. I vomited in the grass. Twice.

But the stinging, the burning on my face never left. It served as a reminder that this gaping hole had been carved through my skin.

"Why?" I groaned, breathing through my nose. "Hector! Did you do this to me?"

In a flash, Hector appeared before me. I glanced up at him. My eyes narrowed—which inflamed the cut on my face.

"You did this," I growled.

Hector watched me, his expression grim. "I didn't do this, Vince. This was your price."

I stared at him. *Price.* For what? For the Call? To pass their little test, I had to get my face cut open?

"Why?" I said again.

"The Call is different for everyone. It responds to our deepest fears and our most basic needs." For a brief moment, Hector's eyes filled with anguish, and I vaguely wondered what *his* test had been.

"I don't remember having a fear of getting stabbed in the face," I snapped.

Hector merely shrugged. "The test usually holds a deeper meaning than what we think."

I stilled at his words. A deeper meaning . . .

I'd wanted to give in, to remove the pain . . . until I remembered what was at stake. The ones I loved.

So, I'd endured. I'd accepted the pain—and the wounds and scars that would come with it.

My price was *myself.* I had to choose between keeping myself whole and unharmed . . . or accepting the damage in order to do something greater. Something more important.

Like preserving the timeline. Protecting the people I loved.

I swallowed hard and found myself nodding. If I had to go back, I would do it all again. I would *die* before giving up Cora and my parents. I would endure a thousand cuts to the face.

"I don't suppose you could heal me?" I asked with a hoarse chuckle before staggering to my feet.

Hector grimaced. "No, sorry. The wound must heal naturally."

I figured as much. Otherwise, what would be the point? I had to suffer through every aspect of this injury—both mentally and physically. And that included the aching slowness of healing without magic.

"You did well, Vince," Hector said, his mouth twitching in a smile.

Discomfort wriggled through me at the sound of this man *complimenting* me. I still hadn't fully accepted him as an ally. He'd done so many despicable things.

"So, what now?" I asked.

Hector's face sobered, and he took a step toward me. "Now, we train."

CHAPTER 3

CORA

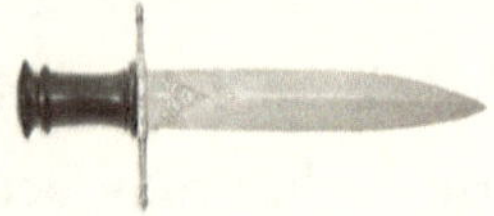

A STUNNED SILENCE SWEPT OVER US AS WE BEHELD THE magnificence and *shock* of the Reaper before us. Red still glowed from Cecile's body, and her chest rose and fell with labored breaths. Her gray eyes surveyed the warehouse until they settled on me.

"Cora." She strode forward.

I tensed, tightening my grip on my daggers. She noticed and froze. Her eyes widened. Her blond hair was in a disheveled bun, and her eyes were haggard. She looked like she hadn't slept in days.

"Why are you here?" I demanded. Unease prickled through me. *Trap, trap, trap,* my instincts chanted. Why else would Cecile be here? She hated me. All the Reapers did.

"You—you called for help," Cecile said, blinking.

I swallowed. This was true—I'd cast a summoning spell

weeks ago in an attempt to reach them—but I hadn't expected anyone to respond. It was a desperate, last-ditch effort because the Reapers wanted to take down Quentin just as much as I did. Enemy of my enemy and all that.

My mouth opened and closed. "Yes, but . . . why are *you* here?" I gestured to her with raised eyebrows.

Cecile's lips pressed together in a thin line, her expression guarded. "Because Vince would want me to help you."

I stiffened. She said that as if he were dead. "Where is he?"

"Last I heard, he was safe in Luke's mind. But it's been a while since I've checked in." She grimaced.

Her eyes were haunted. Something within me stirred in recognition. "What's happened?" I asked quietly, stepping toward her.

"Cora," Piper hissed in warning.

I stilled and glanced at my comrades. Dex, Piper, and Finn all stood at the ready, their bodies poised for battle. Dex's eyes gleamed a hungry red. Finn's fingers curled into fists at his side.

They didn't trust Cecile. Hell, I didn't, either.

But I trusted that she loved Vince.

"Let's hear her out," I muttered before sheathing my knives.

No one objected, but all three of my friends scowled, watching Cecile warily.

"I would've come sooner, but I was being tracked," Cecile said. Her black wings withdrew, receding into her shoulder blades and making her look strangely ordinary. "Then, I lost your trail and struggled to find you again. You cover your tracks well."

I grunted noncommittally and raised my eyebrows, waiting for her to go on.

Cecile exhaled slowly. "My people have been captured."

A lump formed in my throat. "Quentin?"

She nodded. "He—he wants the magic Vince took. He's holding the Reapers hostage, hoping one of them will give away his location."

My blood chilled. I drew closer to her, my nostrils flaring. "They *won't,* right?" My voice was practically a growl.

Cecile shook her head. "Not even I know where Luke is right now. But he's torturing the Reapers. He's already killed one." She clamped her mouth shut, her eyes filling with grief and raw agony.

My chest tightened. Though I didn't care much for the Reapers, they didn't deserve *this.* And they were Vince's people. It would kill him to know what they were going through.

"How did you escape?" Piper asked in a hard voice, her arms crossed. She clearly wasn't swayed by Cecile's sorrow.

Cecile cleared her throat, her eyes moist. "Jocelyn and Gwen created an elaborate distraction so I could get out."

My heart lurched. *Gwen and Jocelyn.* Gwen was tough, but Jocelyn? She'd always seemed so innocent and frail. What punishment had she endured in exchange for helping Cecile escape?

"What about José?" I asked, referring to Vince's mortal father. If Quentin wanted leverage, kidnapping José would be his best bet.

"He's safe," Cecile said with a relieved sigh. "He's taken refuge with a powerful light coven on the west coast."

Thank Lilith, I thought as my chest loosened slightly. I'd grown fond of Vince's dad over the past year. We'd gotten to know each other well after Vince had become a Reaper. "What makes you think I can help?" I asked.

"*You* are what he wants, Cora." Cecile gestured between Piper and me. "You're his daughters. If anyone knows how to defeat him, it's you."

Piper and I exchanged grim glances.

"Even if we *did* know how to take him down," I said slowly, "we don't have enough forces to manage it. We need allies. We need numbers. He has *armies* at his disposal."

Cecile nodded. "I know." She paused and took a breath. "He also has the Timekeepers on his side."

My head reared back. "*What?*" The only thing I knew about the Timekeepers was that they preserved the timeline and played by their own rules. And last I heard, Quentin was breaking the laws of time. How could they side with him?

"They joined out of self-preservation," Cecile said, though her face twisted in disgust. "Quentin had leverage on them. And with his growing power, they knew they wouldn't win a battle against him."

A foul taste filled my mouth. Those damned Timekeepers thought they could do *whatever* they liked without repercussions. They'd intervened with Hector after Damien had died, then refused to help when my father showed up. And now they'd *joined* my father in his efforts to enslave the magical world.

"How?" I asked through clenched teeth. "I thought their one objective was to protect the timeline!"

"It is. In fact, several Timekeepers have . . . been unwell since joining Quentin's forces."

My eyes narrowed. "What do you mean by *unwell*?"

"There have been fits. Episodes of madness. Hallucinations. They're all bound to the timeline in different ways. Those with a stronger bond are . . . suffering for it."

Unbidden, I thought of Vince and that sense of *knowing* he had while time traveling. Would he suffer for the Timekeepers' betrayal as well? I hoped that, wherever he was, he was safe.

"I don't care if it's only the four of you." Cecile stepped closer to me, her eyes pleading. "You're the only one I can turn to. Even if we have no plan, no money, no strength, I will work with you. I'll help you take him down, Cora. Whatever it takes."

There was such open vulnerability in her eyes that my breath caught in my throat. I'd always seen her as fierce—maybe not as callous as Gwen, but still something formidable. A strong, powerful presence.

But now, she looked broken. She didn't know where her son was. She'd had to send her husband away for his own safety. And her people were being tortured and killed.

In her eyes, I saw myself. A kindred spirit. Our losses were so similar that my heart twisted for her.

I found myself nodding before I realized it. "Okay. We'll work with you."

"We will?" Finn asked uncertainly.

"Got any better ideas?" I challenged. "We need allies. Now we've got one. I say let's do what we can." I looked at Cecile. "How did you arrive here? What powers do you still have?" As far as I knew, all the Reaper magic had been given to Vince for protection. Which meant Reapers were as good as mortals right now.

Or so I thought. Somehow, Cecile had Jumped here.

Cecile reached into her pocket and withdrew a long black feather. "Reaper feathers possess magic. It's stronger if it comes from another Reaper, so using my own wouldn't have made much of a difference. Gwen gave me one of hers to use."

My eyes widened. "Does Quentin know this? What if—"

"He can't use the magic from our wings," Cecile said quickly. "Reapers are bonded to the wings by blood and bone. The only way an outsider can access the power of our wings is by using Reaper magic, but . . ." She broke off with a shrug.

But the Reaper magic isn't accessible anymore. My jaw ticked back and forth as I thought about this. "Can you do that again?" I asked. "Teleport like that?"

"No. The feathers have a one-time use. I saved this for when I was certain of your location."

Damn. So the only people who could utilize these magic

feathers were Reapers . . . but Cecile couldn't use her own. We were screwed.

"But I know Quentin's location," Cecile offered. "And I know how many sentries he has posted."

My eyebrows lifted. Well, that was something.

"Even if we can get to him, we still don't have a *plan,*" Dex said sharply. "I doubt the five of us could take him on."

"You're right," I said. "We need to use something else against him. Something he's afraid of."

Piper's eyes grew wide. "Thinkers."

I nodded. "We need to track down Benny."

CHAPTER 4

VINCE

Training, as it turned out, was brutal. Especially with the festering wound on my face.

Hector didn't go easy on me. He was more relentless than my lacrosse coach. We started with strength training and agonizing stretches that pulled my muscles in every direction. Most of the exercises required some form of balance—squats, the chair pose, a one-handed plank, and other strenuous tasks that made me grit my teeth.

"Why am I doing all this?" I growled after what felt like days. I had no way to measure time in Luke's mind, but my entire body was on fire. My limbs felt like lead.

"You have to master balance with your body before you can master balance with your mind," Hector said. He stood on the grass, arms crossed, as he watched me work. He looked perfectly at ease, the bastard.

"Whatever you say, *sensei,*" I spat, not in the mood for his mind games.

Hector rolled his eyes. "Real mature, Vince. But you of all people understand the burden of the timeline inside you. If you have any hope of maintaining control and not completely losing your mind to the power within, you need to work on these exercises."

His gaze darkened, and I paused between squats to look at him. He spoke as if he understood this firsthand—the dangers of going insane. I remembered he once told me it felt like the timeline was constantly whispering in his mind. Voices that wouldn't go away.

I swallowed down my bitterness and continued my exercises.

When I was able to do the chair pose without wobbling, we moved on to mental training. If I thought physical training was tough, it was a picnic compared to my mental workouts. Hector and I sat opposite each other in the grass as he coached me through it. It involved summoning the Call within me, that tiny beam of gold light, and expanding it. In and out, in and out, like I was stretching it. But it took an immense amount of focus—so much that my hands curled into trembling fists and sweat dripped down my face from the exertion. When we finished the exercise, my brain felt like sludge, and I fell backward on the grass with my eyes closed.

"Most Timekeepers aren't able to do physical and mental training back-to-back," Hector said, panting like me. "Well done."

I barely lifted my head to raise my eyebrow at him. "Why are *you* out of breath?"

"I wouldn't be much of a trainer if I didn't do the exercises with you."

I snorted and lay back down. "You didn't do the *physical* part."

Hector remained silent. I rolled over and propped myself up on my elbows to scrutinize him. He had that haunted look on his face again.

"What?" I asked.

"I *need* the mental exercises. Possibly more than you do right now."

I stilled. "Because of the Call? Has it gotten worse?"

Hector nodded. "Migraines every day. That beam of light you describe in your head? Well, for me, it's like a blazing sun beating down on me, off and on all day. And the whispers have grown louder. Sometimes, they scream at me."

I swallowed, uncomfortable with the pity I felt for this man. "Is there any way to fix it?"

Hector shook his head. "Even the strongest of Timekeepers had no solution for me."

An apology formed on my lips automatically, but it died in my throat as I remembered Hector had been about to kill me. Even though it was my fault he had the Call, I wasn't sorry. I'd done what I had to to survive.

I changed the subject. "How long does training last?"

"Until you can use the timeline to travel."

My skin prickled. "I can already travel."

He shook his head. "No, not with your warlock powers. Using *only* the timeline."

My mouth felt dry. I didn't know what to say. The task seemed so daunting I wanted to collapse on the grass again.

Hector seemed to read the apprehension on my face. "Don't worry. It won't be that long. After all, you're able to wear that pendant with ease. It's only a matter of time before you'll be able to handle more power."

I frowned, then remembered the amulet hanging around my neck. The Reaper magic. Somehow, I'd completely forgotten. When I'd first put it on, the burden had been so intense I couldn't stand. Now, I was able to exercise and train without thinking about it. The thought comforted me, making me feel a bit more competent.

"What will happen to the magic?" I asked, glancing down at the shiny gold amulet.

"What do you mean?"

"The whole reason I'm here is to keep this hidden. But once I can use the timeline to travel, I'll have to absorb the Reaper magic to keep it safe from Quentin. How do I do that?"

"The answer will come to you when you solidify your bond with the Call. You'll have a better sense of your power by then. After that, the choice is yours. With the timeline flowing freely within you, you can use your Call to determine the best course of action. As long as it doesn't violate the laws of time, you can do whatever you want."

Whatever you want. The phrase was so casual and off-handed. Like I *hadn't* been chained to a clan my entire life. Like Hector himself hadn't imposed rigid rules and toxic bullying. The reminder made my stomach turn sour, and I dropped my gaze.

"Do you want me to leave?" Hector asked quietly.

The question startled me so much that I looked at him. His eyes were weary. At that moment, he looked so much older.

I almost said yes. I wanted to shout that he was the last person in the world I wanted to see right now, except maybe Quentin.

But if he left, I'd be alone again. And I wasn't ready for that yet.

"If you have somewhere better to be," I said carefully. "It doesn't matter to me."

Hector was quiet for a long moment. "It isn't safe for me out there."

I nodded. "It isn't safe for *anyone*."

Hector leveled a gaze at me. "You don't know?"

"Know what?"

"The Timekeepers have joined Quentin."

Shock rippled over me. My heart lurched, and my blood ran cold. "I—I don't understand."

"He found a way to siphon the Call from a Timekeeper," Hector said, his eyes ablaze with fury. "He threatened to unleash it if they didn't cooperate."

Bile climbed up my throat. "What—what does that mean? Does he have the Call now?"

Hector shook his head. "The Timekeeper didn't survive once the Call was extracted. It's like another form of magic. Almost like a blood ritual. But . . . as you know, the Call responds differently to everyone. If Quentin unleashed it, the consequences would be catastrophic. The fabric of our world would disintegrate. The timeline would fall apart."

I was having trouble wrapping my mind around this. "What do you mean by *unleash*?"

"If a person absorbs the Call by force, the timeline will fight back. Almost like antibodies fighting off a disease. The Call can only be used by mutual acceptance of the caster and the timeline. When used forcefully, it becomes something volatile. Something explosive."

Well, that sounds right up Quentin's alley, I thought bitterly. But the way Hector spoke reminded me of what Mom had told me about Reapers. The vow I swore kept me from using my powers for evil. I could only reap if a soul willed it. Magic could only be parted gently, not by force.

Quentin had extracted magic against the souls' will, destroying spirits in the process. But I'd been able to take it back from him because the magic had called to me—Reaper to Reaper. Quentin might not have wanted to give it up, but his soul had known the power didn't belong with him.

"I thought I sensed something strange in here," said a voice.

I jumped to my feet, my heart racing. Luke stood on the grass, his hands in his pockets and his hard gaze fixed on Hector. Hector stood as well and nodded to Luke politely.

Luke didn't smile. "What're you doing here?"

"Vince is training to become a Timekeeper."

"I know. But why are *you* his trainer?"

Hector's mouth opened and closed. "I—I'm the only one left. The only one available."

I stilled. The thought hadn't occurred to me. I'd figured Hector was my trainer because I'd summoned him.

But this explained why he never left Luke's mind. He stuck around because he knew leaving would put him in danger.

It was smart . . . but also cowardly.

Luke groaned and rubbed his forehead. "It *hurts* having both of you squatting in here."

"Sorry," Hector and I muttered at the same time.

Luke's eyes snapped to me. "I wanted to update you. I reached the coven of Thinkers. They're keeping me safe."

I nodded as relief swelled within me. "Good."

"But I have bad news."

My heart sank. "What?"

"Quentin's imprisoned the Reapers. He's trying to find you—to find *that*." Luke gestured to the amulet.

My throat felt tight. Agony coursed through me as I thought of my mom and Jocelyn suffering at Quentin's hand.

And me sitting here in the grass like there wasn't a care in the world.

"I have to go to them," I said at once, striding forward as if I could actually go anywhere.

Luke touched my shoulder, stopping me. "You know you can't."

"The only reason the Reapers are still alive is because you're safe here," Hector said.

"No, I'm the reason they were captured in the first place," I growled.

"You knew something like this would happen," Luke said. "This was part of the risk. This is why I went into hiding."

I shook my head, my face twisting into a disgusted grimace. *My people . . . trapped with Quentin . . .*

"If you're in hiding, how did you come by this news?" Hector asked, but I was only half-listening.

"My coven tapped into Gwen's mind to keep an eye on things. She's not aware of it. If she were, Quentin would know."

"That's kind of a violation, don't you think?" Hector asked with a raised eyebrow.

"You're one to talk," I spat. Since when had he valued anyone else's privacy?

Hector's face slackened, and Luke said flatly, "Desperate times, Hector." He turned to me. "That's not all."

I groaned, and ran a hand through my hair. "Tell me."

"Your mom escaped."

My mouth fell open, and my eyes widened. A mixture of worry and relief coursed through my chest. "Where is she?"

Luke shook his head. "I don't know. But Quentin's in a rage over it. He's threatening to cut off all their wings."

I shuddered. *Please, Lilith, no.* I focused on my breathing, knowing I was no good to anyone if I had a panic attack. Inhale, exhale. Over and over.

"She must be trying to rally reinforcements," Hector speculated.

"She's going after Cora," I said quietly.

Silence followed my words. Energy pulsed within me as I looked at Hector, my body suddenly taut with anticipation. "Let's get back to training. The sooner I can travel, the sooner I can help."

"Whoa, whoa, *travel*?" Luke raised a hand. "Vince, you can't go anywhere. That's not part of the deal."

"I can't just *sit* here!"

"If you go out there with the amulet, Quentin will find you and steal the magic all over again!" Luke said loudly.

"He can't take it from me if the magic is *inside* me," I argued.

Luke waved his arms in the air, his dreadlocks flopping against his face. "And what, you think once you're a Timekeeper, you'll become this all-powerful being? You don't know what it's like to hold that much magic. It's too risky. You're *staying put.*"

I gritted my teeth. For a moment, Luke and I glared at each other, neither of us backing down.

At long last, Hector said, "Vince *can* absorb the magic."

"Gwen said the burden of that much magic would *kill* him," Luke said.

"Not with the timeline inside him to balance it."

"That's not what the timeline is for!" Luke said hotly.

Hector stared at him calmly. "Let the Call decide. Once Vince masters it, if he senses an issue, he won't do it. But, if the Call doesn't stop him . . ." He broke off with a shrug.

"The timeline doesn't give a damn whether Vince lives or dies," Luke said through clenched teeth. "It has no concept of right and wrong, good or evil. You can't just blindly trust the timeline to keep you alive. The Call only exists to protect the laws of time. Nothing else."

I stilled as I realized something. "The timeline opposes Quentin, right?" I looked at Hector for confirmation.

Slowly, he nodded. "I still hear it whispering inside me, urging me to stop him. Though it's duller in here." He gestured to the field around us.

"If it takes him down, I don't care if it kills me," I said to Luke.

"Vince—"

"Wouldn't you do the same thing?" I challenged. "If the people you loved were being killed and tortured, wouldn't you sacrifice yourself to save them?"

Luke's mouth clamped shut, but his eyes stirred with emotion. I knew he agreed with me. But his pinched brows betrayed his unease.

"Let's just see what happens when you finish training," Hector suggested, glancing between us both.

I almost laughed. In what world had Hector become a mediator between Luke and me? It was just too bizarre.

Luke waved a hand. "Fine. Call me when you finish." Without waiting for our response, he vanished.

Uncertainty swelled inside me. I didn't like being so at odds with my friend. And worse, Hector and I were in *agreement.* That felt even stranger.

Even so, I couldn't just stand by helplessly. It wouldn't take long for Quentin to track down my mom . . . or Cora.

So, I squashed down my worries and focused instead on my resolve. "Let's get back to training."

CHAPTER 5

CORA

"I ASSUMED BENNY WAS DEAD," FINN SAID SLOWLY, HIS dark eyes narrowing as he glanced from Cecile to me.

"So did I," I admitted, dropping to the ground to sit in front of the large bucket we were using to mix spell ingredients. A cauldron would've been ideal, but we could make it work without one. "A locator spell will tell us for sure. If he's dead, nothing will happen. If he's alive, the ember will lead us to him."

"What if he's hundreds of miles away?" Piper asked doubtfully, her arms crossed.

I shrugged. "Then, that's how far we'll have to travel. The ember follows our pace, though, so if we make camp somewhere, we won't lose it." I sprinkled powdered foxglove into the bucket, and a low hiss emitted from the contents.

"Why didn't you do this before?" Cecile asked in a low

voice. Her piercing gaze was fixed on me, but it wasn't accusing. Only curious.

I swallowed down the emotion rising in my throat. In truth, I hadn't wanted to know. If Benny was dead, I wasn't sure I could handle another loss on my conscience. I took a breath and said, "It was too risky. A powerful elixir like this will probably draw Quentin's attention if he has spies lurking nearby. We'll need to move quickly once I cast it, just to be safe." I rested my hands on my knees and inhaled deeply, waiting for my magic to come to life. But it was only a flicker, a mere shadow of its usual power. I was still weak from Dex's feeding.

With a groan, I relaxed and looked at Piper. "I'll need your help."

Piper's brows knitted together, but she plopped down next to me without question. She took my hand in hers, and I closed my eyes before uttering the spell.

"*Magic above and powers that be,*

Guide the way so we may see,

The soul whose presence we now seek.

Find him with the words I speak."

My hands glowed purple, and Piper's emitted an inky black smoke. Our combined magic funneled into the bucket, which rattled. Piper's hand felt hot in my grasp. Energy thrummed around us, tickling my skin. My bones seemed to quiver from the power.

The contents of the bucket glowed purple and then started churning as if an invisible person were stirring it. The gooey substance swirled around and around, making me feel sick just watching. An eerie wind tousled my hair, and I closed my eyes.

At last, the magic faded, and the bucket went still. The ingredients vanished, and in their place was a light purple ember floating in the air.

Cecile sucked in a gasp, and I looked at her. Her face was slack with shock—as if she hadn't believed it would work. Her gaze flicked to me. "I—I thought you needed the essence of a person to cast a spell like that."

"Normally, I do," I said. "But I don't have anything on me that belongs to Benny. I tweaked the ingredients a bit, and it required more power. That's why I needed Piper's help."

"What's stopping Quentin from doing the same spell to find *you?*" Finn asked, glancing around nervously as if expecting Quentin to appear.

I grunted as I rose to my feet. "I based the spell on my emotional connection with Benny. I wouldn't have been able to do the spell on just anyone." My throat tightened, and I swallowed. "Benny is my friend. I'd bet anything that Quentin doesn't share that same connection with anyone else."

Piper stood and shared a grim look with me that confirmed my belief. Quentin took pride in working alone. Yes, he had allies and followers, but he never shared his power.

We all stared at the ember expectantly. It hovered in the air for a moment before floating toward the door.

I exhaled through my lips, glancing at my friends to ensure they were ready. "Here we go."

We strode forward, following the ember out of the warehouse.

The days blurred together. Finn hot-wired a car that we used to follow the ember, which gained speed as if sensing our mode of transportation. When Finn got tired, I took over, claiming I was too wide awake to sleep. Instead of stopping for the night, I drove while the others slept in their seats. Exhaustion tugged at my body, begging for rest, but I kept my eyes on the glowing purple ember hovering over the road.

Sleeping would lose us precious time. I had to keep going.

"You'll wear yourself thin," said a soft voice.

I jumped and glanced in the rearview mirror to find Cecile's gaze fixed on me. Clearing my throat, I said, "I'm fine."

Cecile huffed a laugh. "You may have to put on a brave face for them, but not for me."

I didn't say anything.

"I understand," she went on. "Probably better than anyone."

I gritted my teeth, my fingers tightening around the steering wheel. How dare she pretend like she *knew* me? "Really." I couldn't hide the bite in my tone.

"You want Vince back. So do I. Once Quentin is defeated, Vince can return. Don't tell me it's not on your mind."

Something in me deflated. In a way, she was right. I hoped that once we found Benny, we could take down Quentin and I'd be with Vince again.

But I knew it wasn't that simple. Vince was a Reaper. He'd have to live in another realm once all this was over.

"I also care about Benny," I said in a hard voice. "He's my friend."

Cecile was quiet for a moment. "I understand that too. I had to leave my friends behind to seek out help. If I could, I would go back to them in a heartbeat."

I let out a breath in a low hiss. "What are you doing?"

"What do you mean?"

"Are you trying to *bond* with me or something? Because you sure as hell didn't care about me when we first met. You and your Reaper *friends* were determined to hate me."

More silence. Then, Cecile said, "Vince loves you."

I stilled, and my heart lurched at her words. Though I knew it—Vince had told me himself—it felt different hearing someone else say it. It felt more *real.*

"It doesn't matter what *I* think of you," Cecile went on. "He would do anything for you. And so will I."

Her words jolted something within me, though a shred of doubt lingered in my mind. I wasn't sure I believed her. If my life was at stake, I doubted she would sacrifice as much as Vince would to keep me alive.

"He gave up his Reaper magic," Cecile said.

I stiffened, glancing at her in the mirror again. "He *what*?"

"When we set up the spell binding our magic to the amulet, he touched it first. Willingly. He gave it all up." Regret tainted her voice.

"But he can get it back, right?"

Cecile took a deep breath. "I don't think he'll want to. I saw his face when he lost his magic. He looked so . . . *free*. Unburdened. Unrestrained. I've never seen him look like that."

I swallowed, trying to picture it. Her description reminded me of when I'd first met Vince at his school. He was confident. Casual. Completely at ease. Everything I wanted to be but couldn't because of who I was.

That had all changed when I'd entered the picture. I'd made his life a burden. Ever since he met me, his gaze was always heavy and hard, and he was determined to fix whatever problem he faced.

It was admirable. But it also made me sad to constantly see a war in his eyes.

"Why are you telling me this?" I finally asked, my voice strained.

"Because I think he gave it up for *you*. So he could be with you."

I shook my head, unwilling to let myself go down that path. Hope was a dangerous thing. "It can't happen."

"Maybe it can."

"It *can't*," I snapped. My knuckles turned white from gripping the steering wheel so tightly.

Cecile didn't respond, though I sensed her disagreement. When our eyes met in the mirror again, there was solid understanding between us.

She knew how it felt to hold on to that hope—and to have it shatter into pieces.

So, we settled into silence again. My eyes remained fixed on the purple ember in front of us. And even as we crossed the state line and made our way into New York, the silence continued to press in on me. Smothering me. The purple ember was a lifeline I clung to, but I knew it wouldn't be enough. Not for much longer.

Cecile was right—I was wearing myself too thin. But I would die before giving up. I would die before letting Quentin slaughter anyone else I cared about.

And I would die before giving up on Vince.

CHAPTER 6

VINCE

A FIERCE STORM RAGED AROUND ME. RED LIGHTNING cracked through the sky. And on the ground in front of me, her body limp and unmoving, was Cora. Her eyes were wide open and vacant. The blue within them that had once been so vibrant and intense now stared with startling emptiness.

She wasn't breathing.

I gritted my teeth as grief swarmed inside me. My fingers curled into shaking fists. Sweat formed on my brow.

Remember, I urged myself. *Remember the Call.*

I searched inside for that familiar gold light, but all I saw was Cora's hauntingly lifeless expression. Her body was nothing more than an empty shell. The woman I loved was gone. Dead.

The thought hollowed out my chest, carving my heart

right out of me. Agony split through me, and I fell to my knees.

"Remember," I growled through clenched teeth. "Come *on.*"

But everything felt so real. The wind whipping at my face. The tears streaming down my cheeks.

And Cora . . .

I reached forward. My fingertips brushed her soft hair. Her icy cold skin.

"No," I moaned, hanging my head.

In a flash, I was back on the lacrosse field, my face covered in sweat and tears. My panicked breaths ripped through me again and again. I couldn't get enough oxygen. I couldn't even see straight.

"Vince—" came Hector's voice.

I shot to my feet, ignoring the dizziness that clouded over me. "Again," I said.

"You've already endured the test three times. I don't think—"

"I want to go *again,*" I hissed.

We'd been at it for hours. After physical and mental exercises, I'd finally moved on to a series of tests to ensure I was worthy of the Call. That I would respect it. It reminded me a lot of the vow I pledged as a Reaper—to abide by the laws of reaping magic.

This was similar. I knew that, in theory, my task was simple: I had to set aside my devotion to those I loved in favor of preserving the timeline.

And yet . . .

It wasn't that easy. The whole reason I'd decided to become a Timekeeper was so I could save the people I loved from Quentin. But now the Call was trying to brainwash me into thinking it was *okay* to lose the people I loved.

It wasn't okay at all. Even facing a hallucination, something I *knew* wasn't real—it was too much for me to bear.

We'd already wasted too much time. If I wanted to get to Cora and Mom, I had to pass this test. But it wasn't something I could fudge my way through. The Call lived *inside* me. It knew my thoughts. And even if I told myself it wasn't real, a part of me feared it more than anything.

The Call knew that. It knew that my deepest fear was losing the people I cared about.

"The Call responds to selflessness," Hector said. "Putting the timeline above yourself and everyone you love. If we could manipulate the timeline the way we wanted to, the world would collapse on itself. Parallel universes would be created, intersecting one another until the life we know would be sucked into a massive void of nothingness. The timeline can't withstand that much change. It can only be entrusted to those who would use it properly."

I refrained from rolling my eyes. "I know all this. It's just —easier said than done. Staring at her dead face, I—" I broke off and ran a hand down my face.

Hector crouched on the ground next to me. "Your mother?"

I blinked and looked at him. "No . . . Cora." But as I

stared at Hector, I reminded myself: *He's the reason I grew up without my mom.* Something hard settled in my chest, and I dropped my gaze.

Hector went still as if sensing where my thoughts had turned. And I found myself wondering why it *wasn't* my mom's face I was seeing. I knew I loved her. I would do anything to save her.

But . . . a small voice in my head told me I'd already lost her before. I already *knew* that pain. I'd parted from both her and my dad, believing I would never see them again.

But not Cora. My heart clung to the idea that one day we could live our lives together. Now, the Call was actively trying to crush that hope. After so many months of grasping it in desperation and using that hope to fuel my actions, it was hard to break it.

"Who decided the Call should be in charge, anyway?" I asked bitterly.

I wasn't being entirely serious, but Hector still answered. "It isn't a person. It's an entity. Like . . . magic itself. It's alive and it has a presence, but it doesn't have feelings or weaknesses."

I wrinkled my nose. "Is it like a deity?" The idea made me deeply uncomfortable.

"No. It has no control. It's only a conduit through which others can manipulate things. If the Call lived on its own, it wouldn't be able to do anything. It's just a power source."

I shook my head, my frustration mounting. "It just doesn't

make sense to have access to all this power and not use it to stop terrible things from happening."

Hector was silent for a moment. "There has to be a balance in all things. Sure, stopping a brutal murder would be a good thing. But what if, instead of killing a random person, that murderer went on to kill someone else instead? What if that someone played an imperative part in history and would impact the timeline in monumental ways?"

I exhaled sharply. "But how can we just be *slaves* to the Call? It *needs* us, right? It can't do anything without us! So why can't we—"

"You're not a slave," Hector said in a hard voice. "You made a choice, Vince."

"What, to follow the Call unconditionally?" I snapped. "Even if it kills me? Even if it kills *everyone*?"

Hector sighed and rubbed his forehead. "This is why you haven't passed your training yet. You don't *get* it."

"You're right." I shot to my feet. "I don't." Tilting my head toward the bright sky, I shouted, "Luke! Can we talk?"

Silence greeted my words. I stood there impatiently while my insides squirmed as if trying to escape my body. I felt restless. Agitated. I could barely breathe.

And I was so sick of Hector. I needed to see another face. A *friendly* face.

After a moment, Luke appeared, his eyes tired and his dreadlocks tied behind him. He yawned. "What's up?"

"Did I wake you?"

Luke shrugged, but he didn't seem too angry. "Don't worry

about it. My body's still in bed, so I'm only half-conscious anyway." He grinned sleepily. When he noticed the tension in my face, his expression sobered. He glanced warily at Hector. "What happened?"

I explained my issue with the Call and the timeline and the garbage Hector kept spouting. Luke listened, his brows knitting together as he frowned slightly.

"So, how do you just follow it *blindly*?" I finished.

Luke's jaw ticked back and forth, and his gaze shot briefly to Hector. To my surprise, wariness crept into my friend's eyes as he watched the other man. Hector noticed, and his jaw went rigid.

"You *don't* have to follow everything the Call tells you to do," Luke said slowly, his voice tentative.

I sucked in a breath. Beside me, Hector stiffened, his eyes blazing with shock and anger.

"You—you don't?" I asked in a hushed voice.

Luke shook his head. "It's been a point of conflict between Timekeepers for centuries—how we interpret the Call and how flexible that interpretation is."

"You can't be serious," Hector scoffed.

Luke's eyes hardened. "You're a unique case, Hector. Not everyone hears voices in their heads like you do."

Hector flinched, and his eyes darkened for a moment.

"Tell me," I said urgently, stepping closer to Luke.

Luke sighed and scratched his nose. "It's . . . a long story."

I snorted and spread my arms. "Where am I gonna go?"

Luke shrugged and nodded before dropping onto the

grass, leaning back against his elbows. I followed suit, and, though he wrinkled his nose, Hector did as well.

"You remember hearing about the Great Mage War?" Luke asked.

Frowning, I nodded. All Nephilim learned about it as kids. It was the first great battle between casters and took place sometime in the eighteenth century.

"Timekeepers were a part of that too," Luke said. "It's kept quiet, though—only we know about it, so keep it to yourself. Anyway, it all started when this warlock named Jeremiah started questioning why we couldn't use the timeline to our advantage. Why we couldn't use it to stop terrible things from happening. The leader of the Timekeepers, a woman named Kallista, shot him down. She said that wasn't how Timekeepers work, and his ideas were blasphemous.

"But back then, the only thing they knew about the Call was based on rumors. No one dared defy the Call's promptings for fear the timeline would be ripped from them—or worse, that it would kill them. Early Timekeepers worshipped The Call like a god and offered sacrifices and prayers." He grimaced and shook his head. "So the most pious of Timekeepers feared incurring the Call's wrath and bringing hell to the earth.

"Well, Jeremiah was powerful. And he set up a spell to keep his body preserved and contained in case things went badly. Then, he waited for a nudge from the Call, something urging him to affect the timeline. When it finally came, he refused to obey." Luke paused and took a breath. "And . . . nothing happened."

My brow furrowed. "What?"

"Jeremiah was fine. Nothing happened to him for refusing the Call. Well, Kallista found out about his experiments and labeled him defective, then waged war on him and his followers. Jeremiah was killed, and his followers scattered, afraid of being hunted down and murdered."

Luke's eyes were distant as he went on, "A century later, a small faction of Timekeepers emerged who found Jeremiah's journals and followed his ideals. They, too, refused to blindly follow the Call. They exercised their own judgments, believing that since the Call is different for everyone, it also respects everyone's free will. The series of tests you go through before you solidify your bond with the Call is only to make sure you're worthy of it. After that, you can make the choices you see fit. At least . . . that's what they believed. They called themselves Timewatchers, since their objective was merely to monitor the timeline instead of actively influence it based on the Call.

"The other Timekeepers banished the Timewatchers. And over the next few centuries, the Timewatchers kept popping up and then scattering when the Timekeepers pushed them out. To this day, I don't know where they are, but rumor has it they're out there. I mean, they keep popping up throughout history, so I know they aren't gone." Luke finished with a shrug.

Silence fell between us. I was too stunned to speak. I

couldn't believe how much history was involved, how many battles had been waged over something so simple. Then again, so many wars had resulted from trivial things.

"It's a load of garbage," Hector grumbled.

I looked at him and raised an eyebrow. "How so?"

"Think about the world's population right now. If Timewatchers existed, they would be out in the open like all the other casters. Even demons have their own covens and can live in peace without persecution. So, if the Timewatchers are still alive, where are they?"

I shot him a flat look. "Don't tell me you're *surprised* to learn some magical communities prefer to remain isolated from others." After all, he'd preached the same idea when he'd been clan leader.

Hector had the good sense to look chagrined at that. Pink splotches appeared on his face, and he dropped his gaze. Then, he shook his head and tried again. "I've tried refusing the Call myself. It didn't work. The Call retaliated and practically set my brain on fire. I *had* to follow its orders just to take away the pain."

I winced. I couldn't help it. It was *my fault* he was like this. He was basically a prisoner to the Call.

"I told you, your case is different," Luke said, shooting a nervous glance my way. "No Timekeeper has ever been . . . an *anchor* before. At least, not that we know of."

"Yes, but I'm here in the flesh," Hector argued. "Right in front of you. I'm *proof* that it doesn't work. Where's *your* proof that it does? Where are these alleged Timewatchers?

Have you actually met someone who refused to follow the Call and survived?"

Luke said nothing.

Hector spread his palms, his expression smug as if this settled the argument.

I turned to Luke. "What do *you* think?"

Luke blinked at me. He opened and closed his mouth. At long last, he said quietly, "The Call has never urged me to do something I disagree with, so . . . I've never had to face that kind of problem. Yet." His brows knitted together. Conflict warred in his eyes.

"What if you *did* face that problem?" I urged. "What would you do?"

Sadness stirred in Luke's eyes, and I imagined he was thinking of every horrible scenario—his mom's death, the deaths of his siblings—and what he would do if the Call just let it happen.

His voice was barely above a whisper as he said, "I would refuse."

CHAPTER 7

CORA

"CORA."

My eyes snapped open. Cecile was driving, and I sat in the front passenger seat, my head stuck to the icy window. I peeled myself off the door, feeling groggy and sticky. Rubbing my eyes, I glanced around.

We were in a rural area surrounded by snow-capped hills and trees. Small mountains lined the horizon, and the road was so bare I almost wondered if Cecile had gotten us lost.

Then, I focused on the purple ember. It had stopped right in front of a large, isolated log cabin. Smoke plumed from the chimney.

A knot formed in my throat. "Where are we?" I asked in a croak.

"Roxbury," Cecile said.

I frowned. I'd never heard of it. Then again, this didn't exactly look like a bustling city.

"It's definitely an ideal place to hide," Finn said behind me.

"Benny's not the type to hide," I said, but I wasn't so sure. If he *was* alive, why had he vanished? I cleared my throat. "There's always the possibility my spell didn't work."

"If that's the case, the people who live here are about to get some pretty peculiar visitors," Piper said with a snort.

I wiped my palms on my jeans and took a breath, struggling to awaken my sluggish mind. "Well, let's get it over with." I tried to calm my racing heart, but it was no use. Panicked thoughts kept circling through me. *What if he isn't here? What if he really* is *dead? What if he can't help us?*

I gritted my teeth, forcing myself to get a grip. If Benny couldn't help us, we'd just have to track down other Thinkers. Maybe find the ones Luke went to live with.

This was not over. Not by a long shot.

I was first out of the car. Cecile followed suit, then Piper and Finn. The four of us stomped through the snow toward the cabin, trying to appear nonchalant. With Cecile's wings gone and none of us using magic, we almost looked normal—well, except for Piper's purple hair.

When we reached the door, I knocked firmly and then stood back to wait, my pulse roaring in my ears. The seconds seemed to take forever as we all stood there, teeth chattering. I rubbed my arms, and my breath shook.

Footsteps sounded on the other side. Then, the door swung open.

My heart lurched . . . and then sank.

It wasn't Benny.

Before us was a muscular man who looked about thirty or so. His light brown hair was buzzed almost to his scalp, and his eyes were dark and suspicious as he looked us over. "Can I help you?" he asked.

I swallowed, my throat suddenly dry. Lifting my chin, I said, "We're looking for Benny. Is he here?"

The man's eyes widened, and his jaw went rigid. He glanced behind us as if expecting an army to have followed. "How do you know my brother?" His voice was a low growl.

Brother? Shock flitted through me, but I recovered quickly. "I—he's a friend. We need his help."

The man crossed his arms, his beefy frame easily blocking our view of the inside. "I don't believe you." His eyebrows lifted, challenging me.

My nostrils flared. "Benny was an alpha until his wife, Lynn, died, and he abdicated and joined a demon coven. I'm the leader of that coven."

I heard a sharp intake of breath behind me, but I didn't know who it was. I had no doubt Benny had kept this information to himself, but now wasn't the time to withhold it.

The man dropped his arms and gaped at me. His face paled before he cleared his throat and stood back to let us in.

Apprehension gripped my chest as I strode inside. The cabin was cozy and rustic. A fire crackled in the fireplace. Two small couches faced each other in the living room. A wide window revealed a pristine mountain slope covered in snow.

"He's in the room upstairs," the man grumbled behind us.

We climbed the creaky wooden steps until we reached an open bedroom door. Holding my breath, I peered inside.

Benny sat on the bed, his back to me as he faced the window. His hair was messy and disheveled, and he was hunched over. Even before he turned to look at me, I knew something was very wrong.

He shifted and met my gaze. His brown eyes were full of confusion and fog. His brows knitted together as he stared at me. Dark circles lined his eyes, and his face was drawn and weary.

"Benny," I breathed, exhaling in relief. "Lilith, you look terrible."

I strode toward him, but he tensed, his back rigid and his nostrils flaring. He looked past me to where his brother stood.

"Who is she?" Benny asked, his voice wavering.

I stilled, and my blood ran cold. *He doesn't know me?* My mouth opened and closed.

"Oh, hell," Finn muttered behind me.

I shook my head, refusing to believe it. "Benny, it's me. Cora."

Benny still watched me in bewilderment. His eyes darted to me, then back to his brother. "Gio," he said pleadingly. His voice was so feeble. So unlike the Benny I knew.

At first, I didn't understand what he meant. Then, Benny's

brother brushed past me and knelt on the floor in front of Benny. I realized Gio was the man's name.

"They know you," Gio said softly. "From before the accident. They might be able to help you remember."

Accident? I thought, stunned. *What accident?*

Benny fixed his yellow-rimmed eyes on me again. "Do you know what happened to me?"

My heart rate accelerated, and I suddenly found it hard to breathe. I glanced over my shoulder at Cecile, whose face was pale. She looked at me and shook her head slightly. She didn't know, either.

Finn and Piper had been with me during the battle. None of us had seen what happened to Benny.

I swallowed hard, struggling to find my voice. "What do you remember?"

Benny's eyes grew distant and unfocused. "A wolf. A blast of purple light. And then . . . nothing."

My heart shuddered in my chest. *A blast of purple light.* It had to have been Quentin. He did something to Benny, something to wipe his mind so he would no longer be a threat.

I balled my hands into fists and took a shaky breath. "You were fighting. An army attacked the city. You were probably in wolf form when it happened."

Benny's eyes widened, and for one terrifying moment, I feared he'd forgotten he was a werewolf. But then he said, "That makes more sense. It explains *this.*" He lifted his left arm, and I hissed a breath through my teeth. From his fingertips all the way up his forearm, his skin was covered in burns, red and festering.

What the hell happened to him? My eyes felt hot as I watched this man who'd once been my friend, who was fierce and loyal and determined. This shell of a man was scared and confused and . . . not Benny at all.

My eyes slid to Gio, who watched his brother with regret and anger in his eyes. Slowly, Gio met my gaze. I jerked my head back to the hallway, and he nodded.

Gio and I left the room. Piper took our cue and moved forward to speak softly to Benny.

Once we were out of Benny's earshot, I demanded, "What happened?"

Gio's eyes blazed. "You tell me! He was fighting with *your* coven."

I shook my head. "He wasn't with me. He was on the other side of town. We lost the fight and fled. I couldn't find him after that." I crossed my arms and lifted my chin. "How did he get here?"

Gio pressed his lips together, his eyes guarded. "We share a blood oath, so we can sense when something's wrong with each other. I felt his pain and the trauma in his mind. I tracked him down and found him half-dead on the street. I healed his injuries, but the burns . . . there's something off about them. They won't heal." He shook his head in frustration. "I brought him here, hoping it would help jog his memory. This is the cabin where we grew up. Plus, it's isolated. I figured he was in some kind of trouble, so off-grid seemed best."

Heat climbed up my throat. I closed my eyes as guilt threatened to consume me. "It's—there's"—I cleared my throat and tried again—"It's my father. He's a Bloodcaster and he waged war on our city. He's trying to enslave the entire magical population."

To my surprise, Gio nodded. "I know. My coven was attacked just a few days after I left to find Benny. Covens all over the area are being targeted. It's gotten ugly."

I drew a sharp breath. I had no idea. We'd been in hiding for so long that I hadn't received any news. "Where?" I asked.

"A few covens upstate. New Hampshire and Vermont. Jersey's pretty much gone."

Something hollow settled in my chest. *Pretty much gone.* Quentin had taken over my home. And his forces were already spreading—much faster than I'd feared.

Luke, I thought in a panic. What if Quentin found Luke's coven?

I looked at Gio. "Are you a Thinker?"

He shook his head. "Elemental." I knew he wasn't a wolf, either—his eyes weren't yellow, and I didn't smell dog on him.

I swore and ran a hand through my hair. "Does Benny still have his magic?"

"I don't know. He seems too scared to try. I can smell the wolf on him, though."

I tapped my chin thoughtfully. "Do you have a cauldron? Any potion ingredients?"

"No cauldron, but check the pantry. Mom cooked up a lot of spells in her day. There's probably stuff there you can use."

I nodded and chewed on my lip as I thought. I'd once healed Vince's mind when he'd first come back from the Astral Realm. Maybe I could work on a spell to heal Benny's mind too.

"You can help him, right?" Gio asked. His eyes were fixed on the open door where Benny, Piper, and Finn were talking. Benny still looked confused, and Piper and Finn looked grim. Cecile lingered in the doorway as if too afraid to draw closer.

I inhaled deeply and nodded, trying to appear confident even though my insides were squirming. "I'll certainly try."

A few hours later, my face was covered in sweat, and a few scorch marks singed my arms. Concocting a potion for Benny hadn't been easy. Unlike most of my experiments, this one had a lot at stake. I had no qualms with testing potions on myself. But this was Benny. If it went badly, it could kill him.

Thankfully, I'd dug up a Grimoire from the dusty pantry shelves, along with several helpful ingredients. I used a few drops of my own blood, plus Benny's—which he offered with a painful grimace. The sight of his face scrunched up in fear made my heart twist. *This isn't Benny,* my instincts said. *This is a feeble, frightened man.*

I shoved the thought away, focusing instead on my plan to

cure him. If this worked, I would have Benny back. He'd be a fierce fighter again. And then, we could take down my father.

Piper helped me assemble ingredients. Like before, we channeled our magic together when we uttered the spell. Then, I ladled the soupy purple mixture into a mug and sniffed deeply. I smelled strong herbs plus the sharp scent of my blood. From my experience with concocting potions, it smelled fine. Nothing out of the ordinary.

Even so, my skin prickled with unease.

"What's wrong?" Piper asked, wiping her hands on a cloth.

I shook my head. "Nothing."

"Do you really know how to use *all* these ingredients?" Piper asked, squinting at the label on one of the jars.

"Most of them," I said, sniffing the potion again.

"What's this used for?" Piper lifted a jar of mandrake root and took a whiff, then recoiled with a shudder.

My lips twitched, but I was too nervous for a real smile. "Mostly poisons. Though I've also used it to make this neat elixir that mimics the appearance of death. Really handy for when my enemies track me down and I'm in a bind. They show up, but I'm already dead." Truth be told, it wasn't my favorite way to evade enemies—it felt cowardly to just play dead like that.

I took a deep breath. "Is Benny ready?"

Piper set down the mandrake root and nodded. "He's waiting in the living room."

I swallowed hard, steeling my nerves. *I can do this,* I

thought. With a nod, I gripped the mug tightly and followed Piper out of the kitchen.

Benny sat on the couch, his back straight and his gaze distant as he stared out the window. For a moment, I stood in the doorway watching him. He remained perfectly still. His mind was clearly elsewhere. It looked like he was daydreaming.

The Benny I knew certainly wasn't a dreamer. He was proactive and determined. Always busy with something.

I'll get him back, I promised myself before stepping into the room.

At the sound of my footsteps, Benny looked up, his brown eyes apprehensive. His gaze fell to the mug in my hands. "Is that it?" His voice was timid.

I nodded and sat next to him on the couch. "I'm not going to force this on you. There's a chance this potion won't work." I took a deep breath and looked at him. "It's up to you what you want to do."

Deep down, I *wanted* to force the potion down his throat. But whatever had happened to his mind, this man was still my friend. I could never do that to him.

It had to be his choice.

Benny glanced from my eyes to the mug in my hands. After a moment, he nodded stiffly. "I'm tired of the darkness up here." He tapped his temple.

I offered a tight smile and handed the mug to him. He gulped it down, his face contorting slightly. When he finished, he lowered the mug and winced. "It's a little bitter."

"Sorry."

He set the mug down on the coffee table. Silence settled between us. I held my breath, waiting.

Suddenly, Benny's body lurched forward. He hunched over, roaring so loudly that Gio burst into the room.

"What is it? What's wrong?" Gio hurried forward, kneeling to the floor at Benny's feet.

I flung out an arm to stop Gio from touching Benny. "Wait," I urged.

A violent shudder rippled over Benny's form, and then he straightened, the motion so abrupt that I jumped. Benny blinked a few times, then looked at me. Clarity burned in his brown eyes. The unease and fear had completely vanished. Instead, alarm and anger filled his gaze.

"Cora," he said hoarsely.

A grin spread across my face. "Thank Lilith." I leaned forward to embrace him, but he pushed me back. Frowning, I asked, "What's wrong?"

Benny shook his head. "No. You can't be here. You have to leave *now*."

Stunned, I glanced at Gio, who watched his brother with a hard expression.

"What do you mean?" I asked.

"It's a trap," Benny said, rising to his feet and glancing around as if expecting an intruder.

Bewildered, I looked around as well. Piper, Finn, and Cecile heard the commotion and came into the room, but aside from the six of us, no one else was here.

Had my potion backfired? Had it turned Benny into some paranoid maniac?

I stood and hesitantly touched Benny's arm. His skin was burning hot. "Benny . . ."

"You don't understand." Benny whirled to face me, his eyes crazed. White fur sprang to his arms. He was about to shift to his wolf form. "Cora, it's *Quentin*. He did something to my mind. Something that was triggered by your blood. He's tracking me. And that potion—"

My blood ran cold. Before I could speak, a *pop* echoed in the foyer. My heart stopped. I couldn't breathe.

Slow footsteps drew nearer. And then my father entered the room, smiling widely as if we'd invited him to a party. His hands were in his pockets, and his hair was slicked back. His eyes glinted as he said, "Hello, Cordelia."

CHAPTER 8

VINCE

"Does time pass differently when you're here?" I asked Luke as we sat in the grass. Hector was off pouting a few yards away, clearly still bitter about our disagreement. I tried shoving all thoughts of the Call from my mind, since it made me feel dizzy.

"Kind of," Luke said. "Time is slow for you, but it's even slower when I'm here. You remember when I pulled you in here when you were about to throttle Hector?"

I snorted and nodded. When Cora had been abducted, I went into a frenzy to try to find her. Luke took me into his mind for a few minutes, but when we re-emerged, no time had passed at all.

"It puts you in a kind of . . . stasis," Luke said. "Like a coma. Your mind and body are preserved as long as you're in here and as long as I, you know, don't die."

We both chuckled. I straightened. "So does that mean this will be gone?" I gestured to the long scar on my face, which had scabbed over—but now it was itchy as hell.

Luke winced. "No, sorry. That's permanent. A mark of your trial as a Timekeeper."

I deflated with a sigh, then glanced at Hector. "How long do you think he'll keep brooding over this?"

Luke shrugged. "I think he's questioning everything right now. The Call is *inside his head.* It's different for him. Who knows what would happen to him if he refused? His brain might explode."

I flinched, trying not to picture it. "Right."

Luke seemed to sense the guilt in my tone. He fixed a firm gaze on me, his dark eyes hardening. "It isn't your fault."

"Yes, it is."

"Okay, let me rephrase that. It *is* your fault, but he had it coming. He's lucky he isn't dead."

I nodded, though I wasn't sure I believed it. Maybe death would've been kinder. Instead, Hector was tormented by voices in his head that he *had* to obey.

I changed the subject. "How are things with the coven?"

Luke made a face. "Weird. I've never really been in a coven before. They definitely do things differently. And, I know it sounds childish, but I miss my family." His eyes turned distant and wistful.

I offered a sympathetic smile. I completely understood. Luke and his family were really close. "I've been meaning to ask—do they have magic too?"

Luke shook his head. "No, I'm some kind of anomaly. I had a great-grandfather who was a Thinker. Apparently, the gene was passed down, but it skips a few generations."

A shadow fell on us, and we glanced up to find Hector standing stiffly, his expression tight and agitated. "Ready to try again?" he asked me. The strain in his voice indicated it was the *last* thing he wanted to do right now.

My face softened. The fact that Hector was willing to train with me—despite the earth-shattering revelation that he might be enslaved to the Call for no reason—was pretty admirable. I scrutinized him and the darkness that clouded his eyes. He needed a distraction right now.

So, I stood and faced him. "Sure. Let's go again."

Like before, we sat cross-legged in front of each other. I felt Luke watching us from a distance and tried to ignore his gaze.

"Clear your mind," Hector said softly. "Focus on that beam of light inside you."

The gold light came naturally now. I had to hunt for it before, but now it was effortless. It shone inside me as if it had been there all along, waiting.

Hector extended a hand and brushed his fingertips against my forehead. The gold light intensified, blinding me, spiriting me away, until . . .

I was back in front of a lifeless Cora. Her gaze was empty and cold.

I crouched to the ground, trying to shove down the panic

and grief that gripped me. My gut reaction was to keep thinking, *This isn't real. Try to remember the Call.*

But as I recalled my conversation with Luke, those thoughts slowly faded. Instead of blindly seeking out the Call for guidance, I searched within myself for my own instincts.

If this were real, I thought to myself, *what would* I *do? How would I handle this?*

I closed my eyes. A golden glow resonated inside me, spearing through my uncertainties and fears. For the first time since I started training, I felt peace. I felt whole. The Call grew within me, piercing and pure like a flawless chord sung by a choir.

Emotion climbed up my throat, and tears stung my eyes. The power within me was so intense and so—real.

I'd originally thought of the Call as some innate instinct, guiding me to preserve the timeline. But that perspective had shifted into something strange and mystical and foreign. Something I didn't entirely trust.

Now, I knew my original impression had been right. The Call wasn't its own entity. It lived *inside* me. It was a part of me. The Call couldn't survive without Timekeepers because the Call *was* the Timekeepers. Our impulses and desires and feelings and fears. It was like a magic unique to each of us. Shaped by our past, present, and future.

Clarity burst through the foggy haze that had taken hold of my mind. Seeing the Call as part of myself felt so *right.* Because I trusted myself. I didn't trust this disembodied deity that Timekeepers from centuries ago had worshipped.

But I did trust my instincts.

My eyes opened and fixed on Cora's body once more. But instead of the usual anguish and crippling terror, I clung to that feeling of peace and certainty. Focusing on that gold light inside me—that Call that was a part of me—I extended a hand and touched Cora's wrist. The timeline thrummed within me like a machine. My entire soul seemed to vibrate from the connection. I pressed my fingers to Cora's cold skin.

I breathed deeply. And then, my vision spun.

I saw the timeline flashing before me. But unlike when I Jumped with my warlock powers, I had *control* over it. Like I had a remote to pause and replay at my command. Images and distorted shapes blurred, but when I focused, I could slow it down. I saw Cora fall. The light left her eyes. Using the Call, I pushed time backward, searching for the source of her death.

Nothing. One moment, she was standing in a bedroom. The next, she was on the floor, dead.

Frustrated, I continued backward in time. *Farther back*, I thought.

I kept going. Past Cora and me talking, past Cora fighting with her daggers. I caught a glimpse of my mother. Benny and Luke were there too.

But I didn't stop. I trusted that instinct within me and kept going. Farther. Farther.

A familiar presence stirred in my mind, and I reached for it. It clung to me, tethered to my own mind. I tried focusing on *what* it was, but I didn't want to interrupt the flow of the timeline.

The light inside me lurched, and I stopped. The images slowed until I focused on one thing: Cora.

My heart stuttered at the sight of her, hunched over her desk and surrounded by papers. I tried to reach her, but the gold light held me suspended, unable to move. I knew she couldn't see me because her eyes were focused on the papers in front of her. With a sigh, she pushed her hair out of her face and rubbed her eyes.

The Call wouldn't let me go to her. Why not? I struggled against the invisible vise to no avail.

The amulet, a small voice said inside me.

My eyes dropped to the gold pendant hanging from my neck. *What about it?* I thought.

This is your test, the voice said. *Absorb the magic.*

Alarm and unease shifted within me. *Here? Now?*

As I stared at Cora, I suddenly understood. I was here for a reason. But I couldn't fulfill that purpose until I proved myself.

A knot formed in my throat, and I swallowed. I lifted my arms, expecting that same resistance to keep me glued in place. But the Call relented and allowed me to remove the amulet. My hands shook as I slid the chain forward until my fingers touched the cool metal. My eyes closed.

And a burst of red magic consumed me. Pain ignited in my chest like a wildfire, spreading until every inch of me was scorched. I gritted my teeth but kept the amulet in my grip. Sweat poured down my face and neck.

A presence within me grew and expanded like a bubble. I

held my breath, feeling as if there wasn't enough space for me to inhale at all. The sensation was odd and uncomfortable—like I'd eaten too much and was overly full. But it was no longer painful.

A crackle and an explosion shuddered through me, and I groaned. The Reaper magic roiled, colliding with the Call and my warlock powers.

Balance it, the voice in my head said. I couldn't tell if it was the Call or me. Or both, since the Call was *part* of me.

I inhaled shakily and focused on each deep breath, counting them one by one. As the seconds passed, the tension in my body diminished. My arms relaxed, and I stopped clenching my jaw. My head and chest still throbbed, but I ignored it and kept counting my breaths.

I got to a hundred, and I no longer noticed the collision of magic inside me. Slowly, I opened my eyes. All I saw was gold light.

The Call. Something inside me opened up, embracing the gold light. As it flowed through me, the Reaper and warlock powers swirled together as if the Call provided a chain linking the three of them together.

There was no pain. No discomfort. The three presences could coexist easily within me. Tears pricked my eyes, though I had no idea why, and an insane smile spread on my face. I felt the Call's triumph race through, me almost like a friend patting me on the back and congratulating me.

With a sudden *pop*, the gold light vanished, and I landed on the floor in front of Cora. Papers fell to the floor, and Cora jumped to her feet, her eyes wide and blazing as if she expected a threat.

Then, she saw me. Her jaw dropped. I hadn't realized my dark wings had emerged until her eyes slid back and forth, drinking them in. I hastily slid the amulet in my pocket and faced her.

For a moment, she stood there, completely frozen. Then, she whispered, "Vince."

The sound of my name on her lips stirred something deep in my gut. As I stared at her, absorbing everything about her, I realized something was different. Her hair was a bit shorter, her eyes were tired, and the office looked bigger than I remembered.

Then, I recalled Cora telling me her old office had been burned down.

I'd traveled *back* in time. Farther than I'd anticipated.

Gold light flickered within me, and understanding flooded my mind.

Cora had just taken over as coven leader. I remembered this because when I'd first come here as a Reaper—from the Astral Realm—Cora told me my Mimic had visited her. To warn her to send me back so I could save the Reapers from Quentin's destruction.

I was that Mimic now. And I knew what I had to do.

CHAPTER 9

CORA

In a flash, my daggers were in my hands, my body stiff and poised for battle. My eyes darted behind Quentin, expecting to see an army.

My father spread his arms and smirked. "It's just me. I come in peace."

A low growl built up my throat. "There will *never* be peace between us, Quentin."

Something unreadable stirred in his eyes. For a moment, he watched me with a contemplative expression.

Then, I straightened and chuckled without humor. "What, you wanted me to call you *Dad*?"

Quentin's eyes tightened, and his face smoothed into a pleasant mask. Almost apathetic. He drew closer to me. Dex and Finn stiffened, inching toward me, but I raised a hand to stop them. I didn't need more blood on my hands. I felt Piper completely frozen behind me. Our father had that effect on her. But right now, it was the safest thing for her to remain still. Benny lingered on the couch, his face ashen as he watched Quentin with a hard gaze.

I offered Quentin a cold smile. "I should congratulate you. You clearly went to a lot of effort to find me." I gestured to Benny.

Quentin's eyes gleamed. "You're a hard woman to track. I'm impressed. I don't know many people who can disappear as effectively as you, Cordelia."

My gaze remained on Quentin, but I was aware of everyone in my peripheral vision. Piper, Dex, Finn, Benny . . . Cecile was hovering in the kitchen doorway, unmoving. Her wings weren't out, which was a good thing—I didn't want Quentin to know she was his missing Reaper. Hopefully, he hadn't noticed her yet.

But where was Gio? If things got nasty, I needed to make sure he didn't get caught in the crossfire.

I shrugged and spread my palms. "Well, you've got me. Go ahead. Put me in handcuffs. Drag me to your secret lair."

Quentin cocked his head at me, his dark eyes roving around the room and settling on each one of my friends. I sensed Piper shrinking away from his scrutiny, and Quentin smirked in response. "Aren't you the least bit curious as to *how* I implanted that trigger in your friend's brain? It wasn't easy. He put up quite a fight."

My skin crawled at the delight in my father's voice, and I resisted the urge to look at Benny. If I did—if I saw the agony in his face—I wouldn't be able to keep it together. Instead, I lifted my eyebrows. "What, you want a medal or something?"

"That's the problem with you, Cordelia," Quentin said with an exasperated sigh. "You are so *closed-minded* about your abilities. But I could teach you so much."

"Not interested," I snapped.

"So stubborn. Just like your mother."

"*Don't talk about my mother.*"

Quentin's mouth spread into a wide grin, and I realized my mistake. I'd just given him ammunition. "I can perform necromancy, you know. And once I get those Reaper powers back, I can bring your mother back like *that.*" He snapped his fingers.

I swallowed hard and struggled to keep my breathing even. "I said, *not interested.*"

"You don't even want to know what she looked like? What she thought of you? What her *magic* was like?"

Curiosity coiled inside me, and for a split second, I let myself envision my mother's Bloodcaster magic. I pictured her using her powers for good. Maybe as a healer. Someone so very, very different from Quentin.

"There it is," Quentin said softly, stepping closer to me. "I see that spark in your eye, Cordelia. Don't ignore it. Let me open that door for you. Let me *show* you." He reached out his hand.

"Cora." Benny was on his feet, standing between my father and me. His bulky form blocked Quentin from view, and I blinked, stunned.

I'd clammed up. I'd *completely frozen.*

What kind of fool *was* I?

Quentin sighed again. "You've played your part, little wolf. Step aside and let me talk to my daughter."

"No," Benny growled. The fur on his arms thickened. His hands trembled, and long claws extended from his fingers.

Figures shifted behind me, and then Finn and Dex stood by us, flanking Benny. Piper appeared on my right—as far from Quentin as possible, but still standing with the rest of us. I appreciated the gesture all the same. Even Cecile had joined us, though she hid behind Piper, still trying to avoid drawing Quentin's attention.

"You're outnumbered," I said, finding my voice at last. "Do you really want to wage war right here and right now?"

Quentin laughed. "I'm never outnumbered, dear. I could easily take on all of you." He raised an eyebrow. "If that's what you want."

I read the challenge in his gaze. The veiled threat. He would kill my friends. I knew it down to my bones.

I wanted to hurl my knives at him. To cut his throat and bleed him dry.

But he was right. Even though he was just one man, he would overpower us. Someone would be killed.

But how could I surrender to him? He would sacrifice me, absorb my power, and become even *stronger.* There would be no one left to defend my people.

I needed to draw him away from here. Somewhere I could fight him one-on-one.

Suddenly, Quentin's head turned, his eyes glinting with recognition. I followed his gaze, and my heart sank.

He was looking at Cecile. She stiffened under his scrutiny.

A manic glee shone in Quentin's eyes. "You," he murmured in amazement. I didn't like the disturbingly hungry look on his face.

Cecile lifted her chin, though her eyes were filled with fear. She didn't have her magic. She had no way to defend herself.

I stepped closer to Quentin, drawing his gaze back to me. "It's me you want," I reminded him.

Quentin smiled widely. Purple sparks shot from his fingers. He extended a hand toward Cecile—

The front door swung open with a loud bang. My eyes narrowed as I watched someone step into the house, his frame tall and intimidating. For a moment, I thought it was Gio. But slowly, the figure came into view, and I sucked in a breath.

Great, dark wings spread behind him. And when he emerged from the shadows, I beheld the face of Vince. A jagged scar ran from under his eye to his chin, and I suppressed a shudder. His Mimic had visited me months ago and looked just like this. Scarred. Battle-worn. Hardened.

I'd hated seeing him like that. And I'd vowed to do what I could to prevent whatever trauma he'd endured. But, of course, I was too late.

I felt my friends shift behind me, clearly unsettled by Vince's presence. Cecile inhaled a ragged gasp.

Quentin turned to face Vince and stiffened. "Another Reaper," he breathed, his eyes roving over Vince's mighty wings. "So nice of you to join us." His gaze fell on a large gold amulet hanging from Vince's neck. A feral longing burned in my father's expression.

My blood ran cold. I knew what that was. It was the Reaper magic.

What the hell is he doing with that here? I wanted to scream at him. To shake his shoulders and tell him what an *idiot* he was for coming here.

But at the same time, I also wanted to run into his arms and kiss him senseless.

"I see you've brought a gift," Quentin said, turning his whole body to face Vince. "Would you—"

Before Quentin could make a move on Vince, I hurled my daggers, one after another. They sank into Quentin's shoulder and back, and he hunched over with a groan. Purple blood oozed from the wounds.

Slowly, he glanced at me over his shoulder, his eyes blazing. "Such disrespect," he said in a strained voice. "Don't interrupt, dearest."

I sent a blast of purple magic into him, and he went flying, crashing into a bookcase against the wall. Finn and Dex surged forward, taking my lead. Benny shifted to his wolf form and bounded forward. Red magic exploded from Vince's hands, searing and powerful. It blinded me, consuming the entire room like flames.

Startled, I took a step back. Vince's hands joined together, forming a huge, crimson ball of magic. It spun and twisted as if alive, and then it soared toward Quentin. The magic slammed into his chest, and the smell of burnt flesh met my nostrils.

Quentin collapsed, and I rushed over to him, withdrawing my daggers and holding one against his throat. Before I could slice him open, a voice shouted, "Stop!"

I stilled and looked up to find Gio hovering in the doorway, his face stricken and his eyes wide.

I gritted my teeth. "This isn't your fight, Gio. Let me take care of this."

Gio stepped forward and placed a hand on my wrist. "He—he's got my daughter."

My head reared back. "He—*what*?"

Benny's white wolf morphed until he took his human form again. His face drained of color. "Gio," he breathed. "What have you done?"

We were all so shocked, so taken aback that we didn't notice Quentin shifting from under my blade. When I glanced down at him, he'd uncorked a vial and drank the contents.

"No!" I cried, but I was too late. Quentin rolled away from me, and with a *pop*, he was gone.

A roar of rage ripped from my throat, and I flung my knives to the ground before rushing Gio. I slammed my palms into his chest and pinned him against the wall. He was massive and muscular, and holding him in place made my arms tremble.

"Cora," Benny protested.

"*What the hell did you do?*" I shouted, ignoring Benny.

Gio shook his head, his face crumpling. He looked so pitiful that I relaxed my hold on him. Just a fraction. "He—he took her in the night. I—I thought she was sleeping. I . . . I can't . . ." He choked off as tears rolled down his cheeks.

My nostrils flared, and I wanted to punch him, to scream at him. But instead, I released him, breathing heavily. This was Quentin's style—abducting loved ones to coerce people to work for him. I couldn't blame Gio for having a family.

The tension in the room dissolved. Cecile strode toward Vince, her eyes shining with tears. Her fingers hovered over the scar on his face, which only looked a few days old. Weeping, Cecile grabbed him in a tight embrace. Vince's arms wrapped around her. He was almost a foot taller than she was, and she buried her face into his shirt, weeping openly.

Over Cecile's head, Vince's gray eyes found mine. I was still panting, trying to squash the mounting rage within me. But his gaze steadied me. Grounded me. I swallowed, my mouth suddenly dry.

"Where's he keeping Maddie?" Benny asked in a low voice, drawing my attention away from Vince. I focused on Gio, who ran a shaking hand through his hair.

"I-I don't know," he stammered. "He took her a week ago. I woke up one morning, and she was gone. Then, I got a note from Quentin with instructions."

"What kind of instructions?" I asked. The bite in my voice

made it sound more like a demand. Benny shot me a warning look.

"All it said was, *Wait until I contact you*," Gio said. "Two days later, he asked me some random questions about me and . . . you." His gaze shifted to Benny, and his face twisted in an apologetic grimace.

"He needed information for the spell he cast on you," I said to Benny, who nodded grimly.

"I got another note a few days later explaining that if I told anyone, if I jeopardized Quentin's operation in any way, Maddie would be killed." He broke off with a sob, his shoulders shaking. Seeing this huge, muscular man breaking down like that rattled me. I rubbed my arms as discomfort slithered inside my chest.

"Did he tell you to track down Benny?" I asked.

Gio shook his head. "No. I was telling you the truth before. I knew something was wrong, so I went after Benny, worrying Quentin had targeted him too."

"You weren't wrong," Benny said bitterly.

"I left a note for Quentin in the same place I'd found the others," Gio said. "I outlined my plan to visit my brother. When I got no response, I figured it was fine and I wouldn't be breaking any rules." He shook his head, his face crumpling again. "I-I couldn't lose anyone else. He already had Maddie. If he'd taken Benny, too, I—" He broke off weeping again.

Benny's lips pressed into a thin line as he rubbed his brother's shoulder.

I swallowed down my emotions and asked quietly, "And Maddie's mother?"

"I haven't seen her in years," Gio said, his voice trembling. "She left when Maddie was a baby."

"How old is Maddie now?" I asked.

"Seven."

I flinched, trying not to picture a scared little seven-year-old tied up in someone's basement. The horror of being chained in Quentin's house resurfaced in my mind, making it hard to breathe.

Gio continued to cry, breaking through the traumatic memories that threatened to drown me. Something snapped within me, and I punched Gio's arm. He didn't even stagger backward, but it caught his attention. He went silent and stared at me in confusion.

"Cora," Benny protested.

"Pull yourself together," I hissed at Gio. "Falling apart isn't going to get your daughter back. I know it's hard. But you need a plan. You need to let us help you."

He shook his head. "He'll kill her."

"He'll kill her anyway," Piper said suddenly from behind me. "I know my father. He doesn't leave any loose ends."

"So you're saying my niece is doomed either way?" Benny asked, his voice hard.

"I'm saying her best bet is if we find her," I said. "Do you have anything that belongs to her? I can cast a locator spell—"

"No," Benny said, raising a hand. "He put a trigger on me, alerting him when you gave me your blood. He might've done the same thing to Maddie to make sure you didn't intervene. Someone else needs to do it."

"I'll do it," Vince said, stepping forward. Cecile's eyes widened, and she opened her mouth to protest, but Vince added, "I'm stronger. I have more magic." He lifted the gold amulet, which seemed to shimmer with power.

Cecile's face went pale. "Vince . . . that much magic could kill you."

"It won't," Vince said. There was an eerie calmness in his voice. An otherworldly confidence that hadn't been there before. Something was different about him.

Cecile seemed to sense it too. She fell silent, frowning at her son.

Vince's gaze settled on me, and my face suddenly felt hot. "I can do it. I'll find her and Jump her here."

"You can't just Jump into the middle of Quentin's base of operations," Cecile said, her voice gaining strength.

"Yes, I can." Vince's voice wasn't argumentative. It was quiet, but still commanding. There was such authority in his tone that my head reared back in surprise. Vince looked at his mother, his expression blank. "I have the timeline on my side."

Benny started, his face turning white. Cecile's eyes grew wide, and her lower lip trembled. "Y-you . . ."

"I'm a Timekeeper now," Vince said.

CHAPTER 10

VINCE

GOLD LIGHT FLOWED THROUGH ME, A CONSTANT AND reassuring presence. It seemed to fuel every motion, supply every word I needed to say. From the moment I left Cora's old office to when the Call had sent me here to this log cabin in the middle of nowhere, I felt the solid surety within me: I'd passed my tests. The Call had been fused within me, along with the Reaper magic.

I was a Timekeeper now. And I felt at peace.

Until I looked at Cora. When our gazes locked, a sudden churning broke through the stream of gold light, making everything unsettled and unsure. It was both thrilling and terrifying. I longed for the confidence and assurance of that gold light, but at the same time, the uncertainty, the hot desire within me was . . . exhilarating.

Cora was speaking, and I forced myself to focus. To

channel that inner calmness that demanded respect and attention. Mom had noticed. I could tell. She seemed impressed, but wary.

"If we do this," Cora said to the large, beefy man named Gio, "then we need you to fight with us. We need you on our side."

Gio nodded fervently. "Yes. Get me my daughter, and I'll fight for you. I'll do anything you ask." He sounded so pitiful.

Benny seemed to notice too. He rolled his eyes, and in that moment, I realized they were brothers. Though I had no siblings, I recognized that long-suffering expression on Benny's face. Luke often wore it around his younger siblings.

Benny shoved Gio's shoulder. "Get a grip," he muttered.

"If you had kids, you'd understand," Gio snapped.

Benny's face turned stony, and his expression closed. He dropped his hand, his eyes darkening. I didn't need to ask to know that was a sore spot between them. Perhaps Benny had lost a child.

"We need to do this soon," I said, looking at Gio. "Quentin knows it's only a matter of time before you switch sides."

Gio nodded. "I've got one of her toys you can use." He turned and vanished down the hallway, his heavy steps thudding loudly.

An uncomfortable silence fell among us. I felt every pair of eyes on me. Some watched me with suspicion—like the vampire and the dark warlock hovering near Cora.

I cleared my throat. "Uh, I'm Vince."

"We've met," the vampire said quietly.

I squinted at him and then remembered. He'd fought alongside Cora and me when we'd tried ambushing Quentin.

"So have we," Piper said, offering me a small smile. "Good to see you again, Vince."

"Who are you?" the warlock asked, lifting his chin. His dark eyes narrowed in distrust.

My mouth opened, then closed. Who *was* I? No longer a Reaper. A Timekeeper, sure. I was Cecile's son. And Cora's . . . something. I had no idea what we were.

Cora answered for me, "This is Vince. Vince, this is Finn." She glared at the other man. "Vince is a powerful ally. We're lucky to have him on our side." Her eyes widened meaningfully at Finn, whose mouth snapped shut. His nostrils flared in irritation, but he didn't object.

I looked at Cora, aching to draw closer to her, to pull her aside so we could speak in private. I had so many questions. What was she doing here? What had happened during the battle? How did Quentin find her?

I felt Mom inching closer to me. Though I had questions for her too, the pull wasn't as strong as it was with Cora. My body felt drawn to Cora like a magnet, like I couldn't resist it even if I wanted to.

But Cora wouldn't look at me. She tucked her hair behind her ears. It had grown a little since I'd last seen her. Now it hovered just above her shoulders. Her bangs had grown out too. She ordinarily kept her hair sharp and neat. No nonsense. Just like she was. But now it looked a bit wild and free.

Unkempt, but not unpleasant. It made her look like she'd just woken up . . . which made me feel hot with longing.

I cleared my throat, forcing my gaze away from her and facing Mom instead. "Are the other Reapers all right?"

Grief flared in Mom's face, and she closed her eyes briefly. "I don't know. Gwen and Jocelyn provided a distraction so I could escape. Quentin's already killed one Reaper. I—I fear . . ." She broke off, her mouth trembling.

My heart turned to ice. *Jocelyn.* What if Quentin had done something to her? Killed her. Tortured her. I couldn't bear the thought.

"Vince, what happened to you?" Mom whispered. She raised a hand to hover in front of the jagged scar on my face. I instinctively flinched away from her, though the wound no longer hurt.

"It's a long story," I muttered, avoiding her gaze. I really didn't want to share the details of my Timekeeper tests with the entire room.

"How did you get here?" Mom asked quietly. Her nervous gaze darted down to the amulet around my neck, and I knew what she was thinking. I was supposed to be safe in Luke's mind right now.

I cleared my throat. "I, uh, I'm not entirely sure. Something pulled me here." My eyes met Cora's, and a bolt of desire seared through me.

"It was me," Benny said flatly.

Surprise jolted within me like someone had dumped a bucket of icy water over my head. "Uh—what?" I sputtered.

"Our minds are linked, remember?" Benny said, tapping his forehead. "When Cora unlocked my memories with her potion, our bond must have snapped back into place. That's what called you here."

Disappointment sank in my stomach, though I knew it was ridiculous. I'd just been so certain it was Cora who had brought me here. Almost every time I'd accidentally time traveled, I had visited her.

Gio returned, clutching a doll in his hand. He strode toward me and offered the doll, which had curly golden hair and a too-cheerful plastic face. "Will this work?" he asked.

I turned the doll over in my hands, searching inward for that gold light again. It gleamed eagerly, as if waiting for me to summon it. Closing my eyes, I held the doll tightly and channeled my power toward it. Gold magic encompassed the doll, warming my fingertips. In my mind, I saw the girl's face. Dark hair and eyes, like her father. Olive-toned skin. I found her thread along the timeline and followed it. Watched as one of Quentin's men soundlessly entered the girl's bedroom window as she slept. The man pressed a cloth to Maddie's mouth before slinging her over his shoulder and creeping out of the house.

My eyes flew open, and I gazed at the shocked expressions that were fixed on me. Slowly, the gold light faded.

"I found her," I said quietly. "How do you want to do this?" I glanced at Cora, knowing she was in charge.

"I'll go with you," Cora said at once.

"No," Benny growled. "It's *you* he wants, Cora. He's probably expecting you to show up now that we have Gio. I'll go."

Cora opened her mouth to protest, but Benny went on, "He's afraid of me. He thinks I'm a threat. Otherwise he wouldn't have blocked my memories."

Cora's mouth snapped shut, and resignation shone in her eyes.

"I know Maddie," Benny said quietly. "She trusts me. She'll come with me."

Slowly, Cora nodded and then looked at me. "*Please* be careful." Her voice sounded strained, and I knew how much this was killing her.

"We will," I said, extending my arm to Benny. He took it and looked at his brother.

"I'll bring her back," Benny promised. Gio only pressed his lips together, his eyes full of emotion.

Gold light gleamed in my mind again. My magic surged to life. I spun in place, and Benny and I vanished.

We reappeared in front of a massive building about half a mile from Glen Bridge. The edifice towered over us like a skyscraper, providing shade for us to use as cover.

"The bastard's still in Hinport," Benny whispered, his eyes hardening.

"Of course he is," I muttered. "He knows Cora loves this city. He's trying to bait her."

Benny's eyes flicked to me, his expression unreadable. "Do you know where Maddie is?"

I glanced around. We faced a wide parking lot, and the

entrance to the building was only a few steps away. I closed my eyes and focused on that beam of gold light that connected me to Maddie. After a moment, I pointed toward the entrance. "She's in the building. Third floor."

Benny swore. "We can't get in there unnoticed. Couldn't you have Jumped us straight to her room?"

I shook my head. "Quentin's got wards up. I can't get there with magic. This is as close as I can get."

Benny exhaled through his teeth. "I can shift to my wolf form and make a scene. Use me as a distraction."

"You said yourself Maddie knows you. She won't come with me."

"But *you* are the one connected to her. If I show up on the third floor and face that long hallway, I won't know where the hell to go."

We stared at each other, both our expressions firm and unyielding. At long last, I gave in with a sigh. "Fine."

Benny nodded stiffly. "Wait for my howl." Before I could respond, he strode through the front door, white hair already growing on his arms as he shifted.

I held my breath, lingering in the shadows as I waited. Then, screams erupted from within the building, followed by loud growling and barking. After a moment, a shrill howl pierced the air.

I surged forward, stepping into the building. My eyes grew wide at the chaos around me. Benny the wolf was chasing people down, snapping his teeth and barking madly. Men and women ran in both directions as they tried to get away from him, but he kept turning this way and that, leading them on a wild goose chase.

Stifling a laugh, I hurried toward the stairwell, worried the elevators would shut down from the madness happening on the ground floor. As I raced up the steps, my lungs burning, I clung to that same gold thread within me. I pictured Maddie's face. Urgency pulsed through me. I *had* to find her. I had to.

I reached the third floor, panting and covered in sweat, and threw open the door.

A beefy man stood on the other side. Alarmed, he turned to face me, his dark eyes narrowing in suspicion. "Who're you?"

In a flash, my black wings were out, and I zipped forward, dodging a blow from the man. I struck him in the back of the head, then again in the shoulder. He landed a punch to my gut, and I doubled over as pain radiated through me. Coughing, I ducked and rolled to avoid his next strike.

I couldn't beat him hand-to-hand. He was too powerful. When I rose to my feet, I stretched my arm and back muscles and easily accessed my wings. Turning so my back was to the man, I flapped my wings madly. A fierce wind billowed around me, and the man shouted as he went flying. I pivoted and used my wings to propel myself forward, aiming a kick at the man's head. He collapsed and went still.

Gasping for breath, I straightened, my shoulders and arms screaming in protest. I searched inside myself for that gold light and found it hovering inside me, waiting. A faint glow appeared on the floor in front of me like a gold path lighting my way. My heart raced as I followed it, my steps frantic, until it stopped at a locked door at the end of the hallway.

I took a deep breath and kicked the door in. The crash echoed in the hallway, and I hurried inside.

Three muscular guards surrounded the small dark-haired girl I knew to be Maddie. For a moment, I stood in the doorway and gulped, knowing I couldn't take on all three at once.

The men advanced. Sweat coated my palms as I ducked down low, catching them by surprise. If I could just get to Maddie, just *touch* her, I could Jump—

But no. Quentin's wards would stop me.

Maddie and I would have to outrun these guys.

My brain worked furiously for an escape route as I dodged one meaty fist after another. One guard managed to tackle me to the ground, but I sent a burst of red magic that slammed him into the wall. My heart hammered in my chest as I jumped to my feet and raced over to Maddie. Her feet were tied.

Swearing, I hoisted her up in my arms. She thrashed and screamed through her gag, but I quickly whispered, "It's all right. Your dad sent me. Benny's right outside."

She stared at me with wide, frightened eyes and fell silent. I turned just as a guard hit me in the face. I staggered backward, nearly dropping Maddie. Somehow, I kept her in my grasp as stars danced in front of my eyes. My head spun, and I blinked rapidly, trying to see clearly.

Maddie's muffled scream blared in my ear, and I instinctively ducked. A huge weight collided with me, but I gritted my teeth and held my ground, inching forward to try to escape the mess of tangled limbs as all three of the guards reached for me. I summoned the Reaper magic once more, and an explosion of red light burned against my eyes, bathing the room in an eerie glow. The men screamed, shielding their faces, but for some reason, it didn't affect me. Maddie whimpered and buried her face into my chest. I clutched her close, protecting her from the intensity of the magic as I fled the room and sprinted down the hallway.

From below, another howl echoed. Did that mean Benny was injured? Or was he warning me time was up?

How long would it take for Quentin to intervene? My heart lurched at the thought. I didn't think I could face him *and* protect Maddie.

My feet pushed on and on as I flew down the steps, nearly toppling over in my haste. My body was drenched in sweat. I could barely breathe.

I finally reached the bottom, threw open the door to the lobby, and froze.

There stood Quentin, his arms crossed and his expression amused. The entire lobby had been emptied out. And behind Quentin, bound with silver rope, was Benny—still in wolf form.

Panic raced through me. I surged forward, but Quentin raised a hand to stop me. Slowly, he drew a pistol from within his jacket.

"It's loaded with silver bullets," he said softly. "One more step, and I end this wolf's life."

I swallowed, my throat dry and my heart beating a frantic rhythm inside me. Achingly, my eyes flicked to the door. Only a few steps away . . . All I had to do was get outside and I could Jump Maddie to safety.

But I couldn't risk Benny's life.

"Just let the girl go," I pleaded, my voice barely a croak. "Please. You can do whatever you want with me. Just let her go."

Quentin cocked his head at me, his eyes flashing. "I'll let her go . . . if you hand over that amulet around your neck."

I stilled. My heart stopped for a full beat. *He thinks the Reaper magic is inside the amulet.* I'd forgotten I was wearing it. But of course the Call would urge me to put it on. I had to keep up appearances.

If I gave it up now, Quentin would get suspicious. He would *know* I was hiding something. And I didn't think I was strong enough to fight him off if he tried to extract the magic from me by force.

This was the whole reason why I'd locked myself in Luke's mind—to protect the Reaper magic. Because *no one* was strong enough in a fight against Quentin.

My mind suddenly snagged on something. *Luke's mind.* Was Hector still there? A dozen thoughts passed through me as I considered my options.

"Well?" Quentin demanded, extending his hand. "What's it going to be, Reaper?"

I licked my lips, still wracking my brain. "Actually," I said breathlessly. "I think I should consult my friend first." I took a deep breath and bellowed, "*Hector Moses,* I need your help!"

My voice reverberated off the walls, ringing against my eardrums. For a moment, Quentin shot me a bewildered look as if I'd lost my mind.

Then, a small *pop* echoed, and Hector appeared, looking equally confused.

Quentin whirled to face him, and I snapped into action. My Reaper magic ignited, bursting in the air like fireworks. Quentin yelped as my power slammed into him. A loud clatter told me the gun had fallen to the floor.

I shoved Maddie into Hector's arms. "Take her. Go, *now*!"

Hector's face was pale, his eyes wide with terror, but he nodded. With a *pop*, he was gone.

The red magic still surrounded Quentin. His roar of fury filled the air. I rushed to Benny's side, trying to unravel the silver ropes. But then a blinding purple light pierced through the hazy fog of my red magic, and I knew I was out of time.

Sucking in a deep breath, I wrapped my arms around Benny's torso. Gold light gleamed within me. I focused on it before I Jumped and Quentin's enraged expression vanished from view.

CHAPTER 11

CORA

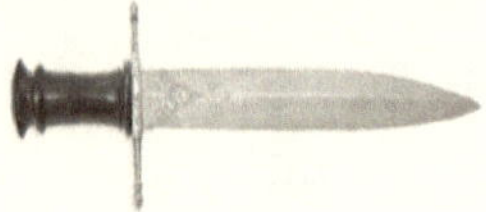

VINCE WAS GONE FOR LESS THAN AN HOUR, BUT WITH THE tension filling the small cabin, it felt like an eternity.

Gio wouldn't stop pacing. His steps were thunderous and incessant, setting my teeth on edge.

Cecile wouldn't stop staring at me. I could tell Vince's presence had shaken her. She was paler than normal and kept wringing her hands together. Her face shifted from regret to anger to fear. A few times, she looked at me and opened her mouth to say something, then changed her mind.

Fine with me. I wasn't about to speak to her first. Especially not if she wanted to blame me for Vince being here. Because I had a feeling that was what she thought.

But it *couldn't* be true. Vince knew what he was giving up when he went into Luke's mind.

So . . . why *was* he back? He was a Timekeeper now, sure, but that didn't explain why he'd left the safety of Luke's mind.

As much as I kept shoving the thought away, part of me *did* wonder if he came back for me. The idea made me feel a mixture of anguish and excitement.

Dex and Finn were muttering to each other in low voices on the other side of the room. They kept casting dark looks toward Gio. I had no doubt they were still bitter about Gio's betrayal. I hadn't exactly gotten over it, either.

If anything happened to Benny or Vince because of Gio, I swore I would kill him.

We couldn't leave the cabin until Vince and Benny got back, otherwise they wouldn't know how to find us. But I was paranoid my father would return, now that he knew where we were.

Piper and I cast protective spells around the cabin to set up wards just in case Quentin came back. All the while, she blathered on about making plans, talking my ear off with suggestions for how to take down Quentin. She outlined every insignificant detail she could remember from living with him. I zoned her out after she spent ten minutes telling me about his eating habits.

As for me, I *wanted* to pace or run to blow off steam, but the cabin already felt so crowded. After Piper told her sixth story about Quentin grocery shopping, I fled the room and locked myself in the pantry to concoct more potions. I figured I might as well make myself useful.

Six potion vials later, I was covered in sweat when I heard

a faint *pop* from the living room. I jumped up so fast I almost knocked over the pot of ingredients. Wiping sweat from my brow, I rushed out of the pantry and flew into the living room, eyes wide.

Vince stood, his dark wings fluttering behind him and his face beet-red. His chest heaved as if he'd run a marathon. At his feet, bound in silver ropes, was Benny—in wolf form.

"*Benny*!" Gio rushed forward, drawing a knife from his belt to cut the ropes. As soon as he was free, Benny shifted to human form and collapsed on the couch, shivering madly. His face was pale and clammy, and his eyes were full of anguish.

"I'll get some blankets," Cecile said before leaving the room.

Gio looked between Benny and Vince. "Where—where's Maddie?" he demanded.

Benny shot Vince a dark look, and I frowned.

Vince opened and closed his mouth, then said, "She's with Hector."

"*Hector*?" I shouted. I hadn't meant to sound so shrill.

"I didn't have a choice!" Vince cried. "I was outnumbered. Quentin was about to kill Maddie or take the amulet from me, and I had to call for help. It was either give Maddie to Hector . . . or leave Benny to die."

I clamped my mouth shut, knowing I probably would've made the same choice. Leaving Maddie was out of the question. But leaving Benny with Quentin? My father would've killed him in seconds. Benny was our only shot at defeating Quentin.

"You . . . should've left me," Benny growled. He still looked weak, but there was fire in his eyes.

"Quentin would've *killed* you," Vince said in a hard voice. "You know it."

Benny clenched his teeth and said nothing.

"*Where is my daughter?*" Gio hissed, stepping closer to Vince. Though Vince was tall, Gio still towered over him.

To Vince's credit, he didn't flinch. He looked Gio straight in the eye and said in a loud voice, "Hector Moses!"

A small *pop*, and there was Hector, clutching a girl in his arms. Hector set Maddie down and fell to his knees, gasping for breath. His eyes were blazing as he glared at Vince. "Don't ever do that to me again."

Vince merely shrugged. I would've laughed if I weren't feeling so overwhelmed.

Gio rushed forward and untied his daughter, then drew her into his arms as he wept. They clutched each other so tightly that I almost felt I was intruding by watching.

Cecile returned with blankets and draped them around Benny, who smiled gratefully at her. Then, she turned to Vince and embraced him. Vince's face slackened in surprise, but he recovered and wrapped his arms around his mother.

Hector straightened and glanced around the room. His eyes widened when he saw Cecile, and she stiffened in response.

"What is *he* doing here?" she demanded, withdrawing from Vince and staring coldly at Hector.

"He's a Timekeeper," Vince explained. "Like me."

"So?" Finn asked, stepping forward. "You said that before. But that means nothing to me."

"Finn," I warned.

"Sorry, Cora, I know you guys are boning or whatever, but that's not enough reason for me to trust him."

My cheeks heated, and I resisted the urge to look at Vince. I balled my hands into fists and drew closer to Finn. "Vince is on our side. Quentin took over his home and enslaved his people. He's as much an ally as Cecile is."

Finn glanced warily at Cecile. "I'm not sure how much I trust her, either."

I threw up my hands in frustration. Lilith, I was so damn *tired.* I just wanted to escape from this mad house and get some rest. "Look, the *only* chance we have is if we work together. Everyone in this house—that's our army. That's *all we have.* You can't be in this halfway, Finn. Either you're with us or you're not."

Finn's mouth tightened. His nostrils flared, but he said nothing. Dex looked equally displeased.

"Before we do *anything* else, we need a new hideout," I said. "Quentin already knows we're here." I let my hands fall on my thighs. "I'm fresh out of safe houses. Anyone have any suggestions?"

Everyone remained silent. Then, cautiously, Dex lifted a finger. "I know a safe house. It's about fifty miles outside of Hinport, but . . ." He trailed off with a grimace.

"What?" I asked, trying to keep the bite out of my tone.

"It's a safe house for vampires," he said. "I frequented it

before joining the coven in Hinport. We might not be alone there."

My jaw ticked back and forth as I contemplated the idea of sharing a safe house with a crowd of vampires. Dex had warned that Quentin owned all the vampires in Hinport. But if this was outside the city, maybe we would be safe.

"Can we still cast protective wards?" I asked.

Dex nodded. "That won't be a problem."

"Then, I say we go." I glance around the room. "Everyone okay with this?"

Finn made a sour expression, and Piper looked deeply uncomfortable. But, nobody had a better idea, so we all agreed. Even Gio consented to bring Maddie there, which surprised me.

A few hours later, Vince had Jumped us all to the safe house, a grungy apartment complex on the east side of New Jersey. Piper helped me cast protective wards around the place, and then we headed upstairs to get situated. We passed by several unsavory characters lurking in the hallway whose sharp vinegar smell marked them as vampires. Though it was a tight fit, all ten of us shared one room. It was safer if we remained together.

Once we got settled, I leaned against the filthy wall. Horns honked outside, and the walls were so thin I could hear people shouting as if they were right next to me. Cecile wrinkled her nose, and Piper rubbed her arms, looking uneasy.

Hector spoke first. "I assume this means you have a plan."

"Nothing concrete," I admitted. "But we know how to take down Quentin."

A hushed silence fell. My eyes shifted to Benny. I hadn't *technically* asked if he was okay with this. But the grimness in his face as he met my gaze told me he was on board.

Benny took a deep breath and said, "We trap Quentin in my mind. Just like Vince was in Luke's mind."

Dex and Finn exchanged confused looks. Gio said, "What exactly does that mean?"

"I'm a Thinker, and I'm a Second Tier demon," Benny said. "My mental ability is powerful. It's the one thing Blood-casters can't replicate, although Quentin's certainly trying. If I get close enough to him to cast a spell, I can keep him housed in a mental prison. He won't be able to use his magic at all."

"And . . . what, he'll just hang out in your head forever?" Finn asked, raising a doubtful eyebrow.

Benny pressed his lips together and shook his head. "No. After we trap him, you'll need to kill me."

I sucked in a breath. Finn blanched, and Dex took a step forward, his eyes hard.

"Absolutely not," Gio growled. Fire blazed in his eyes.

"Benny, what are you talking about?" I hissed, pressing my hand against Benny's shoulder. "We *need* you."

"If you kill me with Quentin in my mind, it'll kill him too," Benny said. "It's the only way, Cora. You know it is."

"Can't you—can't you wipe his mind or something?" I knew I was grasping at straws, but I had to try. "Like he did to you? Make him forget who he is. Then, you can just spit him back out and we can kill him while he's confused."

Benny offered a sad smile, but it just made me angry. How was he being so *calm* about this?

"It'll take a monumental effort to cast the spell to trap someone as powerful as him," Benny said. "I won't have much strength left. You'll have to kill me quickly because I have no doubt Quentin will put up a fight, even without his magic."

"Benny—" I protested.

Gio interrupted. "Can't some other Thinker do this? Why does it have to be *you*?" His eyes were tortured. He still had one arm wrapped around Maddie, who watched our discussion with wide eyes.

"Do *you* know any other Second Tier Thinkers?" Benny challenged. "Even Luke wouldn't be able to handle this. Besides, we don't have time to track down another Thinker. Today was a close call. Next time, we might not be so lucky."

"Can't we use this?" Vince asked suddenly, lifting the gold amulet around his neck.

A few of us shared puzzled looks, but Cecile's face turned ashen. She quickly shoved his arm down and whispered, "Vince, *no*."

"Why not?" Finn demanded. "What *is* that thing?"

Cecile's mouth became thin as she looked fearfully at Finn. Her expression closed off, and I knew she would rather die than expose her clan's secrets.

But I was tired of the tension between us. I was tired of all this division and suspicion. "The amulet holds all the Reaper magic Quentin stole," I said in a tired voice.

Cecile stared at me, her mouth falling open. Shock and betrayal gleamed in her eyes.

Finn's eyes widened, and he whistled. "That *is* a powerful weapon. Add that to two Timekeepers on our side, and I don't see how we can lose!"

"Don't get cocky," I growled. "It's that kind of thinking that'll get us all killed."

"You can't use Reaper magic to kill," Cecile said sharply, still staring daggers at me. "Every Reaper makes a vow to use their magic for the healing and welfare of all souls. The magic doesn't work without upholding that vow."

"I just watched Vince use that magic to kick Quentin's ass," Benny snapped, gesturing to Vince. "No offense, but I don't think the vow applies to Vince anymore."

"Even if that's true, there's no way that magic is enough to stop him," Piper argued. "Kicking his ass and killing him are two entirely different things. If that magic could kill my father, you guys would've done that when you rescued Maddie."

"Can't we use the amulet to steal his magic like we did with the Reapers?" Vince asked.

Cecile shook her head. "It was made with Reaper magic, so it only applies to Reaper magic. And even if we *could* tether some sort of talisman to Bloodcaster magic, it can only be forged by a Bloodcaster. And, no offense, Cora, but you don't have enough power to match Quentin's. It wouldn't be enough."

I sighed. I knew it hadn't been an intentional insult, and I was too tired to care.

Several people started talking at once. Gio shouted something at Benny. Cecile waved her arms toward the amulet while Finn argued hotly with her. Piper raised her voice, trying to talk over us, but it was no use. My mind was a scrambled mess, and I wanted to scream. If I didn't get out of here soon—

A *pop* burst against my ears, and I started, my heart lurching in my throat. Vince appeared just a breath away from me. His wings were gone, and he looked at me, his gray eyes molten. Just his gaze seemed to quell the chaos inside me.

The others continued arguing around us, oblivious to Vince's Jump. Vince took my hands in his and whispered, "Want to get out of here?"

A hysterical laugh bubbled in my throat. "We shouldn't. It isn't safe to leave." As much as I wanted to just disappear with him, it would be reckless and stupid to leave the protection of the safe house.

Vince leaned closer, and his breath tickled my face. I suppressed a shiver of longing as he murmured, "I'm just taking us upstairs. But they won't know that, will they?" He winked.

Desire swirled in my stomach. A slow smile spread across my face, and I nodded eagerly. Vince wrapped me in his arms, spun in place, and with a *pop*, we vanished.

CHAPTER 12

VINCE

I JUMPED US TO AN EMPTY BEDROOM UPSTAIRS. IT WAS small, but it felt spacious compared to the overcrowded apartment below. Though the voices still echoed downstairs, the stillness around us was a relief. I breathed deeply, and the gratitude in Cora's face told me she felt the same way.

"Thank you," she whispered, pressing her forehead against mine. "I was about to murder someone."

I chuckled. "I guess I did us all a favor then."

Cora grinned and shoved my shoulder before sinking to the edge of the dusty mattress in the corner. It creaked under her weight. She buried her face in her hands. "I don't think I can do this, Vince."

I sat next to her so our shoulders were touching. "Yes, you can. You already are."

She shook her head, her face full of agony. "I've already

given up my coven. My *city*. So many are dead because of me. I—I can't lead *more* of my people to their deaths. And Benny —" Her voice cracked, and her face crumpled.

My heart twisted at the sight of her broken expression. I wrapped my arms around her and drew her against my chest. She clung to my shirt, burying her face in my shoulder.

Cora was never like this. And in that moment, I realized she was only breaking down because she was away from the others. She had to maintain the brave face of a leader when she was in charge. But now that we were alone, she could confront the emotions she'd buried deep.

I stroked her hair and pressed a kiss to the top of her head. "It's okay," I said. It wasn't true, but I wasn't sure what else to say. So, I just held her and murmured soothing words again and again. For as long as she needed me to.

After several minutes, shouts sounded from below. They must've realized Cora was missing. I chuckled and shook my head. "Can't believe it took them this long."

Cora snorted, her face still pressed against me. We held each other for a moment longer before she whispered, "Why are you here, Vince?"

My smile faded. "What do you mean?"

She withdrew to look at me. Her face was tired but clear. She scrutinized me, her eyes full of curiosity and wariness. "I mean, why did you escape from Luke's mind? I know you're a Timekeeper now, but *why*?"

My mouth opened and closed. I cleared my throat. "I—I couldn't be helpless anymore. And once I realized that becoming a Timekeeper gave me more options, more *power*, well . . . the decision seemed easy." I dropped my gaze. How could I tell her I'd seen her death over and over and I was desperate to prevent it? I wasn't even sure if it had been real. Hector had called it a test, but after I used the timeline to go backward and *see* the events before her death, it felt more real.

"But the amulet . . ." Cora trailed off and glanced at the gleaming trinket hanging from my neck.

I smiled and removed the chain from my neck, then held it up for Cora to see. She sucked in a breath and recoiled from it as if it might burn her. "I've already absorbed the magic. This is just for show. So Quentin can think he can take it from me."

Cora's eyes widened. "But . . . downstairs, you said . . . and with your mom . . ." She shook her head, exhaling in frustration.

I put the amulet back around my neck and offered an apologetic grimace. "That was also for show. I hate to say this, but I don't trust everyone downstairs." I leaned closer to her. "You're the only one I trust, Cora."

Her cheeks turned pink, and she bit back a smile. "Don't feel bad. I'm not sure I trust all of them, either. But they're the only allies we've got." Her face sobered, and she looked at me in concern. She lifted a hand and brushed her fingertips along the edges of the scar on my face. Though it still itched, it no longer stung, which was a relief. But the gentleness of Cora's touch made me shiver.

"What happened to you?" she whispered. She was so close that her breath tickled my face.

I swallowed, trying to quell the heat rising within me. "It was my first test as a Timekeeper." When she frowned, I added, "I had to prove that preserving the timeline was more important than taking away the pain."

Horror filled her eyes, and her mouth fell open. "They . . . cut open your face? To prove a *point*?"

When she put it that way, it *did* sound pretty ruthless. I shook my head. I didn't want to talk about my Timekeeper tests. If I did, I would have to tell her about seeing her death.

The scar on my face was real. So . . . didn't that mean the vision of her was real too?

I pushed the thought from my mind. "It doesn't matter now. What matters is I have the timeline on my side—and I have the Reaper magic too."

"So, you have *all* of the Reaper magic inside you?" Her voice was hushed. "How?"

I pressed my lips together as I considered this. The weight of the magic didn't feel nearly as overwhelming as when I'd first reaped from Quentin. But I knew the timeline was shouldering a lot of the weight. I wasn't quite sure how it worked, but it made it so much more manageable. "I have the Call," I told her. "That innate instinct that keeps me tethered to the timeline. It somehow grants me more strength. More power."

Cora's lips parted as she watched me, her face full of awe. "It's like you're Second Tier."

I shifted uncomfortably on the bed. Though I knew it was

a compliment in Cora's eyes, only demons could be Second Tier. The idea that *I* could be Second Tier didn't sit well with me.

Then again, when I became a Reaper, I gave up light magic. For all I knew, I *could* be a demon.

Cora read the distaste on my face and laughed. "Don't look so disgusted. If you haven't performed a blood ritual, you aren't *really* Second Tier. The whole point of Ascension is to sacrifice the blood of others to gain more power."

I suppressed a shudder. "Why haven't *you* done it?" I couldn't meet her gaze.

Cora remained silent for so long that I finally looked at her. Her expression was distant. "The excuse I give my coven is that I have no idea what happens when a Bloodcaster Ascends. But . . . if I'm being perfectly honest with myself, I don't *want* to Ascend. I mean, look at my father. What if Ascending turns me into a monster like him? I've heard horror stories of demons becoming addicted to blood magic." Her face twisted in a pained grimace. "I won't risk it."

Emotion climbed up my throat as I stared at the determined gleam in her eyes. My chest swelled with admiration. "I love that about you," I whispered.

Cora blinked in surprise. "What?"

"Even though you're the leader of a demon coven, even though demons are all you know, you still hold on to your principles. You still have lines you don't cross."

To my surprise, her eyes darkened, and she looked away

from me. Her brows creased, and she pressed her lips together.

"What's wrong?" I asked.

"Is that why you want to be with me?" she asked, finally meeting my gaze with tortured eyes. "Because you think I still have morals? I've crossed *every* line, Vince. If you're holding out hope that I can be redeemed, you're wrong."

My head reared back. "Cora, I didn't mean that."

"I'm not some broken thing, some lost cause you can fix."

"I *know* that."

"Really." Her voice was icy. "So, what kind of future do you envision for us? Let's say we *can* be together. Where would we even live? In my demon coven?" Her eyebrows lifted.

Panic raced through me. What the hell was happening? "I—yeah, if that's what you want," I sputtered. "I know how important your coven is to you."

Cora leveled a hard stare at me. "You'd be comfortable living in a city *full* of demons?" Her tone was dripping with doubt.

I shrugged. "Sure."

Her face slackened in surprise.

I offered a tentative smile. "You might've forgotten, Cora, that when I left my Nephilim clan, I abandoned all light magic. As a Reaper, technically, I can live among demons."

"*Are* you still a Reaper, though?" Cora asked softly. "Your mom said you gave up your Reaper magic before you went into Luke's mind. She said you looked so relieved, she'd be surprised if you rejoined the Reapers after all this is over."

My face fell. "She noticed that?" My gut twisted at the thought of Mom's disappointment. She'd been so proud to have me alongside her as a Reaper.

Cora placed her hand on my knee. "She knows you're free to make your own choices, Vince. She's still proud of you. Don't doubt that."

I looked at her in surprise. "Are you really defending my mother right now?" Last I checked, Mom and Cora weren't too fond of each other.

Cora smiled. "Maybe. But that doesn't answer my question. Are you still a Reaper?"

I inhaled deeply before answering. "No. I never felt comfortable around the Reapers and that kind of magic. I'll do whatever it takes to restore their power and their realm, but . . . I'm devoted to the Call now. Being a Timekeeper feels . . . right."

Cora nodded, her eyes full of relief. "Good. As long as that's what you want."

I ran my thumb along the length of her jaw. Her breath hitched. "*You're* what I want," I whispered.

She looked up at me, desire stirring in her eyes. I leaned in until our lips met. Her hand, still resting on my knee, slowly traveled up my leg until my whole body felt like it was on fire. Her mouth roved over mine, exploring as her body pressed up against me. Our kisses turned more urgent, more frantic. Our lips moved with desperation and a raw, feral *need.* Her teeth scraped along my lip, and a low groan built up my throat. Her tongue pressed against mine, gently at first, and then firm and demanding.

Footsteps thundered up the stairs, and we broke apart, gasping for breath. My head spun, and I couldn't see straight. All I could think about was how much I *needed* her body against mine. The wildness in her eyes told me she felt the same way.

"We wouldn't have gotten far anyway," Cora said breathlessly, her face red as she smoothed her hair behind her ears.

The door banged open, and Cora rose to her feet. It was Benny, his face rigid and his eyes full of fury. When he saw Cora standing there waiting for him, he relaxed slightly, though the rage in his face lingered.

"What the hell, Cora?" He lifted his hands in irritation.

"Sorry," Cora said. "I just needed . . . a minute."

Benny's gaze flicked to me. I had myself positioned strategically to hide just how aroused I was, but he saw right through me. His face hardened. "We don't have *time* for this."

Cora crossed her arms. "I said I needed a minute. *You* might be eager to get yourself killed, but I'm not. I had to escape. To process everything. It was either that, or gut someone. Which would you have preferred?"

Benny sighed and rubbed his forehead. When voices echoed in the hallway, he shouted, "I found them!"

Someone swore loudly. It sounded like Finn. Guilt wriggled through my stomach. Maybe it had been reckless to just disappear with Cora.

"It's my fault," I said. "I took Cora. It wasn't her idea."

Benny rolled his eyes. "Don't be a martyr, Vince. Come on. The others are waiting."

Cora shot an apologetic look in my direction before following Benny downstairs. I made for the door, but before I left the room, the air shifted. The sounds drifting from below vanished, leaving an eerie stillness in the apartment. Stunned, I glanced around, looking for the source. The air crackled with magic, powerful and yet unfamiliar.

Someone was here.

I rushed forward and found Cora frozen on the stairs in front of Benny. Their bodies were suspended mid-step as if time itself had stopped.

A small *pop* tickled my ears. I whirled and came face-to-face with a figure in a dark green robe, the hood concealing his face. I recognized the robe. This was what the Timekeepers wore—the *official* Timekeepers. The ones who now worked with Quentin.

My heart lodged itself in my throat. My fingers curled into tight fists at my side. "What do you want?" Thankfully, my voice came out level. But inside, every part of me was shaking.

The figure slowly lowered the hood to reveal a sharp, angular face—a woman's face. She had short, white-blond hair and shrewd green eyes. Her skin was so wan she looked like a ghost.

"Who are you?" I demanded.

"My name is Kallie," the woman said in a firm voice. "I'm a Timekeeper, and I've come to negotiate an alliance with you."

I staggered back a step. "An *alliance*? Are you insane?"

There was no way Quentin would offer that. Unless . . . "Quentin doesn't know you're here, does he?"

Kallie shook her head. "We are not his allies by choice."

Anger surged within me. "I find that hard to believe."

"Believe what you want," she snapped. "I wouldn't expect a boy like you to understand the risks involved. If we angered Quentin and he declared war, the Timekeepers would be obliterated. There would be no one left to preserve the timeline."

"There will *always* be Timekeepers," I said through clenched teeth. "There will *always* be a Call waiting for someone else to be tested."

Kallie lifted her chin, her eyes flashing. "Do not pretend you understand our ways, boy. Passing your tests doesn't make you an expert on Timekeepers."

My nostrils flared. "For someone offering an alliance, you have a funny way of showing it."

Kallie sighed, closing her eyes as if I were a petulant child and she was praying for patience. "If you agree to work alongside us, we can offer the Reapers protection from Quentin Cox."

I frowned. "Work alongside you doing *what*?"

Kallie blinked. "Preserving the timeline. Honoring the Call. It's what Timekeepers *do*." She looked at me like I was insane.

I rolled my eyes. "I know *that*. But I mean, what about Quentin? Will we take him down together?"

Kallie's lips tightened, and her jaw went rigid. Her silence answered my question.

I wasn't entirely surprised by this, but my stomach still sank with disappointment. I offered a cold smile. "Right. Then, consider your offer rejected."

Kallie's eyes blazed as she took a step closer to me. "I don't think you've considered the repercussions here. Quentin *will* find your little band of misfits, and he *will* end you all. I'm offering you a chance to save your people—your *mother*. As a Timekeeper, it's your duty to work alongside other chosen vessels of the timeline."

I straightened. "As a Timekeeper, I don't answer to you. I answer to myself—and to the Call."

Kallie's eyebrows lowered. "We *are* the Call, boy. We serve the same purpose."

I shook my head. "Maybe it's *you* who doesn't understand the Timekeeper ways. The Call is different for everyone."

Kallie's fingers curled into tight fists. "You dare lecture *me* about the Call? You are *nothing*. I've been a Timekeeper longer than you've been alive, than your *parents* have been alive. I know the Call so intimately that I could erase your existence without a second thought."

For one horrifying moment, I froze, my body going stiff with shock as I processed her words. The fire in her eyes told me she wasn't bluffing. And from the flare of gold power emanating from her, I believed she could do it. She could wipe me off the face of the earth.

I held my breath, unable to shake the sense that I was

puny and insignificant compared to this woman. She was right —I *was nothing*. Two days ago, I hadn't even been a Timekeeper. Who was I to challenge her?

But as I focused on that gold light inside me, it burned brighter, as if encouraging me onward. I lifted my chin. "The Call isn't one entity, but a multi-faceted part of every one of us. Unique to each individual. I don't care *who* you are. You do *not* own the Call."

Kallie took a step toward me, and it took all my will power not to shrink away from her fury. "Watch yourself. You're sounding a lot like the Timewatchers. And we both know history wasn't very kind to them."

I stiffened. Another threat—albeit a thinly-veiled one. And how did *she* know I knew the story?

Kallie cocked her head at me, her eyes full of icy rage. "You've made yourself an enemy today, Vince Delgado. I hope it doesn't come back to haunt you."

Before I could respond, she vanished with a *pop*. Time resumed with her departure. The voices downstairs returned, and Cora and Benny's steps echoed on the staircase.

For a long moment, I stood there, frozen, as I stared at the spot where Kallie had disappeared and wondered if I'd made a grave mistake.

CHAPTER 13

CORA

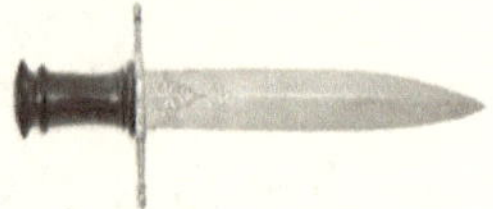

PIPER, FINN, GIO, AND CECILE WORE SOUR EXPRESSIONS when Benny and I returned. Piper's arms were crossed as she said coolly, "Very funny disappearing act, Cora."

I shrugged. I wasn't sorry. They had been arguing like toddlers. "I'm assuming you all didn't form any solid plans while I was gone?"

Silence. I raised my eyebrows, trying not to look smug. "I thought not." I clapped my hands, feeling much more capable than I had half an hour ago. "Let's brainstorm over dinner."

While I searched for my bag, the door opened, and Vince entered. I glanced up at him. His face was pale and drawn, and his eyebrows were lowered. His gaze was hard as he stared distantly at something I couldn't see.

I opened my mouth to ask him what was wrong, but Cecile spoke first.

"You shouldn't have done that, Vince," she chided.

Vince blinked as if suddenly realizing there were other people in the room. "What?"

Cecile let her arm fall against her thigh and shot him an exasperated look. The expression was so motherly, so *normal,* that it made me ache for something as mundane as an argument with a parent. Instead, I was facing world domination from a parent.

"You can't just take your girlfriend and disappear," Cecile said. "You both have a responsibility, and you can't abandon it whenever you feel like."

Vince swallowed and nodded, his eyes still far away. "Right. Sorry."

Cecile seemed to notice as well. She frowned at her son.

I focused on the bag in front of me, digging through until I found the canned goods I'd stolen a few days ago. Finn noticed my movements and said grumpily, "Another feast of canned beans tonight?"

Dex winced apologetically. "Yeah, sorry. Human food isn't really a priority in a vampire safe house."

"Don't worry about it," I said at once, though my stomach growled, and my taste buds *ached* for something fresh.

Instead, I handed out cans of baked beans and ravioli, as well as some plastic cutlery. We all sat in a circle in the middle of the room as if we were camping together. Though Finn wrinkled his nose—and Lilith knew I was also tired of canned food—we still devoured it hungrily.

After a few bites, I got down to business. "The first thing

we'll do is find the spell to trap Quentin in Benny's mind. We can't move forward without it."

Vince exchanged a look with Cecile. "Gwen cast the spell before. I don't remember her exact words, though."

Cecile nodded. "I can jot down what I remember."

"What about ingredients?" I asked.

"I remember what she used," Cecile said. "I'll make a list."

I offered a grateful smile, but she responded with an icy stare. *Still pissed about my vanishing act, I see.*

Dropping my gaze, I said, "We also shouldn't stay here for much longer. The only thing that kept us alive this long was constantly being on the move."

Benny frowned. "But you cast protective wards, right? And we have a Jumper who can get us out of here in a flash."

Vince shot him a flat look. "I can't Jump *seven* other people in one go. Even getting everyone here took multiple trips."

Benny arched an eyebrow. "Really? Your special Reaper magic can't help with that?" He gestured to the amulet.

Cecile stiffened, her eyes tightening, but she said nothing. I knew she was sensitive about how cavalier Vince was about using the Reaper magic. But at this point, we needed every weapon we could get. Reaper vows be damned.

Vince sighed. "It's still a risk. I've never Jumped that many people at once. I can take maybe three."

"Okay, so if Quentin shows up, Vince can take Benny and Cora," Cecile said. "The rest of us are expendable."

A grave silence fell between us. Finn choked on his food and cleared his throat loudly. "Uh, *expendable*?"

Cecile sighed. "Meaning, the war can't be won without them. If Quentin gets Vince, he gets the Reaper magic. If he gets Cora, he gets Bloodcaster magic. And Benny's our only hope of trapping and killing Quentin." When no one responded, she raised her eyebrows. "Am I wrong?"

"You're not," I said quietly. "But I like to think *none* of my allies are expendable."

Cecile stared at me, and I matched her gaze, refusing to back down.

"Either way," Benny said, "I think we're safe for now. No one but us knows we're here."

Vince shifted in his chair. "That's not necessarily true."

I blinked and broke eye contact with Cecile to frown at Vince. "What do you mean?"

Vince pressed his lips together, avoiding my gaze. "A Timekeeper contacted me."

My jaw dropped, and Benny stiffened. "What?" he growled.

"She offered an alliance, but I refused when she made it clear I'd have to join Quentin." Vince's expression soured. "She said I made an enemy of her. I'm worried that she'll share our location with Quentin."

My blood ran cold. "When did this happen?"

Vince finally met my gaze. "Right before we came downstairs."

Shocked, I gaped at him. "Why didn't you say that in the first place? Vince, she could've told Quentin by now!"

Vince shook his head. "I don't think she has. At least, not yet. She seems to be the type who likes to be in control. I can tell she doesn't like working for him. If she has information that could benefit him, she's going to wait until sharing it works in her favor."

"That's not a guarantee," Benny said sharply.

"She had no trouble finding us," Vince argued. "She could've done it earlier and turned us over to Quentin."

"She still might," Benny snapped. "You should've told us immediately."

"You're right," Vince said. "I'm sorry." His eyebrows pinched, and his face filled with regret and confusion. At that moment, he looked so lost and conflicted that I just wanted to wrap my arms around him and hold him close. He'd only just become a Timekeeper. And his first interaction with another of his kind had resulted in a declaration of war.

Suddenly, I stilled. "Where's Hector?"

"He left when you did," Benny said in a tight voice. "I guess he figured if our leader could disappear, then he could too."

I glared at him. "Has no one considered that *Hector* would lead Quentin to us?"

"He won't," Vince said at once. "The Call won't let him."

I refrained from rolling my eyes. The Call might have been real to Vince and Hector, but it wasn't real to me. Repeating Benny's words, I said, "That's not a guarantee."

"It is," Benny said, surprising me. "The Call is ingrained in his brain. He'll literally go insane if he tries to refuse. From what we know, Quentin's very existence is a threat to the timeline. Hector won't do anything for him and risk his brain turning into mush."

I shuddered at the thought, even though a small part of me thought Hector deserved it.

"How can the Timekeepers join Quentin if this . . . Call thingy is so against him?" Finn asked, waving his hand nonsensically as he spoke.

"The Call is different for everyone," Vince said, his eyes darkening. "For some, like Hector, it's physically impossible for them to disobey. For others, it isn't."

Finn frowned as if waiting for more, but Vince didn't go on.

Steeling my nerves, I said, "We'll stay here for three days and then move on. Everyone good with that?"

The others grumbled their assent, and I considered the matter settled.

"Now that we've established who's expendable and whether or not the enemy knows where we are," Piper said in a sarcastic tone, "shall we discuss the big question? *How* do we isolate Quentin and cast this mind spell on him?"

Silence fell between us. Everyone dropped their gazes or shifted uncomfortably on the floor. I couldn't blame them. Every time we'd faced off with Quentin, it had been a disaster. He was always one step ahead of us.

One step ahead . . . My eyes snapped to Vince. "Can, uh, the *timeline* help us?" I felt stupid saying it, but I knew it was a tangible thing for Vince. Like another presence inside him along with his magic.

Vince's gaze grew distant. "Maybe. But it might be difficult because—"

"Because Quentin has Timekeepers on his side," Benny finished. "Vince isn't the only one who can access the timeline."

My insides squirmed at the thought of the Timekeepers altering time to screw us over. And we would have no idea it was happening.

"But if we have Hector and Luke on our side," Vince said slowly, "we might have a better chance."

"You want to drag *more* strangers into this?" Finn snapped. "That's just asking for this to blow up."

I rolled my eyes. "Settle down, Finn. Hector and Luke are already involved. They're on our side."

"Says you," Finn grumbled. Ordinarily, I would bite his head off for that, but I was too tired. We were all on edge right now.

"I'll contact Luke," Benny offered.

"And I can reach out to Hector," Vince said, though he looked deeply uncomfortable with the idea.

I nodded. "Good. Thank you. In the meantime, we all should get some rest. We can brainstorm more tomorrow." I hoped that with the addition of Luke and Hector, we could formulate a plan to incapacitate Quentin long enough to trap him. Maybe Vince could freeze time while Luke did some mind trick on Quentin or whatever. I had no idea how their powers worked. But with so many of us, Quentin couldn't possibly stop us all at once. If we hit him relentlessly, never stopping, never giving him a free moment, surely we had to overpower him.

I tried to believe it . . . but deep down, I feared this mission was already doomed to fail.

CHAPTER 14

VINCE

EVEN THOUGH VAMPIRES DIDN'T SLEEP, DEX STILL MANAGED to find a bunch of dusty sleeping bags in the cellar. After shaking them out thoroughly, we all spread out between the living room and two bedrooms to get some sleep.

It was uncomfortable. And several people snored like warthogs. I was pretty sure one of them was Gio.

For what felt like hours, I lay on the floor, staring up at the dark ceiling. I didn't feel tired at all. I had a feeling Cora was also awake and restless. Though I longed to track her down and talk with her, I forced myself to stay put. She needed rest more than any of us. I had to leave her be.

At long last, I sat up and made my way to the bathroom. After the door was shut, I whispered hesitantly, "Hector? Can you hear me?"

For a moment, nothing happened, and I felt like a

complete idiot. Then, a small *pop*, and Hector appeared. His eyes were tired, and his face was drawn. He crossed his arms and glanced around the bathroom with an arched eyebrow. “Uh, you rang?”

“Sorry,” I said. “It’s just . . . you left, and—well, you’re already pretty untrustworthy.”

Hector rolled his eyes in a very un-Hector-like manner. “There’s a surprise.”

I eyed him warily. “Where did you go?”

“Back into Luke’s mind. I figure it’s the safest place right now.”

My head reared back. “Why the hell are you invading his head like that? Leave him alone.”

Hector snorted. “He says he doesn’t mind.”

I found that hard to believe. Though Luke and Hector were both Timekeepers, it was no secret Luke detested Hector.

Hector’s face sobered. “Look, I’m not proud of it. But I worry if Quentin gets close to me, my brain will—” He tapped his temple, and an anguished look filled his face.

I stared at him. This was the powerful Nephilim who'd had no qualms with banishing his own kind, who stripped *my mother* of her powers, who sought my life. Was he really so cowardly he would run from a fight?

“Don’t look at me like that,” Hector snapped. “I’m not who I was before. The Call changed me. Thanks to you.”

I lifted my chin. Guilt wriggled inside me, but I squashed it down. “You tried to kill me.”

Hector sighed. "Yeah. I know."

An awkward silence filled the space between us. I crossed my arms. "We need to know if you're on our side. If you're willing to fight Quentin with us."

Hector's gaze darkened. "I thought I made it clear I won't go anywhere near Quentin."

I raised my eyebrows. "Really? You'll just keep on letting him wreak havoc and destroy the timeline?"

Hector flinched as if I'd struck him. His eyes were haunted, and he raised his hands to his head. His arms shook, and he gritted his teeth. "N-no," he said in a strained voice. "No, I can't. As much as I want to stay out of this, I . . . can't."

He sounded so pitiful, I almost felt bad for him.

"But I'm not sure how much help I'll be if Quentin has Timekeepers on his side," Hector added.

I stilled, remembering my unpleasant encounter with Kallie. "How many Timekeepers are there?"

"Like in the world?"

I nodded.

"Oh, thousands. But they're scattered all over the globe. Within the official Timekeeper organization, there's just a hundred or so."

I frowned. "Is there a way to contact the others? The ones who *aren't* part of the organization?"

Hector stroked his chin in contemplation. "Maybe. But it would be difficult. You can technically summon any Timekeeper by calling their name, but it will be tricky if we don't know who they are."

I chewed on the inside of my lip as I considered this. Surely, it couldn't be *impossible*. I'd been able to locate Maddie, and she was a complete stranger. But I'd had something that belonged to her. What if . . .

My eyes widened. "What if we locate them *using* the timeline? Sort of like an anchor?"

Hector's face paled at the word, and I didn't blame him. He'd had a rather unpleasant experience as a time travel anchor, after all. "I—I don't know if that's a good idea, Vince."

Once again, I was struck by how *different* Hector was. He was practically trembling with fear. He'd once been powerful enough to strike a person down just by flexing his wings.

"I'm not asking *you* to do it," I said. "But if there *are* other Timekeepers out there who aren't under Quentin's thumb, we need to find them. I want to try. If it's not a good idea, the Call will stop me."

Hector stared at me, his eyes darkening. "I thought you believed obeying the Call was merely a *choice*."

I hesitated before responding. "I haven't fully formed an opinion on that yet." It seemed like the safest answer. I wasn't about to share with Hector the revelation that the Call was inside us and was a part of who we were. Somehow, I didn't think Hector would appreciate knowing his mental trauma was just a byproduct of being *himself*.

Besides, I'd only just become a Timekeeper. Like Luke, I hadn't yet disagreed with the Call. Right now, the Call was on my side. I hoped it stayed that way.

"Just be careful," Hector warned. "If *you* can access other

Timekeepers via the timeline, then others might be able to as well."

"Like Kallie," I muttered without thinking.

Hector blanched. "You've met Kallie?"

I nodded. "Pleasant woman."

Hector shook his head. "Don't underestimate her, Vince. She's *powerful.* She's been a Timekeeper longer than anyone else in the world."

My brow furrowed. "Who is she?"

"She's the leader of the Timekeepers. She's been the head of the organization for at least a decade."

A decade. My heart dropped to my stomach like a stone. I'd only been a Timekeeper for a few days. But she had over a *decade* of experience manipulating the timeline to her advantage.

"Timekeepers like Kallie," I said slowly, "believe in following the Call no matter what. Right?"

Hector nodded. His eyes narrowed slightly in suspicion. "Why?"

I swallowed. "Just . . . trying to understand her. That's all." In truth, I was trying to determine whether or not I could disobey the Call and use that to my advantage. Was I capable of that? Would I be able to handle whatever consequences followed?

I'll cross that bridge when I come to it, I decided. I didn't even know for sure if it would happen.

My eyes shifted to Hector, who still watched me shrewdly.

Clearing my throat, I said, "I'll try locating the other Timekeepers. Stay close. If it works, I may need your help."

Hector watched me, his expression stony. He took a breath, then hesitated. He straightened and said, "I have to tell you, Vince, that if you plan to defy the Call, I can't be your ally." He leveled a stern gaze that reminded me of when he'd been my superior among the Nephilim.

I blinked. "I would never ask you to do that."

We stared at each other for a long moment. I refused to back down, though the fire in his eyes made me want to shrink away.

He's weak, I reminded myself. *He isn't the power-hungry tyrant he used to be.*

"We both want to take down Quentin," I said quietly. "That puts us on the same side."

Hector's expression remained unyielding. "For now."

With a small *pop*, he vanished, leaving me alone in the bathroom. A sense of foreboding rippled over me, but I squashed it down before opening the door.

I came face-to-face with Finn. My heart jolted, and I staggered back a step. My heart pounded madly in my chest. "Uh, hi, Finn. Sorry, are you waiting for the bathroom?"

Finn's eyes narrowed. He towered over me by several inches, and his thick muscles told me I wouldn't stand a chance in a fight. I swallowed and tried looking more confident than I felt.

Finn leaned close and hissed, "I don't trust you, Reaper.

Or your mom. Consider this a warning. You betray us, and I'll slit your throat myself."

I nodded. "Right. Okay. Got it."

Finn didn't move. His jaw was rigid as he stared me down.

I sighed. "I'm *not* going to betray anyone, Finn. I love Cora. I wouldn't do that to her."

Something in Finn's eyes softened, but then his expression closed off again. "Love is volatile. It's dangerous. It makes us do strange things. Things we wouldn't normally do." His voice sounded strained, and I wondered if he'd lost someone. Quentin had razed Hinport to the ground. *Everyone* in Cora's coven had lost someone.

"I won't betray you," I repeated in a hard voice.

Finn blinked at me. We stared each other down, and thankfully, I didn't flinch. At long last, Finn cleared his throat. "Good. Well . . . if you don't mind, I actually do need to take a piss, so . . ."

"Oh. Sure." I stepped out of the bathroom to let Finn do his business.

I lay awake for hours, unable to shake the lingering unease from my conversations with Hector and Finn. After a while, I gave up and climbed to my feet, stepping over the sleeping bodies around me to ensure I didn't wake anyone up.

. . .

A part of me hoped Cora was awake too, but I passed by her sleeping figure. Her brows were knitted together, her mouth puckered in a small frown. Even in her dreams, she was distressed. I wished I could help her somehow. For a moment, I watched her, my mind in agony at the thought of Cora in pain—and me, helpless to save her.

The image of her dead body flashed in my mind, and I flinched, trying to shove the memory away. But once it entered my mind, it festered and throbbed like an infected wound that only got worse. Her wide, empty eyes. Her limp, motionless body. The ghostly pallor of her skin.

Dead. Because I couldn't save her.

My fingers curled into fists and I forced my gaze away from Cora. Fretting over her death—which might not even happen—wouldn't do either of us any good.

I found the food stash and rustled through until I found a bottle of water. With a sigh, I leaned against the wall and took several small sips, hoping my body would magically get tired so I could sleep.

But something odd prickled in my mind, like the nagging feeling that I was forgetting something. A strange stillness surrounded me, a bubble of silence that made my skin tingle.

Suddenly, I straightened, realizing what was wrong. The room was completely silent. No snores. No deep breaths. No creaking of floorboards as someone shifted in their sleep.

Time was frozen.

Which meant a Timekeeper was here. Someone powerful enough to stop time.

A hard lump formed in my throat. I set my bottle of water down and slowly gazed around the room, searching for the newcomer. My eyes settled on a hooded figure in the corner of the room.

My blood ran cold as the intruder drew nearer. Panicked breaths crashed through me violently, but I forced myself to move, to ensure my magic was alive inside me, ready to assist if needed.

Slowly, the figure lowered the dark green hood to reveal a white-haired woman I recognized. Kallie.

My terror abated slightly, but my unease remained. I lifted my chin. "What're you doing here?"

Kallie's green eyes sharpened. "I came to see if you'd reconsidered my offer."

I crossed my arms. "I thought I made myself clear. I will *not* ally myself with Quentin."

Kallie watched me for a moment, her eyes cold and calculating. "I thought you might say that. Perhaps you need a little more convincing." She raised both hands.

My Reaper magic burst forward in defense, but before I could move, Kallie brought her hands together. An explosion of gold light filled the room, blinding me. Spirals of black smoke swirled within the depths of the gold light, like darkness tainting the purity of the timeline. I was mesmerized, stunned and frozen by the sight of it. What did it mean? Was the timeline broken?

Then, Kallie's voice echoed in my ears. "You think you

know power, boy? You know nothing. Look at what I have at my disposal. What I could *teach* you."

A multitude of images slammed into me, blurring together like a sickening carousel. My stomach churned as I tried focusing on each image like I did when I time traveled. But the Call wasn't responding to me. It was like Kallie had frozen that too.

She had complete control. All I could do was watch.

The images slowed until one came into focus. My eyes narrowed as I tried to see what it was.

My heart lurched. It was Luke. He sat huddled in an alley, his hair overgrown and matted with dirt. He shivered against the wind, teeth chattering and limbs quivering. A few people passed by on the sidewalk. Luke scooted closer, begging for spare change, but no one responded. One woman wrinkled her nose and quickened her pace to avoid him.

Dejected, Luke leaned against the muddy brick wall, his expression anguished. His eyes were haggard, and he looked like he hadn't slept—or eaten—in days.

"What is this?" I demanded loudly, looking around for Kallie. But my eyes kept darting back to Luke. The sight of him so frail and miserable chilled me to the bone.

"This is his future," Kallie's voice echoed.

I shook my head. "No. You're lying."

"The timeline doesn't lie, Vince. If you refuse my offer, this is what becomes of your friend. Quentin will wage war. He will slaughter the ones you love. Some will escape, like your friend here, but they will have no allies. No one to turn to.

"But if you join me, together we can reunite the Timekeepers. We can overpower Quentin and change the fate of the world. It's in *your* hands, Vince."

"*Liar*," I growled, my fists clenched so tightly my fingernails dug into my palms. I blinked tears from my eyes as Luke collapsed to the ground, huddling in a fetal position to keep warm. "You expect me to believe someone like *me* can cause a future this drastic? I'm nothing. You told me that yourself."

"You may be inexperienced, but your reach extends farther than you think. You're connected to the Reapers, the Timekeepers, the demons of Hinport . . ." Kallie trailed off, and I swallowed hard, trying not to let her words get to me. "What do you think will happen to your friends if you fail?"

I closed my eyes, trying to block Luke's broken expression from my mind. If we failed . . . if Cora didn't find a way to beat Quentin, then he'd hunt us down. He'd kill us all one by one. Or torture us for information, just like he'd done to the Reapers.

The ground shifted beneath me, and my eyes snapped open. The world spun once more until another image appeared before me.

My mother, sobbing on the floor. Her once magnificent black wings were nothing more than broken and bloody stumps. Feathers surrounded her as she wept, her shoulders trembling. My throat closed, and I couldn't breathe. Even though I *knew* it wasn't real, that Mom was actually sound asleep with her wings intact, I couldn't stop the wretched grief from filling my chest.

"Quentin will find her and cut off her wings," Kallie said softly. "She will live her life as a crippled Reaper as punishment for her betrayal."

My lip trembled. I wanted to shout at her, to tell her I didn't believe her, but my mouth was frozen shut.

The images spun again. Then, I stood in front of my dad, who sat in a filthy prison cell, his hair lank and gray as if he'd been a prisoner for ten years.

Bile crept up my throat. *No,* I thought in horror.

More spinning images. Jocelyn's head was shaved, her arms covered in blood. Her face contorted in pain as she screamed. The image vanished, and then Cora lay on the ground, encircled by demons. They chanted and raised their blades before slicing into their palms. Purple magic filled the air, and Cora's body shuddered and then went still. In the distance, Quentin's laughter echoed as Cora's magic funneled into him.

Dozens of images filled my mind, and I couldn't stop them. Thousands of witches and warlocks enslaved, their hands cuffed in chains. Cities leveled to the ground, armies fighting. Quentin taking control of one coven after another, the Timekeepers powerless to stop him.

"Stop, stop, *stop*!" I roared, covering my face with my hands as I tried to block out the horrors Kallie forced on me.

The air twisted around me, revealing something different. I lowered my hands, my mouth falling open in shock.

Before me stood a group of people. Cora, Mom, Dad,

Luke, and . . . *Kallie.* We huddled together, discussing how to take down Quentin. The group of people grew in size. Hector joined us. Then, the rest of the Reapers. Cora's demons. Soon, we'd amassed a small army to take down Quentin. The images distorted until Quentin's terrified face came into view. He stood before a throng of over a thousand people who were ready fight him. At the head of the army was Kallie, and next to her was . . . *me*.

My mouth turned dry. This wasn't real. It couldn't be real.

"One small step turns into something mighty," Kallie said. Gradually, the gold light melted away, and we stood once more in the darkened apartment, surrounded by sleeping figures. Kallie watched me with sympathetic eyes. "You may think you're nothing, Vince, but you can set off a chain of events that will save the world."

My whole body went cold. I couldn't speak. Couldn't move. Kallie *had* to be lying . . . but I didn't know what to believe. Would the timeline deceive me like this? Was this even the timeline at all? What about my Timekeeper test, when I'd seen Cora's dead body? Had that been real, or a trick just like this?

"If you want to save the people you love," Kallie murmured, stepping closer to me, "you *must* join me. You don't have to like me or follow my practices. But Quentin is our common enemy. And together, we can take him down. From the inside."

I licked my lips and met her gaze. Sorrow and empathy stirred in her eyes. She extended her hand to me, and my fingers twitched in response. My body ached to accept her offer, to save my family. To save Cora.

But as I stared at Kallie, a tiny beam of gold light shone inside me. A feeble attempt to grab my attention.

The Call. It was still here. And as I focused on it, clarity burst in my mind. Kallie's affectionate eyes turned cold and cunning. Her lips curled in triumph. She *knew* she had me.

"No!" I barked, stepping away from her. "You can go to hell, Kallie. I will *never* join you."

Kallie's face slackened in surprise. She quickly composed herself, her jaw rigid and her eyes fiery. "You are a *fool*, Vince. And your friends will suffer for your stupidity."

Her green cloak swirled, and she vanished. Time resumed, and snores and heavy breathing surrounded me once more. My skin felt clammy. I slumped backward against the wall, my heart drumming a panicked rhythm inside me.

CHAPTER 15

CORA

THE NEXT FEW DAYS PASSED IN A SLUGGISH BLUR OF arguments and migraines. Our ragtag group of rebels couldn't agree on *anything*. Finn and Gio wanted to storm Quentin's headquarters immediately, arguing that we needed to take advantage since we knew where it was. Vince, Piper, and Dex argued in favor of infiltrating through stealth and disguises to get as close to Quentin as possible without him knowing. Benny suggested setting a trap for Quentin to lure him out, but I shot the idea down. I'd tried that twice with my father and knew he would see it coming a mile away.

Cecile remained oddly quiet during our discussions. Her gaze was distant, and she often sat with Maddie, Gio's daughter, to keep her company during all this. The haunted and tormented look on Cecile's face told me she was worried for her fellow Reapers. I didn't blame her.

Which made it even more imperative that we strike *soon*. My blood thrummed with impatience. My body itched to fight, to hunt, to *kill*. I hadn't hunted in months, and I ached from that absence. It resonated through me, making everything throb and fester. I often paced the length of the living room while we argued. Finn made an irritable comment about it, but after I held my dagger to his throat, he backed off.

Vince wanted to bring Hector and Luke to our hideout. Finn and Dex hated the idea, claiming they already didn't trust everyone here. Bringing others would only be asking for Quentin to show up next.

But as I watched Vince go quiet, his gaze contemplative, I knew he was planning something of his own. Something related to the timeline.

Two days after we arrived at the hideout, I pulled Vince aside once we broke for lunch. "What're you thinking?" I whispered.

He blinked at me. "What do you mean?"

"Cut the crap, Vince. You're planning something. What is it?" He'd admitted he wore the amulet as an act. If he *was* planning something big, it made sense he would keep it to himself.

Vince sighed and glanced around to make sure no one was eavesdropping. In a low voice, he said, "I want to try to find the other Timekeepers."

I frowned and shook my head. "The ones who are with Quentin?"

"No, the ones who *aren't*. The rogue Timekeepers like

Hector who forge their own path. They're scattered around the world, but if I can track them down, I can Jump them here. It could give us an *army* of people who can manipulate time, Cora. Imagine what advantage that would give us!"

My throat felt dry at the thought. With each passing day, a weight sank heavier in my stomach, reminding me that our odds of success were slim. We likely would all be killed in a week's time.

But imagining an army of Timekeepers fighting alongside us made me feel an alarming amount of hope. And hope was dangerous for me right now.

I swallowed hard, trying to shove the feeling away. "Are you sure you can do that?" Vince was still new at this whole Timekeeping thing.

Vince's brows pinched. "That's the thing. No one really knows how to contact a Timekeeper you've never met before. That's why I want Luke and Hector here. For guidance."

I bit my lip as I considered this. "What do you need from me?"

"Just time." He snorted when he realized his pun. "I mean, when I *do* attempt to reach out, I'll be far from here. Just in case the other Timekeepers are being watched. If they *are,* it'll be a trap, and I want to make sure I don't lead Quentin straight to you."

Worry wriggled in my stomach. "If it *is* a trap, it'll mean you're on your own."

"I know." He held my gaze, unwavering. The scar on his

face and the firmness of his jaw made him look fierce and determined. It was enough to set my insides on fire.

I pressed my hand against his cheek, and his eyes softened. "Do what you need to," I said. "I trust you, Vince. Just be careful."

He smiled and nodded.

After lunch, I decided we'd wasted enough time arguing. Clapping my hands, I got everyone's attention and said loudly, "It's time we make a move. I've heard your suggestions and concerns. And I think we won't get *anywhere* unless we make a choice and stick with it. Right now, the safest option is to get as close as we can and do reconnaissance. Stay undetected. Observe patterns and behavior. We need information. Numbers, weaknesses, plans . . . After we've gathered enough intel, we can decide on another course of action." I raised my eyebrows and spread my arms. "Everyone on board with this?"

Piper and Vince nodded emphatically. Finn and Gio looked doubtful but made no objections.

Another moment of silence, and then my chest swelled with relief. *Thank Lilith we agreed on something.* Clearing my throat, I said, "Great. I'll track down a new hideout for us—somewhere closer to Hinport. Benny and Piper, I need you to start researching the mind spell to use on Quentin. Cecile can help with this."

Cecile looked up, her eyes wide with surprise like a deer in the headlights. I had the distinct impression she thought she'd become invisible.

"We need to have the mind spell ready to go as soon as we

get close enough," I went on. "That way, if Quentin *does* catch us, we can put it into action."

"That's the part where you sacrifice my brother for the greater good, right?" Gio asked in a clipped tone.

Shock jolted through me. A tense, awkward silence filled the room. I shifted my weight from one foot to the other.

Benny shot a warning look at Gio. "I volunteered. You got a better idea?"

Gio's mouth clamped shut, but his eyes blazed.

I exhaled slowly. My throat felt tight, but I forced myself to say, "Right. With this plan in mind, let's pack up and leave by tomorrow."

We adjourned, and everyone started packing up their bags. We didn't have much, but I sensed an eagerness in the air—an excitement about moving forward. It seemed like we'd been in limbo for so long, wandering aimlessly with no plan. It felt good to be proactive. Things were changing. Hopefully for the better.

To my surprise, Cecile approached me, wringing her hands together. Her face was drawn, and dark circles lined her eyes. She looked terrible.

"I don't think we should leave," she said. "At least not yet."

I frowned. "Why not?"

"I think we need a more solid plan first. Maybe send just one person to scope out the area first to ensure it's safe."

I stared at her. Her skin was paler than normal, and she'd lost weight recently. She seemed so *feeble.* It was heartbreaking, but for some reason, it only made me angry.

"You've kept quiet this whole time," I said in a hard voice. "You didn't bother speaking up in *any* of our meetings. And now you suggest we should stay put? Why are you telling me this *now*?"

Cecile opened and closed her mouth, her eyes wide. I raised my eyebrows expectantly, and she pressed her lips together. With a shrug, she muttered, "Just a hunch. Do what you want."

Before I could respond, she walked away. I stared after her, confused. What the hell had just happened? This wasn't the fierce and headstrong Reaper I'd come to know. The woman who was hell-bent on protecting her son from a manipulative demon like me. The woman who'd volunteered herself to be imprisoned in Luke's mind.

What had happened to her?

I watched Cecile disappear into the bedroom and tried to shake off the feeling that something was very, very wrong with her. I turned to Dex, who leaned casually against the wall, his expression pensive.

"I don't suppose you know of any other hideouts near Hinport?" I asked.

Dex grimaced and shook his head. "Sorry."

"Care to join me while I scope out a few places?" I'd found a few good safe houses over the years, but I had to make sure they were still secure.

Dex's eyebrows lifted in surprise. "Me? Why?"

I smiled. "You're a vampire. You know how to stay hidden

and under the radar. We'll grab Vince so he can Jump us there and back."

Dex nodded and straightened. I glanced around the room, looking for Vince. Before I could find him, the front door crashed open with a deafening bang that rattled my eardrums. My blood chilled, my pulse racing as several figures swept into the room. At first, I thought they were vampires from down the hall, but one whiff told me they were various demons—werewolf, dark warlock, dark witch . . . And some of them seemed oddly familiar.

My comrades were on their feet, surrounding me, preparing to fight if necessary. Many drew weapons, and I slid my own dagger out of its holster. Vince appeared beside me, his huge dark wings fanning out behind him. Benny shifted easily to his wolf form and bared his teeth at the newcomers.

More than a dozen demons stood in front of us, bodies poised to attack. And yet, they remained still. I swallowed hard, knowing we were outnumbered. Maddie whimpered in fear, and Gio shoved her behind him, his face taut with fury.

"What do you want?" I stepped forward, hoping to draw their attention to me. I didn't want them seeing Maddie and getting any ideas. She was helpless, and as soon as they knew that, they could use her against us.

Heavy footsteps thudded against the wood floors as one last figure entered the room. I sucked in a breath. It was Quentin. He cocked his head and offered a cold smile. "Hello, Cordelia."

How did he find us? A shiver ran down my spine, but I

straightened and leveled a hard gaze at him. "I see you brought friends this time. Afraid to face me on your own?"

Quentin laughed. "Just leveling the playing field." His eyes glinted. "Don't you recognize them?"

My heart hammered madly in my chest, my instincts screaming at me that something was wrong here. Slowly, my gaze roved over the demons facing us. Then, realization struck me.

They were demons from Hinport. From *my city.* They weren't from my coven—almost everyone else had died—but I still knew them. Some I'd negotiated contracts with. Some had been involved in a few skirmishes with my coven. Neighbors, allies, acquaintances, disgruntled employees, coworkers . . .

Quentin was using *my city* against me.

My nostrils flared and I gritted my teeth, glaring at the smug expression on my father's face. He *knew* this was a blow to me. He could've gotten any number of thugs to flank him here, but he specifically chose demons from Hinport. For me.

My grip on the hilt of my knife tightened, and I stepped forward. "It's me you want. Let's settle this, just the two of us."

Quentin raised his eyebrows with interest. While he was distracted, I slid my free hand behind my back and waved a few fingers, hoping to get Vince's attention. I sensed him stiffen behind me. Frantically, I pointed to Benny and jerked my thumb, hoping he understood my meaning. *Get Benny out of here.*

"Do you really think that's wise?" Quentin asked, his voice laced with amusement. "Our one-on-one scuffles never end well for you."

My ears strained to hear a *pop* behind me, but nothing happened. Instead, Vince stepped forward so we stood side-by-side. The dark feathers of his wings tickled the back of my neck. I couldn't help but glance at him. He lifted his chin, his gaze fiery and defiant as he stared down Quentin.

He wouldn't flee. He wanted to stay and fight alongside me.

Admiration bloomed in my chest, followed swiftly by panic and desperation. He *had* to get out. If something happened to him . . .

And if Quentin killed Benny, we would lose everything. Any shot at defeating Quentin would die with Benny.

Vince's eyes flicked to me. His gaze burned, penetrating right through me. The scar on his face and the rigid posture of his body made him look like a warrior.

And it took my breath away.

Bodies shifted behind me, and I felt my comrades drawing closer. An act of solidarity.

They were all ready to fight.

Quentin chuckled and shook his head. "Touching, really. But your loyalty will doom you all." He snapped his fingers, and his minions surged forward.

I spread my arms, and purple magic exploded from my fingertips, cutting down the four demons closest to me. They collapsed to the ground, and the ones behind them faltered, eyeing me with fear.

Taking advantage of their hesitation, I lunged. My blade sliced into them, flaying open their throats. Before I even took a breath, three more demons went down, their blood pooling on the floor.

I shot a venomous look toward my father, half my mouth quirking in a satisfied smile. But Quentin seemed nonplussed. He waved a hand over his shoulder, and thunderous footsteps drummed against the floor.

My heart dropped to my knees as more demons filled the room, more than I could count. Over their heads, I made out several more figures in the hallway. For all I knew, Quentin could have an entire army waiting for us out there.

My pulse roared in my ears. I cut a glance at Vince, who stared back at me, his expression stony. *We can't win this,* I thought. But how long would it take for Vince to Jump us all out of here?

He couldn't get everyone out. But we had to try.

Several demons advanced. I kicked one down, swiveling so my foot collided with his face. Panting, I glanced at Vince. "Get them out. *Now*."

Vince blasted a demon back with his red magic and met my gaze. "Cora—"

I ducked as a demon swung his fist. I kicked him in the groin and punched him in the jaw, then the stomach. He went down, and I whirled to face Vince. "*Now*!" I roared. "Start with Benny and Maddie. Take as many as you can."

I didn't wait for him to respond. A werewolf lunged for me, but before I could react, another wolf intercepted him.

Benny.

The great white wolf growled at the smaller one, baring his teeth as he advanced. My attacker shrank back in fear, edging away from Benny. For a moment, I marveled at Benny's wolf form as he towered over the other wolf. Benny had been an alpha in his former pack. It had never registered until this moment how *powerful* he was.

Benny lunged, ripping into the other wolf's throat in a clash of claws and fangs. I dived out of the way to avoid a dark warlock's burst of magic. Beside me, Piper sparred with a dark witch. When my sister went down, I flung my dagger into the dark witch. She cried out and fell over. I hurried forward and grabbed my dagger before meeting Piper's gaze. She nodded her thanks before jumping back into the fray.

A small *pop* tickled my ears behind me. *Thank Lilith*, I thought. It meant Vince was Jumping. Nearby, the two wolves still fought. I kept them in my peripheral, ensuring Benny didn't need my help. It seemed he had it well in hand. But he had to get out of here.

Another *pop*. Vince appeared beside me. Benny buried his fangs into the other wolf, who went still. In a flash, Vince wrapped his arms around Benny's fur and vanished with another *pop*.

Relief spread through me. I continued fighting, trying to buy Vince as much time as I could.

"Take down the Jumper!" Quentin roared.

No, I thought in horror. Purple magic shot from my hands, knocking down three demons at once. But the strain wore on me. I was winded, and sweat poured down my face. I couldn't keep this up for long.

My eyes found Vince. He grabbed hold of Maddie and Gio together and Jumped them out. When he reappeared, a dark warlock lunged for him.

"No!" shrieked a shrill voice. Then, glass shattered. A tendril of blue smoke coiled in the air. The sharp smell of jasmine tickled my nose, pricking my memory. It was so *familiar.*

And then, the bodies started dropping like flies. I watched, horrified, as everyone, foe and ally alike, fell to the ground as if passing out. Within seconds, I was surrounded by lifeless bodies. In a panic, I whirled around, and my blood ran cold. My eyes roved around the motionless figures, my heart lodging in my throat. *No, no, no.* My chest shuddered, my arms stiff and unmoving at my side. I couldn't think. Couldn't *breathe.*

My eyes fell on Vince, his dark wings still behind him, his body limp and his arms outstretched. He looked like he could be sleeping.

Wait. My eyes narrowed. His chest still moved. Rising and falling slowly.

He *was* sleeping. The blue smoke had been from a sleeping elixir. *My* sleeping elixir.

My gaze shifted to the two lone figures standing amidst the array of bodies. Quentin—which made sense, since we shared blood and he would also be unaffected by the elixir—and *Cecile.* She held a cloth up to her face to keep from inhaling the smoke that would put her to sleep. Slowly, she lowered the cloth. Her face was still haggard and tormented. But her eyes were dark and determined.

I gaped at her, stunned. "Cecile?" I whispered.

"I'm sorry, Cora." Her voice was full of anguish.

My gaze shifted back to Vince. "Your own son," I hissed.

Cecile flinched. "I don't expect you to understand."

I wanted to scream, to demand *how* Cecile had managed to knock everyone out with *my elixir*. But then my eyes fell to the empty potion vial clutched in her hands. *My* potion vial.

She'd stolen it from my bag. One of the potions I'd made at the cabin while Vince had been rescuing Maddie.

Agony flashed in Cecile's eyes before she smoothed her expression and looked at Quentin. "As agreed?"

Quentin sighed. "This wasn't *exactly* what I had in mind, Cecile." His dark eyes flashed. "We could've easily won this."

Cecile lifted her chin. "You were about to *kill my son.*"

Quentin shook his head and waved a hand. "No matter. You still held up your end of the deal. I'll have your people set free."

Your people. My shock melted away, and rage took its place. My fingers curled into tight fists. "How could you?" I cried.

I lunged for her, tackling her to the floor. My hands clawed at her face. She tried to kick me off, but I pinned her down and clutched at her throat. A choking noise burst from her lips, and her eyes bulged.

A blast of purple magic knocked me down, and I tumbled away from Cecile. I tried to get back on my feet, but Quentin's magic kept me frozen. I thrashed and screamed and pushed against the force, but my body remained locked in place. Inside, I was raging. But I couldn't do anything.

"You can throw your little tantrum back home, Cordelia," Quentin said with a sigh. "It's time to go."

A roar of fury burst from me. My eyes flitted to Cecile, who climbed to her feet, massaging her throat. Instead of looking angry, she stared at me with despair etched into her face.

She traded *me*. In exchange for the Reapers' freedom. I'd never felt particularly close to Cecile, but her betrayal still sliced through me. She was Vince's mother. She claimed she wanted to protect me for *his* sake.

She used her son against me. To get me to trust her.

Magic exploded within me, shooting from my fingertips and colliding with Quentin's force field. A mighty crack split through the air, and Quentin's magic shattered.

I surged forward, shoving Quentin against the wall and raising my dagger to his throat. Before I could bury it into his flesh, he slammed his forehead against mine. Pain radiated through my head, but I managed to duck before he struck me. I kicked. He dodged. My fist swung at his jaw. He caught my arm and twisted. My dagger fell from my grasp and clattered to the floor.

Sparring was usually easy for me. I could have an opponent down in seconds. But Quentin was skilled. And I was already drained from the battle.

The sleeping elixir would wear off in half an hour, and then the others would wake. But I didn't have that long. I had to find a way out on my own.

If I let Quentin take me, his cronies would kill my friends. It was the only guarantee my people wouldn't come after me.

From the corner of my eye, I noticed Cecile bending over Vince's form. At first, I thought she was trying to wake him. Then, I realized she was taking the amulet.

It's just for show, Vince had said.

An idea formed in my mind. I aimed a hard kick between Quentin's legs. He howled in agony and fell to his knees. I hurried to Vince's side and snatched the amulet by the chain before Cecile could put it on.

"Cora." Cecile jumped to her feet, her eyes wide with horror. "Don't—"

Panting, I held the chain up high and turned to face Quentin, who staggered to his feet, his expression wary. "This stops *now*," I said, breathless from the fight. "Or I'll touch this amulet and absorb your precious Reaper magic."

Quentin went very still. Cecile's face turned ashen.

Good, I thought. *I bought myself some more time.* But I needed another plan. It wouldn't take them long to realize the amulet had no magic in it. My bluff would only last so long.

Think, think, think, I urged myself, my mind racing. *How can I wake everyone up?* As far as I knew, there was no antidote to the sleeping elixir.

But . . . I *did* have a Jumping elixir in my bag.

"Be reasonable, Cordelia," Quentin said, edging closer to me. I was out of time.

I swallowed. "I'll go with you. On one condition."

Quentin's eyes narrowed in suspicion. "What is it?"

"Let me leave a letter for Vince. To say goodbye."

Quentin stared hard at me, and I forced myself to hold his gaze. He exhaled and said, "Fine."

"I've got a pen and paper," I said. "They're in my bag." Still clutching the amulet chain, I inched backward toward my bag. My pulse thundered in my ears, sure to give me away.

Quentin and Cecile watched me unblinkingly. I would only have a split-second before they reacted . . .

I carefully stepped around the bodies, edging closer to my bag. Some of my belongings had already spilled loose from the fight. With my free hand, I reached into my bag, searching blindly for the Jumping elixir. I remembered putting it in a fat, round bottle. Keeping my eyes on Quentin and Cecile, I groped through the contents of my bag before I found it. My heart skipped a beat as I clutched it tightly in my hand, working my fingers around the cork to pull it loose.

"*Now,* Cordelia," Quentin hissed, stepping toward me.

With one quick motion, I flung the amulet across the room. Cecile drew a horrified gasp, and Quentin lurched forward, his wide eyes pinned on the amulet.

While they were distracted, I gulped down the Jumping elixir and spun on the spot. The air shifted around me. Gravity pressed in on me. With a *pop*, I vanished and reappeared behind Quentin. I grabbed him by the arms and Jumped again, hauling him with me. My arms strained from the effort. His body stiffened in my grasp.

Mid-Jump, I released him. His limbs flailed as he scrambled to hold on. Before the earth righted itself, Quentin vanished. My body jerked forward, slamming hard into the ground. Sputtering, I scrambled to my feet, gasping for breath and searching for my father.

He was gone.

CHAPTER 16

VINCE

Someone shook me frantically. I groggily shoved them away, but they persisted and hissed in my ear.

"Vince, *wake up*!"

My mind was sluggish as I blinked my eyes open. A heaviness weighed down on my body, trying to keep me on the floor.

Gradually, awareness returned to me, but the haze in my head remained. I could hardly see straight. But I made out the blurry figure of my mother hovering over me. At least a dozen motionless bodies surrounded me.

A bolt of alarm raced through me, and I jumped to my feet. I swayed immediately, my head throbbing, and Mom steadied me. Her eyes were wide, and her face was paler than death.

"What—what happened?" I croaked, raising a hand to my head.

Mom straightened and swallowed hard. "Quentin was here."

I frowned, struggling to remember. Then, my blood ran cold as I gazed around the room. My mouth fell open. *Dozens* of bodies lay on the floor. Some were bleeding out, but others were snoozing softly, as if napping was the obvious thing to do right now.

"He must've cast a spell on us," I muttered, glancing at the others still dozing on the floor and trying to see how many allies we still had. I vaguely remembered Jumping Benny, Gio, and Maddie away from here, so at least they'd been spared. I bent over, scrutinizing Piper's unconscious form to ensure she was breathing.

She was. Along with Hector and Dex. *Thank Lilith.* I searched for the others, but before I found them, Mom whispered, "Vince, you have to get out of here."

I stood and faced her. Her eyes brimmed with tears. Regret shone on her face, and her lips quivered.

I stilled, my stomach clenching at the sight of her like this. "What happened?" I repeated, my tone laced with suspicion. My eyes roved around the room again, and with a start, I realized Cora and Quentin were missing.

"He took her," I said, striding toward the door, prepared to Jump across the world to find her.

Mom grabbed my arm, stopping me. "Vince, *don't.*"

I stopped and whirled toward her. The guilty look on her face made my skin prickle with unease. "What did you do?"

"I didn't escape from Quentin. He set me free. I struck a deal with him. He agreed to free the Reapers in exchange for Cora."

My blood boiled. "You *betrayed* us?" My voice was practically a shout.

A few people on the floor stirred from my outburst, and Mom shushed me. "The Reapers are my family, Vince. I did it for them—for *you*."

"You were lying to me this whole time!" I cried, waving my arms. "You were supposed to help us *take down* the murderous psychopath, not *hand him* what he wants on a silver platter!"

Mom flinched, and I enjoyed a sliver of satisfaction before my anger took over again.

"After everything Cora did for you, how could you do this to her?" I growled, stepping closer to her. "You *know* what she means to me, Mom! And you still turned her over!"

Mom gritted her teeth, her gaze hardening. "You are still so *closed-minded*. You don't *get it*. Without the Reapers, the souls of the dead will be overwhelmed. They'll spill over into the mortal realm and start taking over the bodies of the living! Don't you realize how catastrophic that is?"

"About as catastrophic as a madman trying to enslave the entire magical population," I snapped.

"It was the lesser of two evils!" Mom shouted. "At least the mortal realm will stay intact."

"*Lesser of two evils?*" I repeated, my voice rising in pitch. "There's *one evil*, Mom. It's Quentin. And you're *working for him*!"

Mom flinched again.

At my feet, Dex groaned and mumbled something incoherent. A few others shifted and tried to rise.

Mom's eyes widened in panic as she glanced around at the sleeping figures starting to wake up. The terror on her face quelled some of the fury raging inside me. My body ached to lunge, to *move*, to do something, but in this moment, I knew my mom would be seen as an enemy. People like Finn were already suspicious of her.

As angry as I was, I didn't want to see her killed.

"Go," I hissed.

Mom blinked at me. "What?"

"Get *out* of here, Mom," I said sharply. "If they wake up and learn what you've done, they'll *kill* you."

Mom's mouth fell open, and her face turned ashen. She backed away a few steps, her arms trembling. "I'll—I'll find the Reapers and come back for you, Vince."

"Don't bother," I growled.

She recoiled as if I'd slapped her. "You're my son. I'm not abandoning you."

"You did that when you sided with my enemy. You chose him over me. Besides, I'm not a Reaper anymore. I'm a Timekeeper. And I have to clean up your mess now. So *leave*."

Horror and hurt shone in her eyes so intensely it made my heart twist. But I shoved down my guilt and turned away from her to help Piper to her feet. Behind me, I heard Mom's frantic footsteps as she left the apartment and hurried downstairs.

Piper groaned and rubbed her forehead. "What the hell's going on? Why were you two fighting?" She glanced around, her eyes clouded. "Where—where's Cora?"

In a hushed whisper, I filled her in. Fury mingled with confusion in her eyes. "Cecile did *what*?"

A few of Quentin's demons started to wake. I grabbed Piper's shoulders. "I need your help. We have to get our people out of here before this army wakes up."

Dazed, Piper nodded, her face pale. "Right. Okay. What can I do?"

"Start getting everyone up and ready to Jump." I glanced at Dex, who staggered to his feet. Without preamble, I looped my arm through his and Jumped.

We arrived at an abandoned gas station just outside of Hinport, where Benny, Gio, and Maddie awaited.

Benny, in human form, stomped toward me. "What happened?" he demanded.

"Later," I grunted before vanishing again. Exhaustion tugged at my body as I found Piper trying to rouse Finn. I stepped forward, then froze as Piper glanced up at me, her eyes shining with tears.

"He's gone," she whispered, her voice shuddering.

A hard lump formed in my throat. Finn's eyes were wide open, and blood pooled underneath him.

He's gone. And it was my mother's fault.

A growl sounded behind me. A werewolf stalked toward us, eyes bloodthirsty.

We were out of time. I grabbed Piper and Jumped just as the wolf leapt toward us.

Gio, Benny, Maddie, and Dex surrounded us, their expressions rigid with concern. Benny glanced behind me as if expecting more people to pop up. "Where are the others?"

I wiped sweat from my brow and quickly filled everyone in. Gio swore loudly and ran his hands through his hair, but Benny's steely gaze remained fixed on me. His eyes narrowed. "You let her go."

"She's no longer a threat to us. We know she's a traitor, and she has no magic."

Benny's eyes tightened. "And she's your mother."

I nodded. Benny's gaze fell on Gio, who was pacing frantically. Something softened in Benny's eyes, and I knew he felt what I did: *You don't always get to choose your family.*

"I don't care whose mother she is," Dex growled, his voice soft and his red eyes gleaming as he watched me. "She betrayed us *all.* Finn is *dead* because of her. And now we can't avenge him because *you* let her go."

I raised my hands. "Look, you guys can yell at me, beat me up, whatever you want—but I have to find Cora first."

Dex said nothing, his expression stony. After a moment, he nodded stiffly. I glanced at the others, who remained silent as well. They would let me go. For now.

I closed my eyes and searched inside myself for that

familiar golden presence. It gleamed within me, eager and ready to help. With Maddie, I needed something of hers to connect me to the timeline. But I knew Cora better than I knew myself. All I had to do was picture her face, and the gold thread inside me lurched forward, yanking me along with it. My world spun like a roller coaster, and I clenched my teeth, trying to remain upright. My stomach churned as gravity pressed in, squeezing the breath out of me.

Then, I slammed into the ground, landing on my hands and knees. Gasping for breath, I shook my head violently to clear the dizziness and rose to my feet. I was in some wide and empty field about a half mile from the main road. I recognized it as a stretch of farmland just outside of Hinport.

A few feet ahead of me stood Cora, her body rigid and her hands in tight fists. She whirled, her eyes wild and feral when they settled on me.

Shock slackened her expression, and her body straightened. "Vince," she whispered. She blinked in confusion and then raced toward me, launching herself into me. Her arms wrapped around me, clutching so tightly I couldn't breathe. I held her, breathing in her lilac scent and relishing the feel of her, solid in my arms.

"Thank Lilith," she breathed with a half laugh, half sob. "I wasn't sure how I'd get back."

We broke apart, and I looked around in alarm. "Where—where's Quentin?"

"I dropped him."

My brow furrowed. "You *what*?"

"I grabbed him, then Jumped. And . . . I let go of him mid-Jump." She grimaced.

My head reared back. *Holy hell.* I wasn't exactly an expert on Jumping, but I knew the number one rule was if you traveled with someone else, you *never let go.* To be honest, I wasn't entirely sure what happened if you *did* let go.

"We can't assume anything," I said quickly. "He's powerful and clever. I'm sure wherever he is, he's found a way to carry on."

Cora nodded, and an uncertain expression crossed her face. "Vince, you don't think I . . . *time traveled* with him, do you?"

"Not unless you were clutching some kind of object." I flinched, remembering how I'd used *Hector* as an anchor through time. The uncertainty in Cora's face told me she was thinking the same thing. "You have to have a different kind of mentality to time travel," I clarified. "It isn't the same as normal Jumping."

Cora nodded again. Then, her eyes grew wide, and she grabbed my arm. "Vince—your mom—"

"I know," I said grimly.

Stunned, she dropped my arm. "You . . . know?" For a split second, suspicion crept into her eyes, but she quickly shook it off. "Are you okay?"

"No," I said honestly. "My mom screwed us over. Screwed *me* over. But there's nothing I can do about it now. She's gone."

Cora stepped back, her eyes narrowing. "What do you mean, *she's gone*?" Her tone was hard.

"I let her go."

Cora's nostrils flared, and her jaw tensed. "Why the *hell* would you do that?"

I spread my arms. "She's my *mom*, Cora. And she's no longer a threat to us!"

"The hell she isn't! She knows *all* of our plans, Vince! Everything we said in front of her will go straight to Quentin!"

"So what, you wanted me to just *kill* her?" I shouted.

Cora shrugged and gave me a look that said, *well, duh*.

My blood chilled, and I drew away from her. "Cora . . ."

"It is what it is, Vince. She's my enemy now. If she's not with me, she's against me."

My mouth felt dry, and I swallowed hard. "She's my *mother*."

"And Quentin is my father!"

I shook my head. Though I was still pissed at Mom for what she'd done, I couldn't stand the thought of Cora—the woman I loved—hunting her down and slaughtering her. "She did it to protect her people."

Cora's face contorted with rage and disgust. "How can you be *defending* her right now?"

"Wouldn't you have done the same thing?" I cried. "You would've given *her* up if it meant protecting your coven, right?"

Her lips pressed into a thin line, and she glared at me, her eyes icy. "Maybe," she said, her voice dangerously quiet. "But I never would've given *you* up, Vince. Not in a million years."

Something loosened in my chest, and my mouth fell open in surprise. The fight inside me vanished like a popped bubble, leaving a sickly feeling in its wake. Cora still stared at me with venom in her eyes. Like I was a stranger. No, an *enemy*.

My mouth closed, and I struggled to breathe evenly. "What—what will you do with me?"

Surprise flickered in her eyes, and she lifted her chin. "*You* didn't betray me, Vince."

"I let my mom go. Isn't that just as bad?"

She smiled without humor, her expression cold. "You're on thin ice. But I know you're still with me." Uncertainty flashed in her eyes. "Aren't you?"

My eyebrows lifted. "What? Of course I am!"

"So, if it comes down to the Reapers or me, you'll be on my side, right?"

I didn't even hesitate. "I already gave up the Reapers, Cora. For *you*."

She blinked. For a moment, her anger melted away, and something soft glittered in her eyes, reminding me of that familiar heat between us. But in an instant, her expression closed off again, and she nodded stiffly. "Okay. Good." She cleared her throat. "We should probably get back to the others and get everyone safe again. Would you mind?" She stretched her arm toward me, her movements tense and reluctant as if I were contagious. As if it caused her physical pain to be so close to me.

The thought made my insides shrivel up and cave in on themselves.

I forced the despair from me and extended my arm, looping it through hers, before I Jumped us back to the hideout.

CHAPTER 17

CORA

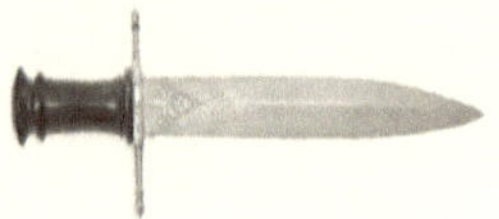

THE AIR WAS TENSE WHEN WE ARRIVED. GIO PACED furiously across the length of the pavement of the old gas station while Maddie sat cross-legged nearby. Benny's arms were crossed, his expression hard and distant. Piper chewed on her fingernails, her face paler than normal.

When we arrived, everyone stiffened. Then, Gio's dark, angry eyes slid to Vince, and his body went rigid. "You," he snarled, stomping toward Vince.

I stepped between them and shoved Gio's shoulder before he could strangle Vince. "Easy," I hissed.

Gio's nostrils flared as he fixed his venomous gaze on me. "Finn is *dead,* Cora! Because of *him.*"

Shock rippled through me, and my mouth fell open. Slowly, my gaze shifted to Vince, whose eyes closed with regret. Why hadn't he told me? Bile climbed up my throat. I couldn't see straight.

Finn was dead.

I swallowed hard. *Get it together, Cora,* I told myself. I couldn't lose it here. Not now.

"This has gone on long enough, Cora," Dex said softly. "You can't keep defending him."

Gio grumbled his assent. "I didn't trust him before, but now because of him and that other Reaper, we're *screwed*."

Dex grunted in agreement. Even Piper looked like she wanted Vince dead.

This is not *good,* I thought. I suddenly preferred the tedious arguments from a few days ago. At least then, we'd been on the same side. We'd been united, if a bit contentious.

Now, our small alliance was crumbling. It had already been rocky to begin with.

Damn Cecile and her misguided loyalty. I wanted to wring her neck for what she did to us. To Finn. To her own *son.*

And he'd defended her.

I swallowed down the regret in my throat and lifted my chin. "Vince didn't betray us. Cecile did."

"He let her get away!" Gio roared. "He's her *son*! Do you really think he's completely innocent in all this?"

"What would you have done if it had been me?" Dex challenged. "Or Gio?"

I pressed my lips together, cursing myself. He was right. If it had been anyone but Vince, I would've thrown them out with no mercy. Maybe even killed them.

A warm hand gripped my arm, and the air shifted. The

people around me froze as if someone had pressed pause on a remote. The soothing lull of cars rushing past was gone. Everything was eerily still.

I sucked in a breath, and the sound felt odd amidst the sudden silence. Slowly, I turned and found Vince watching me, his hand still holding my arm. He met my gaze with a grim expression.

"Did you—" I whispered.

He nodded. "I stopped time."

"I—I didn't know you could do that."

He glanced around, his eyes full of awe. "Honestly? I didn't, either. I'm not certain, but something tells me if I let go of you, you'd freeze too."

My mouth felt dry as I glanced down to where he touched me. A familiar spark of heat surged within me, but it was tainted by anger.

"You have to kick me out," Vince said.

My eyes snapped to his. "*What*?"

"You'll lose them if you don't."

I gritted my teeth. "I *told* you I won't give you up. Not for *anyone,* Vince."

Vince's eyes softened, and his expression warmed as he drew closer to me. My body ached for him, yearned to close that distance between us. "I know," he murmured, raising his free hand to brush his fingertip along my cheek. I closed my eyes and suppressed a shiver of pleasure. "But we need all the allies we can get. And . . . I need to leave anyway."

My eyes widened, and my heart sank. "You do? Why?"

"To find the other Timekeepers. After Mom—after what happened, I can't put it off any longer. We need help."

I sighed and nodded. It made sense, but my insides twisted at the thought of parting from him.

Vince drew closer and pressed his forehead to mine. His breath tickled my face, and I breathed him in, memorizing his minty scent.

"I'm still pissed at you," I muttered.

He laughed, and a huff of air blew against my face. "You have every right to be. I'm not sorry for defending my mom, but I *am* sorry for what she did. I wish I could've stopped it."

My chest tightened at his words. He wasn't sorry for defending her.

But what did I expect? She was his mother. He'd grown up with her, loved her. Their relationship was very different from my relationship with Quentin.

For most of my life, the only person I could rely on was myself. Then, I met Vince, and that all changed. I put him first. He was everything to me. He was my priority. I'd thought he felt the same way about me, but he didn't. Not quite. He had a family—parents to protect. I didn't. How could I make him choose between me and them? It wasn't his fault he had loved ones.

Even so, my stomach soured. I couldn't think about this anymore.

Vince read the conflict in my eyes and tilted my chin up so I met his gaze. "I'll come back," he promised. "And we'll finish this together. I swear it."

I nodded. A lump formed in my throat, and warmth stung my eyes.

"I love you, Cora."

I closed my eyes, relishing the sound. Even though I knew this, it was still a relief to hear the words. To remind myself that I was loved. "I love you too," I breathed.

He kissed me, his lips moving slowly and tenderly, like I was the most precious thing in the world. His free hand cupped my chin, bringing me closer. I pressed against his chest, drinking him in, fusing my mouth to his. For this moment, we were one. Sharing the same breath. The same heart. The same soul.

Then, much too soon, he pulled away, and I felt like someone was sawing off half my body. Like with Vince leaving, he was taking a chunk of me with him. A gaping hole settled in my chest, permanent and endless. It hurt to even breathe.

"Ready?" he asked.

No, I thought. But I forced myself to nod. Just as I turned away from him to face my coven, the air shifted again. Everything slammed forward, and a cacophony of noises erupted around me. It hadn't seemed that loud before, but now my eardrums were throbbing. Vince released my arm, and my skin felt cool in his absence.

Dex watched me expectantly, his eyebrows raised, and I realized he was waiting for a response. I cleared my throat and stepped toward him. "You're right."

Dex's head reared back, and his mouth fell open. He exchanged a bewildered look with Gio. Piper's brow furrowed, and Benny frowned and cocked his head at me in confusion.

I spread my arms, gesturing to the group at large. "I'm sorry, everyone. You're absolutely right. I've put my own interests above yours. But no more." My heart drummed anxiously in my chest as I turned to face Vince. He watched me with a solemn expression. His eyes were full of affection, but his face was taut and rigid.

"Vince," I said, struggling to keep my voice even. "It's time for you to go."

He swallowed, and his throat bobbed. "Cora—"

I raised a hand. "Don't make me force you. Because I will."

We stared at each other, neither of us backing down. In my mind, I pleaded, *Please don't make me. For the love of Lilith, don't make me fight you.*

At long last, Vince dropped his gaze, his jaw hardening. "Fine," he bit out, turning away from me.

"Vince is our only Jumper," Benny said in a slow voice.

"So what?" Gio snapped. "Cora can make a Jumping elixir. It's not a big deal."

Benny's mouth clamped shut, and his questioning eyes met mine. I knew he didn't care much for Vince, but he didn't hate him, either. And Benny also knew how *I* felt about Vince.

"It's fine, Benny," I said quietly. "It needs to be done." Briefly, I widened my eyes at him, and his expression smoothed. Even if he didn't know Vince and I had spoken privately, he still knew *me.* He knew how precarious my leadership position was. And he knew how unstable things already were.

Vince was right. This had to happen.

Vince met my gaze, then glanced at the hostile crowd. “Good luck to you all. I’m sorry. For everything.”

And, with a *pop*, he was gone.

CHAPTER 18

VINCE

I ARRIVED IN THE SAME FIELD I'D BEEN IN WITH CORA. THE space seemed to stretch on forever—an endless void of loneliness.

I swallowed hard, trying to stifle the regret pulsing within me. In a loud voice, I shouted, "Hector Moses!" My voice echoed in the vast emptiness before me.

After a moment, a *pop* alerted me to Hector's presence. He frowned and glanced around the field. "Where *are* we? And where are the others?"

"Gone," I said in a hollow voice. "I—I left. My mom betrayed everyone, so I was no longer welcome."

Hector's eyebrows lifted, his mouth opening slightly. A dozen unreadable emotions crossed his face, but I wasn't paying close enough attention to care.

"I see," was all he said.

A strange silence fell between us. My thoughts turned to Mom and where she was now. She claimed she'd betrayed everyone for *me.* But she hadn't shared her plans with me. She hadn't told me *anything.* She'd lied to me just as she'd lied to Cora and the others.

Suddenly, I didn't feel so bad about keeping things from her too. Like the truth about the amulet. Although, based on Cora's story, Quentin and Mom already knew.

"So, what are we doing here?" Hector asked. "Are you going to return to Luke's mind?"

"*No,*" I said firmly, rubbing my forehead. When Hector remained silent, I peered at him curiously. He watched me, his eyes questioning.

He was looking to *me* for answers. The idea was so unsettling that I couldn't speak for a moment.

I cleared my throat and shook my head. "Um . . . well, we actually *do* need Luke. I want to try to find the other Timekeepers."

Hector's face drained of color. His eyes filled with fear. "Vince—"

"Do you want to hide forever, Hector?" I snapped. "Because Quentin is taking over the *world.* If he wins, he'll enslave everyone—including you. And then those voices in your head will be screaming at you for the rest of your pathetic life, and you won't be able to do a damn thing about it."

Hector's face took on a greenish tint. His expression twisted into a horrified grimace. He licked his lips and asked in a shaky voice, "What about other covens? Can't we find witches and warlocks—hell, even *demons*—to help us? We can't be the only ones who want to stop Quentin."

I shrugged. "Maybe. But we don't have time to travel from coven to coven, asking for them to just hand over their armies. We can't pay anyone. We can't offer anything in return. The other Timekeepers are the only magical beings who would benefit as much as we would. With Quentin destroying the timeline, they will be as motivated to stop him as we are."

"Unless you believe Luke's little story about Timewatchers," Hector pointed out, his gaze hardening.

I fell silent. He had a point. If the "rogue" Timekeepers believed as the Timewatchers did—that the Call was merely a suggestion, not an order—then they could easily refuse. "We don't know for sure that they follow the Timewatchers." But my voice sounded uncertain.

Hector arched an eyebrow. "What other reason would they have for defecting from the Timekeeper organization?"

"What's *your* reason?" I challenged. "You defected, didn't you?"

Hector's jaw went rigid, and he lifted his chin. "I did. Because they—" His mouth clamped shut, and a sliver of satisfaction wriggled through me.

"Because they were ignoring the Call," I finished, trying not to feel smug. "Right?"

Hector's mouth formed a thin line, his eyes flashing with irritation.

I sighed. "Look, we won't know unless we try, all right? If you want to run and hide, be my guest." I gestured vaguely to the empty field behind him.

Hector's expression hardened. His eyes blazed with that familiar fire I remembered from when we lived in the clan. For a moment, he was the old Hector again. Unafraid. Commanding. Powerful.

"I'll stay," he said tightly.

I nodded once. "Good." I closed my eyes and imagined the lacrosse field. It felt like I hadn't been there in ages. But it still appeared in my mind as easily as if I'd been there moments ago.

And Luke stood there, waiting for me, his eyes wide. "Vince," he breathed in relief. "You all right?"

"I'm fine. Where are you right now?"

"Back home." He shook his head, looking at me in exasperation. "You shouldn't have left like that, Vince."

"It was . . . kind of an accident," I said with an apologetic grimace. "But I could use your help, if you're up for it." I quickly filled him in on my plan.

His face turned a shade paler. "That's a really risky idea, man. What if Quentin's Timekeepers catch you?"

"That's where you and Hector come in. I want to tether my magic to you so you can yank me out if there's trouble."

"Yank you out of *where*?" Luke asked, but the horrified look in his eyes told me he already knew.

"The timeline."

Luke shuddered. "You gotta be careful, Vince. Using the

timeline to do something as powerful as locating hundreds, maybe *thousands* of other Timekeepers? It won't be easy." He paused. "And the Call might try to stop you."

I nodded. "I know."

"And you still want to go through with it?"

"Yes." I didn't have much of a choice. Cora needed numbers. This was the fastest way to get them. If it didn't work, I silently vowed to go with Hector's plan of traveling to different covens and begging for help.

It was better than being enslaved to Quentin.

"So, are you with me?" I asked tentatively. Luke and I had our differences, but he had always been there for me. My heart twisted at the thought of him walking away now.

Luke watched me pensively for a moment. Then, his face split into a wide grin. "What the hell? Sign me up."

Relief spread through me, and I beamed at him. "Thank you. Can I summon you like I summoned Hector?"

Luke shook his head. "It's different for Thinkers because we manipulate the timeline in our minds. We can travel mind-to-mind, but that's it."

"No problem. I'll come get you."

In a flash, I was back in the grass with Hector, his expression perplexed as he stared at me. I quickly explained the plan to him, then Jumped to Luke's house. After saying a quick hello to Luke's mom, I grabbed Luke and Jumped us both back to the field with Hector.

Winded, I collapsed on the grass, struggling to catch my

breath. My stomach grumbled, and I realized I hadn't eaten in over a day.

"You're weak," Hector said.

"Thanks," I snapped.

"I mean, you can't move forward with the plan until you've taken care of yourself." He gazed upward, squinting against the afternoon sun as if looking for something. "I'll be right back." He vanished with a *pop*, leaving Luke and me alone.

Luke shifted his weight. "I heard what happened with your mom."

I raised an eyebrow. "You *heard*?"

Luke grimaced and tapped his temple, and I sighed. Right. Our minds were connected. I wasn't sure I'd ever get used to that.

A heavy weight settled in my chest, and I averted my gaze. I really didn't want to talk about this.

"I'm sorry," Luke said quietly. "That can't have been easy."

I only shook my head. A lump formed in my throat, and I tried swallowing it down.

"Quentin was torturing Reapers," Luke said. "He cut the wings off one of them. He's probably killed others."

"What's your point?" I couldn't keep the bite out of my tone.

"My point is, if it had been your Nephilim clan—you know, the one you grew up with—wouldn't you have done anything to save them? Jocelyn's there. She's one of his prisoners."

I flinched, picturing Jocelyn's innocent face. What horrors

had she endured? Bile crept up my throat, but I let the images take over my mind. I deserved it. I deserved to torment myself by imagining the worst. Jocelyn dead. Jocelyn with her fingers cut off or her face carved up like mine.

I should be with them, I thought. Agony ripped through me with the crippling realization of my guilt. It should've been *me.* Instead, I'd been safely tucked away in Luke's mind, complaining about being helpless and powerless. All the while, the other Reapers literally *were* powerless and had to submit to Quentin's whims.

What the hell was wrong with me?

Rage quivered through me, and I slammed my fist against the grass. It did nothing to alleviate the anguish within me.

I couldn't condemn my mother for what she'd done. The Reapers were her family. She'd been with them longer than with me.

But I also couldn't stand by her. I still felt a shred of loyalty toward the Reapers—especially Jocelyn and my mom—but my first priority was Cora. It was always Cora.

Luke heaved a deep breath and sank to the grass next to me. "You're in a tight spot, dude."

I glared at him. "Are you reading my mind?"

"Some feelings radiate from you. The stronger the emotion, the easier it is for me to sense it. Even without trying to get in your head. It's how I knew about your mom—the strength of your emotions was pulling at our bond." His face sobered. "Your most powerful emotions will always alert me, kind of like a distress signal telling me something's wrong.

It's vague, though. I can never tell *exactly* what you're thinking unless you allow it. I would never violate you like that, Vince."

I stared at him for a long moment. "You've never read my mind before?"

"Any time we were on that lacrosse field together, that was essentially me reading your mind," Luke said. "But that was only after you invited me. When you access the field, you access our link. It opens your mind up to me."

I nodded contemplatively. Even though I hadn't always known this—for a while, I thought Luke was just in my imagination—it still didn't bother me. There was nothing I wanted to hide from Luke. And that thought brought me a sliver of comfort.

"Thanks for always being there," I muttered. My eyes burned, and I couldn't look at him.

I heard the smile in his voice when he said, "Don't mention it."

A few minutes later, Hector arrived with takeout, and we all sat in the grass together to share a meal. It felt ridiculous. Hector had used the timeline to get fast food, and we were having a picnic out here in the middle of nowhere while the people we cared about were risking their lives.

Not the people Luke and Hector care about, I reminded myself. They probably didn't give a rat's ass whether Cora and the others lived or died. But they both wanted Quentin gone. At least on that front, we were united.

After we finished our burgers, we sat in silence. The sun lowered in the sky, creating a pleasant orange hue that warmed my face. I wanted to bask in it. To lean my head back, close my eyes, and just enjoy the nothingness of the moment.

But I'd already wasted enough time.

With a grunt, I rose to my feet and wiped my hands on my jeans. "You guys ready?"

Luke and Hector both stood. Luke looked uneasy, while Hector looked nauseous. I wondered if eating right before doing this had been a good idea . . .

"Remember, *I'm* the one going through the timeline," I said. "I just need you two as anchors." When Hector blanched, I quickly amended, "Uh, I mean as a safeguard." I exhaled slowly and pressed my hands together, summoning my magic. It was strange to have so much inside me. My warlock powers now mingled with the Reaper magic, forming something completely new. They'd merged, both blue and red, Jumper and Reaper. No longer two separate entities.

I'd only heard Cora utter the spell once, but I could still remember the words. After a deep breath, I muttered,

"*Magic above and powers that be,*
Link these two to the magic in me.
Bind our powers to hold me steady,
And bring me back when I am ready."

It was the spell Cora and I were supposed to use to go back in time to the Demon War and save my mom. Cora had offered to bind her powers to me to help boost my magic. Only . . . it hadn't worked out that way. We'd never gotten to use the spell.

So, I wasn't prepared when jets of red magic flew from my fingertips and encircled Luke and Hector, coiling around their waists like snakes. Luke grunted and struggled against the vise, and Hector crammed his eyes shut, his face turning green.

Panic rose inside me. I stepped forward, intent on helping, but the red magic faded. Luke and Hector relaxed, breathing heavily, though Hector still looked ill.

Then, I felt it. A swelling sensation in my chest. Like my lungs were expanding and I could take in more air. My body felt larger—more flexible. I sucked in several enormous gulps of air, feeling more powerful with each breath. Gold light gleamed within me. And as I searched my magic, I found the barest hint of Luke and Hector, like faint and flickering lights.

They were tethered to me. I could sense Luke's surprise and Hector's unease. I couldn't exactly read their minds, but I *felt* them.

"You all right?" Luke asked.

I hadn't realized I was gaping like an idiot. My mouth clamped shut, and I nodded numbly. My throat was dry as I whispered, "Yeah. It worked." My heart drummed an erratic rhythm in my chest. The vast magic within me quivered in response. I sensed the Call lingering, waiting. Almost as if it were impatient to get started.

Clearing my throat, I spread my hands and wiggled my fingers. My eyes closed, and I gently tugged on that coil of gold light inside me. The timeline.

And then it consumed me. Beams of ethereal light blinded

me, obscuring everything from view. A presence stirred in my mind—the Call.

I focused on my objective: *Find the other Timekeepers.* The timeline rippled before me as if it would mold to fit the shape I commanded. Excitement flared inside my chest. This could work.

But as I reached forward to grasp the timeline, a voice in my mind whispered, *No.*

I froze, my arm still outstretched toward the beams of light, ready to grab hold and find the missing Timekeepers. I was so close . . .

Don't do it, the voice whispered. And deep down, I knew it was the Call.

Icy fear climbed up my throat. Dread pooled in my stomach at the thought of what I had to do in order to succeed.

I had to defy the Call.

I'm sorry, I thought in response. *But I have to do this.*

My fingers wrapped around the timeline's thick rod, and it fused itself to me. My fingers burned as if the rod were on fire. I couldn't let go even if I wanted to.

A scream ripped from my throat as I lurched forward. In the recesses of my mind, I registered Luke and Hector's presence still clinging to me, but it felt fainter than before. The timeline yanked me like a rag doll, tossing me about until I thought I might hurl.

Then, it stopped. I slammed into the ground, and something cracked within me, leaving me feeling cold and clammy.

Had I broken something? I tried to rise, but I was locked in place by some unknown force. I remained face-down on the ground. The air smelled of dust and decay.

The back of my neck prickled. *Someone's watching me,* I thought. My skin crawled as I tried to move again, but my body was motionless.

"It's a shame," murmured a voice, "that someone as foolish as you was given so much power."

My heart jolted in my throat. I knew that voice . . . I gritted my teeth, trying to fidget or squirm or do *something.*

"You'll move once I release you," the voice said. It was a woman, her tone commanding and assertive.

My blood ran cold. It was Kallie.

Hector had warned me someone might be watching the timeline. But I was still anchored, right? I could get back to Luke if I . . .

A coil of despair sank in my stomach, dragging me down into a black hole. Whatever had cracked when I'd landed—that was my bond to Luke and Hector. Because now, I couldn't feel them at all.

It was just me. And Kallie.

"You wanted to find the Timewatchers?" Kallie whispered, her voice closer than before. "Well, here they are."

Something crashed into my mind, and I roared in pain. Black spots danced in front of my eyes. With a groan, I shifted—and then realized I could move. I jumped to my feet, my head spinning. But instead of Kallie, I faced a large crowd standing in front of a row of houses. The street looked similar to where I'd lived in my Nephilim clan.

My mouth fell open as I gazed at the people watching me with bewildered expressions. Some were about my age, but others were old enough to be parents and grandparents. A few children clung to their parents and stared at me with wide eyes.

"Where—where am I?" I croaked, my head still throbbing.

The man in front had black hair that fell past his shoulders, speckled with gray. He looked to be about fifty years old. His green eyes were haunted and filled with regret. He said in a deep voice, "You're trapped. Just like we are."

CHAPTER 19

CORA

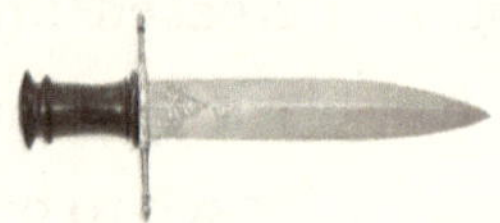

I USED MY LAST JUMPING ELIXIR TO GET US TO OUR NEXT hideout—an abandoned farmhouse just outside of Hinport.

Our tiny group of six felt bare compared to what we'd had before. Even though I knew Vince, Luke, and Hector were still on our side, their absence still throbbed inside me.

Well . . . one absence in particular. I hated that Vince and I had left things so uncertain between us. Though I still resented his decision to let his mom go, I understood why he'd done it. And, despite my anger, I still loved him.

I had to trust his feelings for me were strong enough to overcome our argument. It should've been a no-brainer: *Of course Vince still loves you, Cora*!

And yet . . . a small, dark part inside me told me it was inevitable. That I'd pushed people away my entire life and was destined to be alone. That I would eventually become just like Quentin and manipulate and torture those closest to me.

I'd never been in love before. Hell, I hadn't even had a steady boyfriend. Damien hardly counted—he and I had been casual at best.

I had no idea what I was doing.

Then again, as I glanced around our group—all of us covered in dirt and sweat, our expressions bleak—none of us knew what we were doing.

The farmhouse smelled like mold and wood rot, along with the lingering stench of pigs and animal excrement. But it was cleaner than the old warehouse we were in before.

Gio and Maddie slumped to the floor, leaning their heads against a wall. Benny peered through the windows, no doubt searching for enemies nearby. Dex paced the length of the dining area, his jaw rigid.

Piper wiped sweat from her brow and glanced at me. "Ready to put up the wards?"

I nodded, feeling dejected. What was the point? Quentin had still found us, even after we'd put up wards at the last place.

Because of Cecile, I reminded myself. *It wasn't your fault, Cora.*

That didn't do much to assuage my guilt. I shouldn't have trusted Cecile right away. Lilith knew she didn't trust me. I'd let my feelings for Vince blind me.

My movements were stiff and robotic as I followed Piper out of the farmhouse. We clasped hands and muttered the same enchantments we'd spoken at the last several hideouts.

My magic felt feeble and frail compared to the power I'd felt while fighting Quentin.

I was hollow inside. Nothing but an empty shell.

When we trudged back inside, Dex stopped pacing and met my gaze, his eyes grim.

"I hope we didn't ruin things for you back at that vampire hideout," I muttered. My chest ached at the thought of Dex burning bridges with his vampire allies just for associating with me.

Dex's eyes softened. "What we're doing is worth it, Cora."

Is it? I wondered. How many other lives would Quentin take before this was over? Even if we *did* succeed—which seemed less and less likely—Quentin could kill everyone I loved. He could even kill *me* before we defeated him.

Would it be worth it then?

"So, what now?" Gio asked in a hard voice. Accusation laced his tone, and I knew he still hadn't forgiven me for letting Vince go. As I watched how tightly he held Maddie against his chest, I understood why. My mistake had endangered his daughter.

I sighed, rubbing my eyes. "Now, just focus on resting. We'll come up with a plan in the morning."

Silence greeted my words. Everyone seemed too exhausted to respond. Maybe that was a good thing. It meant no one had the energy to argue right now.

But something inside my chest ached, almost *yearning* for an argument or a fight. I still hurt from the battle, but my body itched to run, to fight, to kill something.

The battle had been a failure. And I wasn't accustomed to failure.

I left the room, stomping upstairs and shutting myself in an empty bedroom. Gritting my teeth, I pressed my head against the wall and closed my eyes.

You still have a job to do, Cora, I told myself. *People are still counting on you.*

A firm knock sounded on the door, and I stifled a groan. "I'm resting," I snapped.

"Let me in," Benny shot back.

I huffed in exasperation before throwing open the door and glaring at him. Benny glared right back. He strode inside and shut the door, then faced me with raised eyebrows. "All right. Let it out."

I frowned. "What the hell are you talking about?" I really wasn't in the mood for this.

Benny raised his fists and shifted his feet so they were shoulder-width apart. "Fight me."

I almost laughed in his face, but something deep inside me roared with satisfaction. Benny knew me. Probably better than I knew myself.

He knew what I needed right now.

So, I swung my fist. It was a wide, obvious strike that he easily dodged. But it got my blood pumping and my body *moving.* Adrenaline pulsed through me as we sparred. I aimed several well-placed jabs at his stomach, but he retaliated by kicking my shins and hooking his leg under mine so I slammed backward against the floor.

We kept at it for an hour. Sweat dripped down our faces. A trickle of blood oozed from Benny's nose. But he never backed down.

And neither did I.

When we couldn't keep going—when pain and sweat and blood took over completely—we both collapsed to the floor, winded and groaning. Though every inch of me throbbed with exhaustion and agony, inside I felt alive. I felt a sense of peace and release.

I can do this, that familiar voice rang out in my head. *I can do this.*

"I really needed that," I said breathlessly, staring at the ceiling.

"I know," Benny said.

My eyes shifted to him. My body protested from the movement as I turned my head to look at him. "Thank you," I said softly.

He grunted his response, avoiding my gaze.

After a moment, I whispered, "Are you really planning on sacrificing yourself?" A naïve part of me felt like if I never said it, it would never happen.

Benny finally looked at me, his expression solemn. "If it's the only way? Then, yes."

I found myself nodding, despite how my chest caved in from his words. I didn't know when or *how* it had happened, but Benny was my best friend. My trusted comrade. I couldn't do this without him. I couldn't do *anything* without him.

But hadn't I just been thinking the same thing he was?

That I should give myself up to stop the war, the slaughtering of my people? That it would be easier if I were taken out of the equation?

I couldn't begrudge Benny for making the same choice. In my heart, I knew it was better for Benny to die than *everyone* I cared about.

A lump formed in my throat, and I swallowed hard. "If that's your decision, then I'll stand by you." My voice was strained, but I forced myself to look at him, to convey the truth behind my words.

Benny held my gaze for a long time. "I'm doing this for you, Cora. It's all for you."

My breath caught in my throat. My face warmed, but I couldn't look away from him. I wanted to—I knew nothing good would come from this conversation. As much as I wanted to force myself to feel something for him, I couldn't.

And Benny knew that.

I licked my lips and took a shuddering breath. "You shouldn't say that."

His brow furrowed. "Why not?"

"Because you know how I feel."

His expression didn't change. "You love Vince."

I nodded.

"I know that. But if I died before telling you, I would never forgive myself."

Oddly enough, his words infuriated me. Before I could stop myself, I snapped, "So you want me in as much agony as possible when you die? Is that it?"

His eyes widened. "What? Cora, no—"

"It's hard enough losing my friend, but now you have to add this to it? You have to profess your undying love for me and give me that burden of guilt along with everything else?"

Benny groaned and looked away from me, fixing his gaze on the ceiling. "It's not like that, and you know it. Stop biting my head off for feeling something you don't want."

I sat up and gaped at him. A nasty retort rose in my throat, but then he sat up and looked at me, his eyes earnest. The softness in his expression startled my rage until it dispersed completely. Shame took its place.

I was such an asshole.

I shook my head. "Sorry," I muttered. "You're right. That was unfair." I drew my knees to my chest and wrapped my arms around my legs. With a heavy sigh, I said, "And I *am* sorry. For not feeling the same way. I wish I could choose who to love."

Benny smiled wryly. "Me too. You think you've got it bad? Try being in love with someone who's dead."

I flinched, feeling even worse.

Benny read the despair in my face and said, "It's fine, Cora. I've made my peace with it. In fact, dying means . . . I'll get to be with her again."

I looked at him in surprise. "You believe that?"

"Don't you?" He arched an eyebrow. "With everything we know about magic and spirits, you don't believe there's something after death?"

I didn't know what to say to that. I'd definitely had experience with communicating with the souls of the dead, but I'd never considered it as an afterlife before.

I opened my mouth to respond when a loud *bang* echoed from downstairs. In a flash, Benny and I were on our feet. He threw open the door as something else crashed below. We flew down the stairs and found Piper sparring with a masked assailant. He was tall and wiry and covered in black from head to toe—like a ninja.

And he moved like one too. His arms sliced through the air, easily evading Piper's clumsy blows. Dex and Gio jumped to her defense, surrounding the ninja, but he jumped into the air, arcing high above them as he twisted lithely and danced out of reach. He landed on his feet and swiveled to face me. Something shifted in the dark eyes I could barely make out from behind the mask.

Then, he lunged for me.

But I was ready for him. Purple magic shot from my fingertips, engulfing him completely. My muscles strained as I froze him in place. He thrashed and struggled. With each movement, my arms quivered from the effort of holding him. I was already so weak.

"I've got it," Benny said, hurrying forward. As soon as he stood in front of the ninja, I released my magic and doubled over, wheezing.

Benny snatched the man's arms and pinned him against the wall. The man grunted in pain, his face pressed up against the wall.

"Who are you?" Benny hissed.

The man spat in his face. Benny didn't even flinch. He twisted the man's arm until I heard a sickening *crack*. The man cried out, the sound strangled.

"I can kill you quickly or slowly," Benny growled. "Your choice."

He pressed harder until the man choked out, "All right! The—the Guild sent me."

"What Guild?" Benny asked.

"The Guild of the Unmarked!" the man cried, his voice turning hysterical. "We call ourselves the Unmarked!"

Benny made a low sound of impatience and pressed against the man's twisted arm until he screamed.

"Wait," Gio said suddenly, stepping forward. "I know what he's talking about. Release him. He's mortal."

My mouth fell open. *Mortal?* "What the hell is a mortal doing here?" I demanded.

"Benny," Gio said, gesturing to the man.

With a sigh, Benny released the ninja, who slowly lifted his mask to reveal a narrow face with wide-set brown eyes.

My gaze shifted from the ninja to Gio. "What is this *Guild*?"

"The Guild of the Unmarked," Gio said. "It's a group of mortals who know about magic and are sworn to secrecy. It started out as a way to unify with mortals in the same situation—they have no magic, and yet they have to carry that secret around with them. It's usually the loved ones of casters. My wife's family was a part of the Guild."

Ninja-man nodded, looking relieved. He cradled his

broken arm against his chest. "Yes. Some of us train so we can defend ourselves if need be. Many of us have seen darkness firsthand. Our enemies love to exploit mortals as a form of coercion." His face twisted in a disgusted grimace.

I immediately thought of Vince's dad, José. Vince had been terrified that Quentin would find his father and torture or kill him. That was why José had gone into hiding. He obviously didn't know about this Guild—none of us did. Most of our families possessed magic, so we had no reason to know about an alternative lifestyle. But it made sense. Whether we liked it or not, some mortals were a part of this lifestyle.

I shook my head. "But *why* are you here?"

Ninja-man rubbed the back of his neck with his good arm, his cheeks turning pink. "To, uh, kill you."

I stiffened. Then, an insane laugh burst from my lips. I couldn't help it. The thought of this scrawny man killing *me* was just too much. When the man scowled at me, I covered my mouth and forced a serious expression. "I—sorry." I cleared my throat. "Um, why? Why were you trying to kill me?"

"One of our benefactors put a bounty on you. If we killed you, we could collect."

I frowned. "A benefactor?"

Ninja-man shrugged with one shoulder. "Many of them are anonymous. I don't know who it was."

"Why would a benefactor of an organization of mortals want you dead?" Piper asked me, her brows furrowing.

My first thought was Quentin. But he didn't want me

killed—he wanted to sacrifice me himself. This couldn't have been his doing. He likely didn't even know about the Guild, just like us.

"It could be unrelated to Quentin," Dex said softly. "Cora has lots of enemies."

My eyebrows lifted as I acknowledged this. "True." My gaze shifted to Ninja-man. "But how did you find us?"

"We have trackers," the man said. "Devices that detect areas of high magical activity. My device led me here. Your magic couldn't keep me out, since I'm a mortal."

I rubbed my forehead. As if things weren't bad enough, now I had assassins to look out for. Thank Lilith they were only mortal. Even so, this man had put up a decent fight. I groaned and glanced at Benny. "What do we do with him?" Killing a caster was one thing. But killing a defenseless mortal? Despite all the blood on my hands, that felt like a step too far.

Benny shook his head slowly. "We can't risk him coming back."

"Please," Ninja-man begged. "I won't come back. I swear it."

Regret climbed up my throat. Even if I wanted to believe him, there was no way to prove he wasn't lying. A caster could sign a blood contract that would physically prevent him from following us. But this man was mortal.

"There is another way," Dex said in a low voice, his red eyes gleaming. "If I drink from him, it will take him several days to recover."

The man's face paled. "D-drink from me?"

I waved a hand. "Relax, Dex is one of the good ones. He knows how to control himself." My jaw ticked back and forth as I considered this. Generally, Dex offered a Donor his own blood to help quicken the healing process. But if he abstained and let Ninja-man's body take care of itself, it would buy us enough time to disappear.

I looked at Ninja-man. "It's your call." On principle, I couldn't condone a vampire feasting on an unwilling human. He had to consent to it.

"What are my options?" the man said uncertainly.

"Death or give him some blood," I said in a flat voice.

The man blanched. "Uh, I'll give him my blood."

"I thought so," I grumbled, gesturing for Dex to come forward. While Dex explained to the man what would happen, I glanced at the others and jerked my head toward the kitchen. They followed me into the wide-open space and circled around me. My eyes flicked from Piper to Benny to Gio, with Maddie standing behind him.

"First of all," I said in an undertone, "are any of you hurt?"

Gio shook his head, and Piper said, "He gave it his best effort, but I'm fine."

"And Maddie?" When I looked at Maddie, she shrank away from my gaze.

Gio nudged her, and she muttered feebly, "I'm fine."

"Good." Relief spread through me, but confusion and fear soon took its place. "Second of all, *what the actual hell*? Now mortals are after me? It doesn't make any sense. What do they gain from it?" Other casters hunting me made sense—they wanted my blood. But my blood didn't do squat for mortals. So, why would someone send them after me?

"Quentin owns the magical population," Benny said slowly, rubbing his chin. "At least, the covens in the area. It's possible someone tried to get around him to take you out."

"Yes, but *who*?" I asked, gritting my teeth in frustration.

"We can't be the only ones who want to stop my father," Piper said quietly. "Maybe someone wanted to take you out so he couldn't get stronger."

"And they covered their tracks by using mortals," Gio said, catching on. "Because Quentin would kill them if he found out who ordered the hit."

I nodded, my brow still furrowed. It made sense. But it didn't narrow down the suspects at all. It still could be anyone —even someone I hadn't met.

"The question is," Benny said slowly, "does this change anything? Do we still move forward with our plan?"

Silence fell between us as we all exchanged uncertain glances. After a moment, every pair of eyes settled on me.

It was my call to make.

I took a deep breath. "This doesn't change anything. We'll need to be more cautious moving forward, but this only makes me *more* eager to finish this. We end Quentin, we end all these threats. I'll scope out a new hideout, and then we'll set a plan in motion to kill the son of a bitch once and for all."

CHAPTER 20

VINCE

I STARED NUMBLY AT THE OLDER MAN, MY HEART DRUMMING an erratic rhythm in my chest. "What do you mean, *trapped*?"

The man with the long dark hair sighed and ran a hand down his face. "It's a rather long story. Come inside and I'll tell you everything." He stretched his hand toward the nearest house, an unassuming two-story home.

I stilled, my skin prickling in suspicion. "I don't even know who you are."

The man straightened, dropping his hand. "I apologize. My name is Jeremiah." He pressed a hand to his chest. "I can introduce you to the others, but it would take a very long time. Kallista has trapped enough of us here to populate a small town."

Recognition pricked the corners of my mind. *Jeremiah . . . Kallista . . .* "You mean Kallie—"

"Kallie is Kallista the Timekeeper. From the Great Mage War."

My head spun, and I blinked rapidly to try to clear it. But in my mind, questions swarmed. Kallie was Kallista—the Timekeeper from Luke's story. The one who had waged war against the Timewatchers.

Which meant Jeremiah . . . was the first Timewatcher. The one who had first defied the Call.

"Please," Jeremiah said, reaching his hand toward me again. "Let us go and sit down."

I nodded absently, my tongue turning to sandpaper in my mouth. Jeremiah led me through the crowd toward his front door. My eyes shifted to each person with a new, unsettling perspective—*what time period are these people from?*

The questions formed in my mind faster than I could keep track. I suddenly felt dizzy and worried I would faint. Jeremiah seemed to sense I was unsteady, and he gripped my arm firmly as we went inside.

We sat opposite each other on the couches. A coffee table sat between us. A large TV hung on the wall. I gazed, open-mouthed as I drank in my surroundings.

"It's so . . . *normal*," I said.

Jeremiah chuckled. "Yes. The town adapts to the present day. When I was first trapped here, the homes were made of slabs of concrete and we had no running water."

I stared at him with wide eyes, unable to form words.

"What's your name, son?" Jeremiah asked gently.

"Vince Delgado." My voice was strained.

Jeremiah offered a small smile. "A pleasure to meet you, Vince." He cleared his throat and leaned forward, propping his arms on his legs. "How much do you know of the history of the Timekeepers?"

"I know you angered Kallista by resisting the Call, and she wiped out the Timewatchers."

Jeremiah nodded. "That much is true. But Kallista didn't wage war because I defied the Call. She waged war because I defied *her*."

I frowned and cocked my head. "Did you try to usurp her?"

"Not at all. I wanted to form my own organization with the Timewatchers—an organization with more freedom and flexibility, where following the Call was optional. We could each preserve the timeline as we saw fit."

I stared at him. Shock and numbness still gripped my body, but a small sense of understanding swelled in my chest. The organization Jeremiah described was exactly what I wanted in my life—a way to use my magic and be *free*.

"Kallista enjoyed being in charge," Jeremiah said. "She wanted all Timekeepers to work under her—to *report* to her. Those who didn't were banished here."

My jaw dropped. "She . . . *trapped* you here? Because you wouldn't be her slaves? How did she do it?"

"Less slaves, more like subordinates. And she trapped us in a time loop. We live the same day over and over again. Aside from a few changes here and there as technology advances, everything is the same here. The weather, the homes, the whole town. The area is sealed by a barrier we cannot cross."

"Can you use magic?"

He shook his head. "Our magic doesn't work in the loop. We've tried. We've been here for hundreds of years. Trust me, we've tried *everything.*"

I licked my lips, my heart thundering as I realized what he meant. *My* magic wouldn't work here, either. I was trapped like everyone else. In desperation, I searched inside myself for Luke and Hector, clinging to the feeble hope that they'd remained tethered to me.

I felt nothing but stillness in me. Emptiness.

My magic—the Reaper magic—was gone, leaving nothing but a hollow shell.

"Our food replenishes itself daily," Jeremiah went on. "We want for nothing here. But we are still prisoners."

"Why?" I finally found my voice. "Why wouldn't she just . . ."

"Kill us?" Jeremiah smiled wryly. "The Call won't let her."

I scoffed. "But it let her *trap you* here?"

Jeremiah shrugged. "I'm sure you know already I don't believe the Call's orders are absolute. It's possible Kallista believes the same. The Call is different for everyone, but I know that taking a life has severe consequences. Kallista may be willing to defy the Call for her own benefit, but she won't risk the Call's wrath if she murders innocents. It's a crime against humanity and against the timeline. She risks losing the Call completely."

"But her whole belief is that—"

"That the Timekeepers should follow *her*," Jeremiah said slowly. "She doesn't care about the Call as much as history suggests. She only cares about control and power. Every magical community has an organization, whether it's a coven or a pack. The Timekeepers are the only loose organization where its members are scattered around the globe with no defined leader. Kallista wanted to settle us in one unified community. It was a good idea, in theory, but she learned the hard way that you cannot force people to follow you."

I rubbed my forehead, trying to ward off the growing headache. "She's insane."

Jeremiah nodded. "She is. But living forever will do that to a person."

"How? How is she so young?" Granted, Kallie had had white hair when I saw her, but still—the Great Mage War took place in the 1700s.

Jeremiah took a long, slow breath. "It took us years to figure it out, but once we acquired a few skilled warlocks, we were able to piece it together. She uses this time loop to fuel her. It . . . keeps her young."

Horror coiled in my stomach. "She's . . . *sucking* the life out of you?"

He laughed. "Lilith, no. She's sucking *time* from us. We're frozen in time, you see. Living the same day again and again. She's stolen our future from us, using it to give her youth. As long as she keeps imprisoning people, she'll have an endless supply of time. She's essentially immortal."

My mouth turned dry. "How?" I asked weakly. "How does she possess enough magic for something that powerful?"

"Well, for starters, she was a Second Tier demon before she became a Timekeeper."

My heart lurched. *Second Tier Demon.* Merciful Lilith . . . Then, I remembered Kallie's horrifying display of magic when she'd shown me the consequences of not joining her. Black and gold magic had swirled together—the timeline, mingled with her dark magic.

"And secondly, even the most powerful spells are easier to cast if you tether them to an enchanted talisman."

I thought of the amulet I'd worn around my neck. That was how Gwen had bound the Reaper magic to me. It made sense that Kallista was doing something similar so she could keep her enemies imprisoned here.

Bile climbed up my throat at the thought of *my adult years* being stolen all so Kallie could live forever.

I was trapped here. I couldn't get back to my mom, to Cora, to the impending battle with Quentin . . .

My gaze snapped to Jeremiah, and I leaned forward urgently. "What do you know of Quentin Cox? Why is Kallie working with him?"

"Out of necessity. She knows he could easily destroy her and her carefully cultivated followers. But she doesn't like following orders, as you may have guessed. She has no loyalty to Quentin."

"Why doesn't she just trap *him* here?" I asked, breathless with the notion that the answer was staring me in the face.

Could Kallie end this whole thing for us, right here and now?

"The timeline doesn't work the same way with Quentin," Jeremiah said, rubbing his chin in contemplation. "He's defied the laws of time, so they no longer apply to him. I'd wager Kallie fears if she tries to trap him here, it won't work—or he'll be able to use his magic to escape and then kill her."

"How do you know all this?" I asked. "I doubt Kallie would just tell you."

"No, but each time a new resident appears, they give us information. About Kallie, about the magical world, everything."

I froze, my brain working furiously to form a plan. "Who's the most recent addition?"

"Gloria. She lives down the road."

"Can I speak with her?"

Jeremiah frowned at me. "Why?"

"She might be the key to figuring out how to take down Quentin—*and* Kallie."

Jeremiah shook his head. "You can't escape here. It's useless."

"*You* said you tried for years," I snapped. "But I just got here. At least let me try. I can't give up and accept my fate just yet." Besides, Kallie didn't know I had the Reaper magic in me. Maybe I could find a way to access it.

Whatever I did, I couldn't sink into despair. No matter how the panic swarmed in my chest and threatened to consume me.

I'll find a way out, I vowed. *I have to find a way out.*

Jeremiah offered me a patronizing smile that I'd often seen Hector or the other Nephilim officials wearing when they looked at me. It set my teeth on edge, and I balled my hands into fists.

"Sure," he said at long last. "Do whatever you need to do."

I stood, and Jeremiah's head reared back as he gazed up at me with wide eyes.

"Now?" he asked, rising to his feet.

I resisted the urge to shout at him. "*Yes.* What else am I gonna do?"

"I don't know. Sit for a moment. Process this. You have all the time in the world." He let out a wry chuckle.

I stepped closer to him, gritting my teeth to keep from punching him in the face. "*You* might. Because you've been alive for hundreds of years. But the people I love out there are *dying*. They are relying on me. I have to *do something.* Now."

Jeremiah pressed his lips together into a thin line. Disapproval glinted in his eyes. "Look, you're just a kid. We have some of the most powerful witches and warlocks trapped here. What can *you* possibly do that we can't? Just take a breath. Relax. Digest this information. There's nothing you can do." When my expression remained unyielding, he sighed in exasperation. "You strike me as the type who doesn't like to follow orders."

My temper flared inside me. Before I could stop myself, I hissed, "*You* strike me as the type who *enjoys being in charge.* Just like Kallie." My eyebrows lifted with a challenge.

Jeremiah's cheeks reddened, and his jaw went rigid. "How dare you?"

I lifted my chin. Even though it was petty, in this moment, I was grateful I stood taller than him. "How dare I? I don't even know you. For all I know, *you* could've trapped me here and you're just manipulating me into thinking you're my ally." I drew closer until my gaze bore into his. "Trust is earned, Jeremiah. So show me I can trust you."

Jeremiah's nostrils flared, and rage boiled so fiercely in his eyes I thought he might hit me. Then, he inhaled deeply, and his face smoothed. He forced a pained smile and stretched his arm toward the door. "Of course," he said tightly. "Let me show you to Gloria's house."

I nodded stiffly. Relief spread through me, but it was fleeting. Anger and terror overshadowed it, clawing at my chest like a beast. As I followed Jeremiah out the door, my mind scrambling to find a way out, I feared I had just doomed myself forever.

CHAPTER 21

CORA

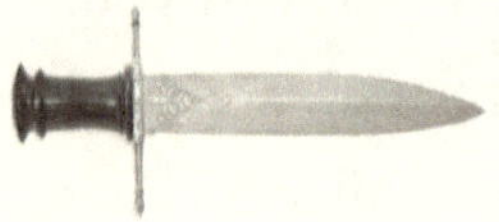

WE FOUND A RUN-DOWN HOUSE IN FORECLOSURE ON THE outskirts of Ravenbrooke—right by the Glen Bridge. It was risky being so close to Hinport—and so exposed—but we no longer needed to be cautious. It was time to make our move.

We spent a full day outlining our plan in painstaking detail, ensuring everyone knew their part. By the end of the day, my head was splitting. Nightmares of blood and death plagued my dreams, and I got little sleep. My insides churned with unease and apprehension, but the time for waiting was over. We had to strike *now.* No more waiting for help that wouldn't come.

It was just us now.

We ate our breakfast of granola bars in solemn silence. Piper kept glancing my way, her face pale. Benny stared hard into the distance, his eyes grim. Gio kept his arm around

Maddie and kept giving her unconvincing smiles. Dex sat cross-legged, his eyes closed as if in prayer.

There were so many holes in our plan. We all knew our chance of survival was slim. One misstep and Quentin could sic his entire army on us. Plus, who knew what Cecile had told him? We also hadn't gotten her input for the spell to trap Quentin in Benny's mind—I'd had to write it from scratch, with help from Benny and his knowledge of Thinker spells.

"Remember, if things go south, you all *get out*," I reminded everyone as we gathered by the front door, preparing to leave. "Quentin wants me. You aren't a threat to him, so you can go free."

"We're with you, Cora," Dex said quietly. "Until the end."

Regret pulsed within me in sickening waves as I remembered the words we'd shared when we first fled Hinport. *I'm with you. Until the end.*

But now, I regretted those words. I was perfectly willing to give myself up if it meant they could live their lives. But if *they* died for my sake? I wouldn't be able to handle it.

Closing my eyes, I took a breath. "If I know you all are safe, I'll be at peace. Please, just give me that." I forced myself to meet their gazes, my eyes pleading. Never before had I laid myself bare before my coven. But these five people were my friends. They risked their lives by fighting alongside me.

They deserved openness from me. No matter how uncomfortable it made me.

So, I kept my gaze level, despite the heat burning behind my eyes and the lump lodged in my throat. "If this plan fails,"

I said in a strained voice, "I need to know I succeeded in *something*. That you all got out. That I'm not—" My throat tightened, and tears stung my eyes. A breath shuddered through me. "That I'm not a complete failure as your leader." My voice broke on the last word, and tears trickled down my face. I ground my teeth against the chagrin swelling within me. I *hated* crying. And I'd learned early on to never let anyone see my tears.

But today was different.

Benny drew closer to me, his eyes moist. "You aren't a failure, Cora."

The others nodded their assent, even Gio, who technically didn't belong to my coven.

"I swear to you, I'll get everyone out," Benny said in a low voice. "If it comes to that."

"But it might not," Gio said, his brow furrowing. "Right? We don't even know if Quentin survived your Jumping stunt."

I grimaced. A normal person might've died from slipping between Jumps, or been dismembered. But with someone as powerful as Quentin, I had no doubt he survived.

And he was *pissed.* I was counting on it. I'd slipped through his fingers again. His deception with Cecile had failed him.

He needed the upper hand again. So, we'd give it to him.

"You're right," I said. "We don't know. That's why Dex will do reconnaissance first. But the rest of us need to stay close in case there's trouble. Quentin's wards will be powerful, even with my cloaking elixir." I met Gio's gaze. "Is Maddie's hideout lined up?"

He nodded. "A family healer lives nearby. She's ancient—and alone. Off Quentin's radar. I'll leave Maddie with her."

"Make sure she seals the wards with blood magic," I said. "That way only you or Benny can get in."

Gio's eyes tightened, and I understood why. Blood magic would require the healer to cut Maddie. But it was her best protection. Stiffly, Gio nodded. My chest constricted, my limbs stiff and motionless. I knew it was time—there wasn't anything left to do—but I didn't feel ready.

I balled my hands into fists. *I'm a fighter. A killer. I can do this.*

But as many times as I'd told myself this, I knew things were different now. I shared a bond with these people. We were comrades. Friends. Family. I'd never felt a connection this strong before.

I was no longer alone. My own survival wasn't as important to me anymore.

So, I altered my thinking. Instead of empowering myself, I said the words aloud. "We are strong. We are powerful. And we can do this." I arranged my expression into something fearsome and cruel, the face I reserved for my enemies. My icy gaze drilled into each of them, daring them to defy me. "Don't underestimate yourselves. *You can do this.*"

Piper's chin lifted. Benny's eyes gleamed. Dex's mouth curled into a half-smile. And Gio nodded, his jaw rigid and his eyes determined. Even Maddie glanced around the group, her eyes full of awe.

Pride swelled in my chest. The feeling was so unfamiliar to

me. I was accustomed to being proud of myself and my own accomplishments. But never other people. Never those I was charged with protecting.

It was both terrifying and humbling at the same time.

Swallowing, I adjusted my bag, ensuring all my elixirs were in place. Then, I gestured to the door. "All right. Let's go."

Traveling on foot was bizarre. We'd grown used to the luxury of Jumping. The thought made me ache for Vince. I wondered if he was okay and if he'd found the other Timekeepers.

Or if Quentin had found him first.

I knew Vince would want me to wait for him. But I couldn't sit around, hoping others would come to my aid. I was never one to stand by and let others fight my battles. This one was mine. And only I could end it.

Benny showed us the way to Quentin's base of operations, since he recalled the building from when Vince had taken him there. Dex used my shadow elixir to canvass the area while the rest of us remained hidden in the alley between buildings. Piper and I had cast a cloaking spell, but I wasn't holding my breath. My insides churned with anxiety as I expected Quentin to pop up any second and grab us.

An hour later, Dex returned, panting. Blood dripped down his chin, but when I scrutinized him, I realized his fangs were red. He'd had to take someone out. My heart lurched in my throat as I watched him lean against the wall, winded.

"What happened?" I asked.

"A few guards gave me some trouble, but I took care of them." Dex closed his eyes and took a deep breath.

"Did anyone else see you?" Benny asked.

Dex shook his head. "Everyone who did is dead. I shoved their bodies in a closet. Should buy us some time."

"And the building?" Gio asked.

"A dozen sentries posted outside," Dex said, opening his eyes. "There's a stairwell on the east side. If you take it out, the whole building will come down."

That was our ace in the hole. Gio had several of my most explosive elixirs on hand. While Benny and I were with Quentin, Gio would rig the building to blow it up.

All we needed was a moment's distraction. One split second when Quentin wasn't on guard, and we'd have him.

"Dex, you and Piper stay here," I said. "Benny, Gio, and I will go in, and you two will be our second wave in case anything goes south. Stay hidden."

Piper and Dex nodded. Piper looked a bit pale, and I knew facing our father was difficult for her. Hopefully, she wouldn't have to see him at all.

Hopefully, he'd be dead before she got the chance.

My eyes roved over the group. Gio ensured my elixirs were secure in his belt. Benny double-checked his weapons. I peered into my bag and counted my vials to verify all my potions were accounted for. When we all looked up, I asked, "Everyone ready?"

Solemn and determined gazes fixed on me. Though our group was small, we were warriors. Fighters. We'd either destroy Quentin or go down fighting. Either way, it ended today.

My heart lodged itself in my throat as I realized I'd never gotten to stay goodbye to Vince. If I died today, he wouldn't know.

I swallowed down the agony in my throat and forced the thought away. This was more important.

Benny met my gaze and nodded slowly. His eyes hardened, blazing with a ferocity that made me tremble.

He's going to die today, I thought. *Even if we succeed, he'll be dead.*

His eyes saddened, his face filling with regret. I forced myself to hold his gaze for just a moment longer, though the yearning in his face made me want to look away. I shoved away my discomfort and schooled my expression into something full of affection and admiration. Benny deserved that. Even if I couldn't give him what he longed for, I could give him that. I was proud of him. Despite the tragedy in his life, he'd become a fierce warrior and a loyal friend.

I took a deep, cleansing breath and broke eye contact. Benny and I crept to the edge of the alley. Unfortunately, I was all out of my shadow elixir, but Benny and I knew how to stay out of sight. Plus, my cloaking spell would help us blend in with the shadows.

We pressed up against the building, edging closer to the entrance. When a sentry appeared, I slit his throat in one swift motion. He didn't even have time to scream before he crumpled in a heap, his blood pooling on the ground. Benny dragged the body out of sight, and we crept onward.

Getting inside undetected would be a struggle. From what Dex described, the lobby was *filled* with people.

So, instead of going through the front, we broke into the back door that led to the stairs. It would make Gio's task easier if the door was already open anyway.

We climbed upstairs, pausing when a door banged open or loud footsteps echoed nearby. Each time we came across someone, we hid, then killed them quietly and hid their bodies. We needed the element of surprise on our side. If any of Quentin's men found a dead body, they'd sound the alarm.

By the time we reached the top, sweat covered my face. My legs burned, and blood coated my hands. My dagger gleamed with the crimson blood of my last kill, and my heart hammered an excitable rhythm in my chest. I'd missed this. The thrill of the hunt. It was different this time, but the adrenaline felt the same.

Benny, also wheezing and covered in sweat, shot a quick glance my way before he eased open the door with a loud creak. We both froze, waiting for someone to come investigate. But silence echoed around us.

Benny hoisted open the door all the way and let me pass first. The hallway was eerily empty. My grip on my knife tightened as we edged along the sides of the narrow passage. My skin prickled with suspicion. I was about to suggest to Benny that we turn back—that this was a trap—but then, I heard muffled voices. I raised a hand, and Benny stopped. We both approached the closed door next to us and listened.

The voices were unfamiliar. Not Quentin. But at least it meant there were other people here. It *could* still be a trap, but it was less likely.

I waved my hand, and we kept moving. Benny had only been on this floor to grab his niece, but he'd told me there were dozens of offices here. And Quentin had protective wards over all of them.

If Quentin wasn't here, something important definitely was.

We reached the end of the hallway, and an office door stood ajar. I peered inside and found a luxurious suite with two pristine sofas, a large and ornate desk, and a figure perched behind it, huddled over paperwork.

My heart shuddered. Had it really been this easy? There he sat, alone and unguarded. Completely unaware.

My father.

I widened my eyes at Benny, and he drew the potion vial from his pocket and nodded.

Together, we strode inside.

CHAPTER 22

VINCE

GLORIA WAS AN OLDER WOMAN WITH DARK BROWN SKIN and wild, curly hair. Jeremiah told me she'd only arrived a few days ago and was still shell-shocked. I found her drinking tea on her porch, her hands shaking as she surveyed the neighborhood. She hardly blinked at my approach.

I cleared my throat. "Are you Gloria?"

Her wide, dark eyes fixed on me, and her expression clouded. "Yes. Why?"

"I'm Vince. Can I ask you a few questions?"

She arched an eyebrow, and brief clarity burst in her eyes. "What are you, the police?" She scoffed and looked away, dismissing me.

Irritation and impatience swelled inside me, but I forced a smile. "I want to know what happened to you."

Gloria's eyes tightened. "You know what? So do I." Her nostrils flared.

Clearly, being polite wasn't getting me anywhere. I lifted my chin. "Look, I get it. You're pissed that you're stuck here. I am too. But you're not going to fix that by sitting here and being bitchy to everyone who tries to talk to you."

Gloria's mouth thinned, and she set her tea down on the table so forcefully it sloshed out of the cup. Slowly, she rose to her feet and drew closer to me. "Don't play with me, *boy.* If I had my powers, I could toss you around like a rag doll."

I raised my eyebrows. Now, we were getting somewhere. "What kind of powers did you have?"

Gloria straightened, and pride gleamed in her eyes. "I was a Pusher."

Was. The word jolted inside me. She spoke as if her powers were a loved one who had died. Like she would never see them again.

I swallowed. "I was a Jumper."

Her eyes softened. "I guess it doesn't matter, does it? In the end, our powers weren't strong enough to save us." With a sigh, she shakily sank back into her chair and stared into the distance as if our conversation had ended.

I sat in the wicker chair next to her and leaned forward, my eyes intent. "Why did Kallista send you here?"

Gloria blinked and looked at me, her expression dazed again. Hardness settled in her features as she watched me. "Kallista," she growled. "That madwoman has been a thorn in my side ever since I became a Timekeeper."

"Why?" I couldn't keep the impatience out of my tone.

"She approached me with an offer to come and work for her," Gloria said, her tone laced with bitterness. "But I prefer to work alone. The Call and I . . . we have a special relationship. It almost feels like I'm doing the Lord's work."

I stilled, trying to hide the disdain from my face. Here was someone *else* who believed the Call was some kind of deity.

"I know what you're thinking," Gloria said with a chuckle. "It isn't like that. I know my personal version of the Call belongs to me and me alone. But . . . the Call is something otherworldly, you know? Even though it's a part of us, it *knows* things we don't because it *is* the timeline. I can't explain it." Her gaze turned distant again, but her eyes filled with awe as she spoke.

My derision melted away, and my chest loosened at her words. I could understand her thinking. I was in awe of it too. It still felt surreal, the idea that I could manipulate the timeline. It was even *more* unbelievable that there was some inner . . . *presence* looking out for me.

"Anyway, Kallista showed up again later," Gloria went on. "She claimed she wanted to see how I did it—how I used the timeline. And, as soon as I reached out to the Call, as soon as I interacted with the timeline"—she snapped her fingers—"I was dragged here by Kallista herself." Her expression soured.

I took a shaky breath. Just like me, Gloria hadn't been caught in Kallie's snare until she'd used the timeline. It was like Kallie had been waiting for her. Monitoring the timeline, not for those violating the laws of time, but for those who refused to bow down to her.

"She's a tyrant," I growled.

"Got that right," Gloria muttered.

I shook my head, knowing my anger would get me nowhere. "Is there anything . . . unusual you noticed about Kallie—I mean, Kallista? Was she wearing some kind of talisman or trinket?"

Gloria frowned as she thought about this. "Now that you mention it, there *was* some kind of weird silver chain around her neck. It had this crescent moon at the end of it. Super gaudy, if you ask me. She wore it every time I saw her and it did *not* go with her outfits." Her face twisted in disgust.

I wracked my brain, thinking back to my first conversation with Kallie. Had she been wearing the chain? I couldn't remember.

"Do you think you can stop her?" Gloria asked quietly, her expression somber.

I sighed. "Some people have been trapped here for hundreds of years. The most powerful witches and warlocks haven't been able to escape."

"That doesn't answer my question." Her gaze sharpened as if she could see right through me.

I swallowed. "I'm going to try. My powers are different from others."

"How so?"

"Well, for starters, I'm a Reaper." I offered a wry smile. "So I have Reaper magic. And for another, my mind is linked to . . ." I trailed off. My blood turned to ice in my veins as I realized what I'd been about to say.

My mind is linked to Luke.

My breath caught in my throat as the faintest ray of gold light shone in my mind as if lighting a path I never saw before. Luke and I were linked at a young age. But why? All Luke knew was that a powerful witch had enchanted him, binding him to me. Luke had never questioned it—never asked why, never tried looking for the witch, never challenged the act . . .

Because he'd *known*. The Call had told him this had to happen.

What if the powerful witch who cast the spell was someone with a unique magic? Someone with the ability to cast spells of enormous power?

Someone like Cora?

And what if the *reason* Cora cast that spell was because a Jumper, who *also* had the Call, had time traveled with her to enchant Luke's mind and link it to mine?

Because the Call *knew* I would need that link.

Right now. At this moment.

I drew a shuddering breath, my mind a torrent of clarity so intense it made my head throb. A ringing blared in my ears, and I couldn't hear anything but the pounding of my pulse.

Everything made sense now. This was why I had the Call—why Luke and I both had it. So we could save all these Timekeepers. So we could take down Kallie.

"You all right, son?" Gloria asked softly, jolting me from my startling epiphany.

I was bound to Luke's mind. Because at some point, I would travel with Cora to the past so she could make it happen.

Gold light gleamed in my mind, affirming this. As if the Call had been waiting for me to realize it all along.

My eyes stung, and it took me a moment to realize tears were brimming. I sniffed and wiped my nose, hoping Gloria hadn't noticed.

She had. Her eyes were tender as she said, "I know it's unfair, to be trapped here."

A hysterical chuckle bubbled from my lips. "That isn't it," I said thickly. "I've just realized something that . . . well, it changes everything."

Gloria frowned at me, but I wasn't paying attention. I thought about my connection to Luke and what that meant here in this time loop. Magic was gone—*my* magic. But not Luke's.

So I couldn't access the timeline. But the Call was still active. I could *feel* it.

I needed power. If Luke's mind was still linked to mine, the bond was faint because of Kallie's prison.

I needed the other Timekeepers to help me.

Jeremiah begrudgingly gathered the hundreds of Timekeepers in the neighborhood park. He tried to flat-out refuse my request, but for some reason, Gloria backed me and threatened to kick Jeremiah's ass if he didn't comply. I wasn't sure how or why, but Gloria and I had bonded on her porch, and now she was an unlikely ally. Whatever the reason, I was grateful she was in my corner.

The crowd of people watched me doubtfully. Many of them looked wary and slightly irritated. But the majority looked simply tired. Like they were exhausted from living for so long, trapped here. I couldn't blame them.

Nervous, I cleared my throat and tried to project my voice. "I won't take much of your time. But if this works, it means freedom for everyone here. It's worth a shot, right?"

A few grumbled in disagreement, but many watched me with curiosity gleaming in their eyes—along with hope.

I knew how dangerous hope could be. This *had* to work.

"Your magic is gone," I said, "but the Call still remains. You just can't act on it. The Call is a part of *you.* I'd wager that belief is one of the reasons many of you are trapped here: because Kallie—Kallista disagrees. She doesn't want us following our instincts. She wants us to follow *her.*

"But the good news is, she can't take *everything* from us. She can take our magic and our lives, but she can't take what's *inside* us. You may not believe me, but I *know* the Call is still here. And, hopefully, this will prove it."

I paused and surveyed the crowd. Almost everyone stared attentively at me.

I took a deep breath. "I'm hoping that we can all channel the Call collectively and use it as a power source. It will be faint, but if we can access it, with our strength combined, we should be able to reach out for help."

"Reach out to *whom*?" asked a sharp voice from within the crowd.

I licked my lips. "My mind is linked to a powerful Thinker. It's a bond that's lasted for years, and it transcends even my magical abilities. As long as *his* magic is intact, I should be able to reach him."

The man scoffed, and I finally made out his features among the many faces in front of me. He had a long nose and dark, humorless eyes that watched me with doubt. "So our freedom hinges on some teenager's friend to magically whisk all three hundred of us out of here?"

"Pipe down!" Gloria barked, her voice booming louder than mine. "You got a better idea?"

The man fell silent, and gratitude spread through my chest. I shot a smile at Gloria, who nodded encouragingly. Her brow was furrowed, as if she wasn't sure where I was going with this.

But she was willing to try.

Confidence burst in me as I said, "If we all join hands and try to summon the Call, this might work. But you need to trust the Call. It's like a living thing. If it senses your doubt or disbelief, it won't emerge. Please try this with me. People out there are dying because of Kallista's treachery."

Solemn gazes rested on me. A few people shifted uncomfortably.

"I'll do it," Gloria said, lifting her chin. Several others muttered their assent as well.

Gradually, murmurs rippled through the crowd like waves as each Timekeeper agreed to give my plan a shot.

Thank Lilith, I thought, my chest swelling with relief. Jeremiah stepped forward and directed the crowd to form a massive circle around the park so there would be enough room for all of us to join hands. When Jeremiah's eyes settled on mine, he nodded stiffly. Hesitation lingered in his gaze, but he, like the others, was willing to try.

It was tedious, gathering everyone like sheep and ensuring we were all spaced out appropriately. But at long last, we stood in a giant circle, hands clasped and waiting for a miracle. I stood at the front, between Gloria and Jeremiah. My heart drummed an erratic rhythm inside me, and I found it hard to breathe.

Inexplicably, I thought of Cora. The way her eyes blazed with determination. The unyielding sharpness of her face. The way she carried herself with confidence and power.

Be like Cora, I told myself. *You can do this.*

"Everyone, search inside yourself for the Call," I said, raising my voice to be heard. Several people in the circle straightened and closed their eyes, their expressions going slack. I did the same, bringing that shocking epiphany back to the front of my mind.

Luke. Cora. The Call. My bond with Luke. The timeline.

A feeble ray of gold light gleamed in my mind, and I grabbed hold of it, clinging desperately. My jaw went rigid, and my hands shook as they struggled to hold on to the Timekeepers on either side of me. Warmth tickled my palms. Gloria's hand was sweaty, and her whole body trembled. But the heat from her skin told me it was working—she'd found the Call.

A light buzzing thrummed around the circle, and a euphoric thrill shot through me. It was working.

Still grasping the ray of light in my head, I tentatively reached out for Luke. My mind returned to the lacrosse field. The smell of grass and sweat surrounded me. My fingers now gripped the crosse as I faced the empty net in front of me.

Come on, Luke, I thought. *Find me!*

I focused on the adrenaline, the excitement of the game, the strategy and exertion. Faint shadows appeared on the field, marking the shapes of my faceless opponents. I surged forward, my eyes fixed on the goal before me. My focus honed in on that singular objective: get to the goal.

Magic crackled in the air. In a flash, Luke appeared as if he'd fallen out of the sky. He collapsed on the grass, coughing and gasping for breath.

"Luke!" I shouted, so startled I almost lost my grip on the Call—and the field. Sweat trickled down my face as I struggled to hang on. If I lost this connection, the plan would fail. I *had* to hold on.

Stiffly, I approached Luke, ensuring my focus remained on the power pulsing inside me. Luke heaved a rattling breath and gazed up at me, his face drawn and haggard. He looked like he hadn't slept in days.

Maybe he *hadn't.* I had no idea how time worked in the loop I was stuck in.

"What happened?" I asked in a strained voice.

Luke staggered to his feet, still winded. "I've been trying to reach you . . . for three days! Where the hell did you go?"

"Kallie trapped me in a time loop," I said quickly. Fatigue tugged at my body, coaxing me downward. I wouldn't be able to hold on much longer. "*All* of the Timewatchers are here. Everyone who's defied her. Three hundred people, Luke. Can you help me get them out? We don't have our magic. My link to you is our only hope."

Luke's face paled. "Dude, I'm already drained from trying to get to you. But *three hundred people*? That many souls in my mind would kill me."

I gritted my teeth. "There must be *something* you can do! Is Hector still with you?"

Luke's gaze grew distant, and he waved a finger at me. "That . . . might work. If I use Hector as a sort of conduit to channel power, I might be able to use my mind as a bridge for the Timekeepers. As long as they don't stay in my head for too long."

I nodded eagerly. "Okay. What do I do? We're all connected right now. How do I summon them here?"

"Hang on," Luke said, and then he vanished.

I groaned, sinking to my knees. My mind strained to hold onto the Call, but it was growing more and more faint. *Hurry,*

Luke, I thought. Waves of agony crashed over me, and my head started throbbing.

A few minutes later, Luke appeared with Hector alongside him. Hector looked at me, his eyes filled with an unreadable emotion that made my chest tighten. After a moment, I realized what it was: concern. Hector had been *genuinely* concerned for me.

I wasn't sure how I felt about that.

"How can I help?" Hector asked. Once again, I was struck by how *odd* it was that he even bothered to be useful. But the tightness of his eyes made me wonder if it was just the Call urging him onward. That made more sense—that Hector would only help others if it kept the Call at bay. If it kept his mind free.

"It's the same spell I used before," I groaned, squeezing my eyes shut against the pain. "Do you need me to repeat it?"

"No," Luke said quickly. "I remember. Hector, take my hand." After a moment, Luke muttered the spell.

"*Magic above and powers that be,*
Link this man to the magic in me.
Bind our powers to hold me steady,
And bring me back when I am ready."

I cracked my eyes open and saw a beam of blue light. My heart jolted in my chest at the sight of my friend's face lighting up from the glow of his magic. I'd never seen Luke cast a spell before. Even though I should've been used to it by now, it still jarred me to watch my friend use magic.

Hector sucked in a breath in a low hiss, his body going stiff. "It didn't feel like that before."

Luke grimaced. "Vince didn't need as much power as I do. He had all the Reaper magic to lean on."

Hector nodded, his expression strained. "It's okay. I can do it."

"Ready?" I asked, glancing from Luke to Hector. Luke took several deep breaths, his face pale. Hector's eyes closed, his expression slackening as if he were meditating. Luke met my gaze and nodded stiffly.

I exhaled long and slow and then shifted my mind back to the park with the other Timekeepers. The air swiveled around me, and my stomach churned. Gravity slammed into me with full force, and it took every ounce of strength to keep my grip on Gloria and Jeremiah's hands. Panting and covered in sweat, I opened my eyes and found Gloria watching me anxiously.

"It's time," I wheezed. Exhausted, I looked up at the massive circle of Timekeepers.

As if reading my mind, Gloria took it upon herself to shout, "Everyone, get ready! Here we go!"

I shot her a grateful look before pulling both arms with a sharp *tug* and dragging Gloria and Jeremiah back into Luke's mind.

CHAPTER 23

CORA

"HELLO, CORDELIA," MY FATHER SAID PLEASANTLY, AS IF WE were meeting for lunch. He glanced up from his papers with a mild smile on his face. "I'll admit, I'm surprised to see you here."

Well, at least that was something. But it wasn't nearly as satisfying as the utter shock I was hoping to find when we stormed his headquarters. In fact, I'd anticipated *anger.* As I watched him, I could tell something was off, but I couldn't put my finger on it.

I resisted the urge to check my watch. We had two more minutes before Gio would detonate the explosives. I had to make sure Quentin was within reach when that happened.

"Where are the Reapers?" I asked.

Quentin's brow furrowed. "I'm a man of my word, Cordelia. I let them go."

I snorted. *Yeah, right.* No way would he just release the captives who had seen his headquarters.

"I had no quarrel with them once they turned you over to me," Quentin said, rising from his seat. Then, I realized what was different about him. His hands were trembling, and his eyes were unfocused. He looked on the brink of insanity, though he spoke with perfect clarity. "Especially after your little stunt revealed that amulet was nothing more than a piece of junk." His cloudy eyes darkened for a moment, betraying his anger.

Good. I lifted my chin. "I can't believe you didn't already know. How can someone as powerful as you not detect that an object has no magic?" I arched an eyebrow and gave him a bemused expression.

Quentin's eyes flashed, but his face remained calm. "I had no reason to suspect the amulet was useless. After all, that *boy* shouldn't have been able to handle that much magic." He cocked his head at me. "How *did* your little boyfriend manage it?"

I knew what he was doing, and it wouldn't work. He couldn't bait me like I was trying to bait him. "I don't know," I said, and it was partially the truth. Vince had said the timeline gave him more power, but I wasn't entirely sure what that meant. "But surely a little boost of magic like that is insignificant compared to your power, right?"

Quentin offered a patronizing smile, but it only tugged at half his face. The other half remained slack. "Oh, Cordelia, you have so much to learn. You probably think your pitiful reserve of magic is satisfactory." He leaned over the desk to stare at me. "Your abilities are *nothing* compared to what you could become."

I suppressed a shudder. *What* I could become . . . not *who.* That implied I would become some *thing.* Some creature of darkness. Something inhuman.

I forced myself to give my father a level look. "I know," I said softly. "But I make my own choices, Quentin. I don't want to become like you. Ever."

Quentin went very still, his expression frozen. His eye twitched, and he gave me a pained smile that looked more like a sneer. "Your loss." He dropped his gaze and shuffled papers on his desk as if dismissing me. But I didn't miss the tremor in his hands.

"That Jump did something to you, didn't it?" I asked, trying not to sound smug.

Quentin stilled, his nostrils flaring. I realized *that* was what angered him the most: that I had crippled him. Nevermind the amulet or my escape. Somehow, against all odds, I'd *weakened* him. "As you can see, I still function perfectly. So, your efforts were unsuccessful."

"I got away, didn't I? So did my people. That's a success to me."

Quentin's jaw quivered, and he looked at me with fire in his eyes. "Is that all you came here to say?"

I barked out a laugh. "Are my comments bothering you?"

"Hardly," he snarled. "But I don't think you came here just to gloat."

I stared at him, grinding my teeth. *He needs to come out from behind that damn desk.* I estimated I had about a minute left. Goading him hadn't worked. If we rushed him, he'd blast us backward, even if he *was* weakened.

Time for a new tactic. I glanced at Benny, who had remained completely silent. His stony gaze was pinned on Quentin as if he could kill him with his icy stare. Slowly, Benny's eyes shifted to meet mine, and he nodded ever so slightly. *Time for Plan B.*

I looked back at Quentin. "I came here to give you information."

"Cora," Benny said sharply.

"We're losing," I snapped at Benny. "This information will put an end to everything once and for all."

Quentin straightened, his eyes glinting with interest. "What is it?"

I opened my mouth, but before I could speak, Benny crashed into me, tackling me to the floor. I grunted, pretending to struggle, but he held me in place, pressing his knees against my legs.

"Stop!" Quentin roared, darting out from behind his desk with a limp in his step. "Garrett! Kent! Get in here, now!"

Dammit, I thought. I'd feared he would summon his goons. Our time was up.

As soon as Quentin approached, Benny jumped off me and pressed his fingers to Quentin's temples. Quentin's expression immediately went slack, his eyes rolling back until they were all white. Benny grunted, his body stiff and the veins and tendons standing out on his neck. I had no doubt that keeping Quentin subdued would completely drain Benny.

I grabbed Benny and my father by the shoulders, closed my eyes, and uttered a hasty spell.

"*Magic above and powers that be,*

Protect us from harm and injury.

Seal a barrier to shield us here,

Conceal us from the danger near."

Purple wisps of magic surrounded us, wrapping around us like ropes. Heavy footsteps echoed as Quentin's henchmen made their way toward us. I shared an alarmed look with Benny, but before the men arrived, a deafening *boom* shook the building.

Gio had done his part.

The floor quivered. The glass windows rattled. Tremors rocked us, but my spell held us in place as if an invisible hand kept us steady. The quaking intensified until something shattered, and I flinched away instinctively, even knowing my spell would protect us. Shards of glass burst in the air. Bookshelves toppled over with a crash. Screams filled the hallway.

Then, the building swayed. I closed my eyes. I couldn't watch this part.

But I could still hear the screams.

I knew Quentin held prisoners here. There just wasn't time to free them. They would die along with everyone else.

Gravity shifted around me. My stomach dropped, and bile climbed up my throat. Dust and ash tickled my face. My fingernails dug into Benny and Quentin's arms, desperate to hold on. The ground trembled and then gave out completely, leaving us suspended mid-air. And still, I kept my eyes shut tight, even as I felt weightless, like on a roller coaster just before a drop.

A blinding light burned against my eyelids. The commotion settled, and the air gradually went still. Slowly, my eyes cracked open. The three of us stood in the vast, empty parking lot, surrounded by a pile of rubble that had once been a magnificent building. Bodies were strewn about, some wriggling and shrieking, and others not moving at all. Flames burned nearby, though I couldn't see through the haze of ash that drifted in the air like snow.

"Cora," Benny moaned weakly. I glanced at him and found him covered in sweat, his face pale as he kept my father unconscious.

My body snapped to action. We didn't have much time. But as I took a breath, preparing to recite the spell we'd rehearsed, a lump lodged itself in my throat.

This was it. This would kill Benny.

But it would also kill Quentin. If I were in Benny's shoes, I would make the same sacrifice in a heartbeat.

Benny met my solemn gaze and nodded. He'd made his peace with this.

My voice shook as I uttered the spell.

"*Magic above, and powers that be,*

Hear my call, and answer me,

Seal this man and trap him inside,

Let him in the mind reside.

Hold him there, and leave him be.

Imprison him for eternity."

My hands glowed purple and surrounded Benny and my father. The glow burned against my eyes, stinging me. I bit my lip, realizing the pain in my eyes was from oncoming tears that I could no longer hold back. They spilled down my face. Sobs broke against my throat as I watched Benny stiffen. With a *pop*, Quentin vanished, and Benny collapsed on the pavement.

I rushed to his side, cradling his head in my lap. His wide eyes stared at the sky above us, still filled with ash.

"Cora," he groaned incoherently. His body convulsed, and he gagged as if something strangled him.

"I'm here," I choked, weeping freely.

"Y-you have to do it," Benny grunted. He stiffened again, the veins so stark against his skin I thought they would burst free. "*Now.*"

I inhaled a rattling breath. *Oh, Lilith, I can't do this. I just can't.*

"All the p-people you've killed," Benny croaked, "and you c-can't kill me?" Faint amusement sparked in his eyes, but it vanished as he seized again.

My tongue felt like lead in my mouth.

"You owe me," Benny said, his voice weak. "Remember? W-when we defeated D-Damien together. I—I told you I'd c-call in a favor."

My mouth opened in surprise. I'd forgotten all about that.

At the time, I assumed he would have me kill someone for him.

My face crumpled as I realized that's exactly what he *was* asking.

"This is it," Benny rasped. "This is my price. Do this, Cora. Y-you have to."

Agony swelled in my chest. All I could do was shake my head as Benny convulsed, his face going taut.

"He's f-fighting," Benny whispered. "Please, Cora. Please."

Let him be a hero, I told myself. *Let him do this.* I stroked the hair out of Benny's face and pressed a kiss to his forehead. He closed his eyes, his jaw rigid and his limbs trembling.

I drew in a deep breath, my insides quivering. "Go to her, Benny. Go to Lynn. She's waiting for you."

Benny nodded. His body still strained, but a momentary look of peace crossed his expression.

I firmly clasped the hilt of my dagger and raised it high above me.

A sob broke through me as I plunged the knife into his heart.

I knew exactly where to bury it. Years of killing taught me the best places to end a life immediately—and the best places to make the agony last.

Benny choked once more, his eyes wide with shock. Then, he slumped backward, his mouth slightly agape and his eyes still open. Blood pooled from beneath him, and his chest stopped moving.

I remained there with his blood staining my lap. I wasn't

sure how much time had passed. But I was waiting for my father to resurface. I had to ensure Benny hadn't died in vain.

So, for what felt like hours, I sat there, crying like a baby. Tears and dirt mingled on my face, forming a sticky paste. The ash burned in my throat, but I didn't care. My chest felt like it caved inward on itself, crumbling to dust just like the building around me.

Benny was gone. My best friend was dead.

A small *pop* echoed nearby. I raised my head, my heart lurching in my throat. Vince? Could it really be him?

A figure appeared in the ash, tall and slim. Definitely not Vince.

I hastily swiped particles out of my eyes so I could see better. "Who's there?" My voice cracked, but it was loud and commanding.

"I must congratulate you," said a deep, female voice. "Though I knew your interference would be beneficial, I had no idea it would be *this* grand."

My eyes narrowed. As much as I didn't want to leave Benny's body, I knew if this woman killed me because I was on my knees, Benny would never forgive me. Slowly, I shifted his head off my lap and rose to my feet, ignoring the dampness of blood on my shirt and pants.

"Who are you?" I snapped.

The figure emerged from the shadows, revealing a tall, graceful-looking woman with white-blond hair and brilliant green eyes. Her sharp, angular face looked like it could cut right through me. She offered me an icy smile, her eyes dancing with smug amusement. Like she knew something I didn't.

"*Who are you?*" I growled, gritting my teeth. My knife was still in Benny's chest, but I had no qualms about killing this woman with my bare hands. Lilith knew I could blow off some steam right about now.

"My name is Kallie," the woman said, inclining her head. "I'm the leader of the Timekeepers. And now, thanks to you" —she gestured to Benny's body—"I'm also the leader of Quentin Cox's army."

I stared at her, my brows furrowed. "What the hell are you talking about?" But my pulse drummed an erratic rhythm inside me as if warning me.

"Did you really think I *wanted* to work alongside Quentin?" Kallie cocked her head at me, her cold eyes calculating. "I joined him out of necessity. To protect my people from his wrath. But my connection to the timeline has its . . . benefits." Her thin lips curled into a cruel smile. "At first, I thought you needed to be dispensed with, so I took precautionary measures. But when that failed, I looked a bit more closely at the timeline to see just *how* much of a nuisance you would be.

"It turned out, your little friends were planning something big. Something that could benefit *me* as well. So, I stood back and let you take the lead. I made sure everything you needed was in place and nothing would obstruct you." She laughed, the sound like broken glass. "And you performed your task brilliantly."

Something in my mind snagged at her words. *You needed to be dispensed with, so I took precautionary measures.* "You—you sent the assasins. From the Guild."

Kallie scoffed. "I had little faith in them, but it was the only way to get around Quentin."

My skin prickled as I processed this information. She'd been pulling *all* the strings. This whole time. Horror pooled in my stomach, and my instincts screamed at me to run, to get as far away from her as possible.

But Benny . . . Gio had asked me to bring his body so we could give him a proper burial. A hero's memorial.

I swallowed hard, gathering my wits. *Stay on top of this, Cora,* I told myself. A quick glance over Kallie's figure told me she didn't have any obvious weapons. But the timeline itself was a weapon with her. I couldn't get too close.

"So, you're exactly like my father then," I said coolly.

Kallie's nostrils flared. "I am *not*."

I shrugged. "You want to control the world, right? You wanted *his* army and *his* authority. How are you any different?"

"I don't want to crush the minds of innocent casters," Kallie hissed. "I have no quarrel with the magical community as long as they don't hinder me."

"Hinder you from *what*? You already have everything. You've *won*! Congratulations." I clapped slowly, fixing a sarcastic stare on her.

Kallie's eyes burned with rage. "Don't patronize me, girl. You have no idea what I've endured. You know *nothing*."

I spread my arms. "You're right! So I'm no threat to you.

As you said, you have no quarrel with the magical community, right?"

Kallie's expression smoothed into an unreadable mask, and she drew closer to me. I stepped back. "Not necessarily," she said softly. "You are a Bloodcaster, after all. Your very existence is a threat to us all."

I laughed, but I placed my arms behind my back and wiggled my fingers, ensuring my magic was at the ready. "I've been on this earth for more than two decades and no one's batted an eye." Not necessarily true, but whatever. "I just want my city back. That's all. Take your army, take the *world* for all I care."

Kallie stepped closer, and I edged away from her again. "Unfortunately, I can't take your word for it. I've lived for centuries and learned the hard way that words mean nothing."

I stilled, my skin tingling. *Centuries?*

Kallie lunged for me. My shock delayed my response, but I managed to duck before a blast of black magic spiraled toward me. White-hot flames seared the top of my head, and I scrambled back to avoid another spell. Purple light exploded from my fingertips. Kallie waved it away like it was nothing more than paper. I raised my hands again, but Kallie flung burst after burst of black magic, an onslaught more powerful than I could have imagined. I ducked and jumped, trying to evade her power, but one blast caught me in the chest, sending me flying. I collided with a pile of rubble, the rocks scraping against my skin.

Coughing, I tried to rise, but her magic pinned me in

place, holding me steady. In that moment, I knew: she was Second Tier. After my spell on Benny, I didn't have the strength to defeat her on my own.

Kallie drew closer, her arm outstretched as her magic pinned me to a hunk of concrete on the ground. I thrashed against her power, but it was useless. I was completely frozen.

Kallie's mouth spread into a wide, insane smile, her disheveled hair making her look crazed. "Goodbye, Bloodcaster."

A burst of gold light, and the ground gave out beneath me. I was flying through the air, flying through *time,* until everything went dark.

CHAPTER 24

VINCE

GUIDING ALL THREE HUNDRED TIMEKEEPERS THROUGH Luke's mind felt like herding cats. And each person I passed through weighed down on my body as if I were benching a hundred pounds over and over. Within minutes, I was drenched in sweat. An hour later, I was ready to pass out.

Luke wasn't much better off. He sat on the grass of our mental lacrosse field, overseeing everything and checking in with us here and there. But I sensed his distress. Occasionally, the ground rumbled, or the sky above me darkened—proof that his mind was taking a hit from all this activity.

But every time this happened, he glanced my way. Though his face was haggard and pale, his eyes were clear as he nodded reassuringly.

Hector popped back and forth, shepherding people from Luke's mind to the outside world. I couldn't imagine what the

Timekeepers were experiencing as they breathed fresh air for the first time in centuries.

"What will happen to Kallie?" I asked as I passed on another Timekeeper. Hector appeared with a *pop*, his eyes tired, and grabbed the Timekeeper before vanishing again.

"You mean when everyone leaves?" Luke asked, his voice hoarse. He shook his head. "From what I understand of talismans, as long as there is still an energy source attached to it, it still works. So, once everyone is out of the time loop . . ."

"It'll stop working," I finished. Relief bubbled up inside me. "Will she just . . . I don't know, wither away? Will the years come back to her?"

"I'm not sure. As long as the talisman is intact, the spell will still be in place. The years she's stolen will remain hers. But . . . with the Timekeepers living in present day, utilizing the timeline once again, I'm sure that would disrupt things for her." He scoffed and ran a hand down his face. "We've never seen anything like this before, Vince."

"I know." If I weren't so exhausted, I would marvel at the cruel, impressive power of it all. Kallie was essentially *immortal* because she kept trapping people in her own personal time loop. In a way, that made her worse than Quentin. No amount of magic could make Quentin live forever. But as the oldest Timekeeper, Kallie had access to all kinds of dangerous possibilities.

Which was why she *had* to be stopped.

I wasn't sure how much time passed when we finished. But Luke's arms were trembling, and blood trickled from his nose when I passed on the last Timekeeper. My body felt like lead as I trudged over to him and put a hand on his shoulder.

"You all right?" I asked.

Luke looked at me through half-lidded eyes and teetered slightly. "I'll . . . be fine. Let's get you through so I can rest."

I nodded, but then something shifted in the air. I stiffened and glanced around, trying to pinpoint what was different. A faint voice shouted my name. Hands gripped my shoulders, and my body jolted. My mind spiraled, and suddenly, I was no longer in Luke's mind.

I was back in the park in the time loop. The wide expanse of grass seemed so empty without all the Timekeepers crowded around each other.

Someone was shaking my shoulders violently as if trying to wake me from a deep sleep. Gravity pressed in on me, dragging me downward until I collapsed, staring up at the bright sky. A figure hovered over me, but I could barely make out the words being shouted at me. Dazed, I blinked, trying to clear my head.

I sat up quickly. Too quickly. A bolt of pain speared through my head, and I winced, clutching my forehead.

"You all right?" a voice asked.

I sucked in several deep breaths and looked around. My heart shuddered in my chest.

Cora. She crouched next to me in the grass, her eyes wide. Dust and dirt covered her body, smearing along her cheeks and arms. A pool of blood stained her pants and shirt.

"Cora," I breathed. "What—what the hell are you doing

here? What happened?" My voice rose in pitch as I realized what this meant: Cora was stuck in the time loop.

Cora stood too, her expression darkening with fury. "That Timekeeper bitch sent me here." She rubbed her arms and looked around. "Where *are* we, anyway? And how did *you* get here?"

"I don't have time to explain." I grabbed her hand. "Come on." I closed my eyes and thought of the field again.

Nothing happened.

With a grunt, I closed my eyes and tried again, focusing with all my might on the field, the goal, the crosse, the opponents around me . . .

A jet of purple magic sparked, and Cora yelped next to me. Something hot burned our hands, and I jerked away from her on instinct. We stared at each other, gaping.

"What was *that*?" Cora asked.

I opened and closed my mouth. The magic had been *purple*. I'd assumed it was her, but she seemed just as confused as I was. Shaking my head, I said, "Maybe—maybe Luke passed out or something. Or maybe all this is too much for him. Let me try on my own." I took a deep breath, shut my eyes again, and tried once more.

In an instant, I was back on the field. Stunned, I gazed around, looking for Luke. He still sat on the grass, right where I left him. He raised his eyebrows expectantly. "You okay, man?"

My mouth felt dry, and I couldn't breathe right. I gestured nonsensically next to me where Cora had stood just moments before—but she wasn't here now. "I—Cora. Cora's in the time loop."

Luke's eyes widened. "What? How?"

"Kallie got her."

Luke's face drained of color. He licked his lips. "Vince—this is bad."

"I *know*."

"No, you don't get it. Cora can't get inside my mind."

My brow furrowed. "Why not? If it's because she's a Bloodcaster, then—"

"It's not." Luke rose to his feet, his legs wobbling. I grabbed his arm to steady him. "It's part of the failsafe built into the spell linking our minds. If she comes here, the spell will recognize her presence and it'll be nullified. Her magic cancels it out."

My blood ran cold. I stared at Luke, not seeing him. My mind spun as I tried to process this information.

Slowly, the pieces slid into place. "Because Cora cast the spell," I whispered.

Luke pressed his lips together, his eyes full of guilt—but also confirmation. "I'm sorry I didn't tell you before. I *couldn't*—"

"No, I understand. I . . . actually figured it out earlier. But—" I glanced behind me as if Cora herself might appear and solve this whole predicament.

But she wasn't here. And deep down, I knew she never could be. If she showed up here, my connection to Luke would be lost. Which meant there was no way out of the time loop.

"How do we get her out?" I asked. Fear coiled inside me like a snake waiting to strike. Panic pulsed in my chest. *I can't leave her behind.*

Luke shook his head weakly. "I—I don't know, man. Maybe Benny can do something. He's Second Tier, so his link to you might be strong enough to withstand her magic."

I nodded as a tendril of hope curled within me. I clung to it before shifting back to the time loop—back to Cora. My head throbbed, and my whole body ached. But I forced myself to face her, to figure this out.

"Where's Benny?" I asked.

Cora blinked at me. Then, her face crumpled. "I—he—" She broke off with a shuddering gasp and covered her mouth with both hands.

Oh, Lilith. My heart dropped like a stone as Cora's eyes filled with tears. I'd never seen her cry before.

I stared at the blood on her clothes, finally realizing it wasn't hers. "He's dead, isn't he?" I breathed.

Cora sobbed and nodded, sucking in ragged breaths. "He —he died to save us all f-from Quentin."

My chest tightened at her words, though I had no idea why. Then, realization hit me. "Quentin—Quentin's *dead*?"

Cora brushed tears off her cheeks and sniffed. "Yes. The mind spell worked. But . . . Kallie was using us. She *wanted* us to kill Quentin so she could take over his armies."

Horror numbed my body, freezing me in place. "Mother of Lilith," I hissed, running a hand through my hair. Now Kallie had even *more* power at her disposal. We hadn't even known she was a true threat until a few days ago. She'd played a clever game, lurking in the shadows undetected for so long, biding her time until the perfect moment came along . . .

"What happened to Luke?" Cora asked. "Is he all right? Can he get us out?"

A lump formed in my throat, and I swallowed hard. "I—" The words choked me, and I closed my mouth. How could I tell her she was trapped here with no way out? Instead, I raised a finger. "Hang on one second."

And then, I was back on the field, standing in front of Luke. He watched me, his brows knitted together.

"What happens if we destroy the talisman while people are still in the time loop?" I asked.

Luke winced. "If you break a talisman that's tethered to a living soul, that soul will die."

My blood chilled. *Cora will die.*

I shook my head. It wasn't an option. Even if it meant taking out Kallie, I would *not* sacrifice Cora. Never.

"You go rest," I told Luke. "Tell Hector what's happened. Maybe he has some ideas. You two can put your heads together and research to find us a way out so we can stop Kallie."

Luke's jaw went rigid as he stared hard at me. "What're you going to do?" But his tone told me he already knew.

I took a deep breath. Resolve filled me, and I knew without a doubt this was what I had to do. "I'm staying here. With Cora."

CHAPTER 25

CORA

WHEN VINCE RETURNED FROM LUKE'S MIND, HE SAT ME down on a park bench and told me everything—about Kallie, the time loop, and the other Timekeepers.

After losing Benny, I didn't think things could get worse. But I was so very wrong.

For several minutes, I sat there, staring numbly at the winding sidewalk in front of us. My muddled brain struggled to keep up with everything. Just processing the information made my whole body ache.

"I don't understand," I said at long last. "Why are *you* still here? You can use Luke's mind to get out of here!"

Vince hesitated, his eyes guarded. Then, he lifted his chin. "I'm not leaving you here."

I groaned and hunched over, grabbing fistfuls of my hair. "Dammit, Vince! What the *hell* are you thinking?"

"I let you down before, and I won't ever do it again." His voice was hard.

Startled, I sat up and looked at him. His jaw was firm, his gaze unyielding as he stared at me. "Saving your own life wouldn't be letting me down," I said quietly.

"It would," Vince said. "At least for me."

"I can take care of myself."

"I know that."

Our gazes held, neither of us backing down. The certainty in Vince's eyes told me I couldn't change his mind. With a groan, I broke eye contact and rubbed my forehead. "Okay. Since you're being a stubborn ass about this, what's your brilliant plan for getting us both out of here?"

Vince chuckled. "Honestly, right now, I'm too exhausted to think of anything. I told Luke to find help. I'll check in with him after he's rested."

I arched an eyebrow, eying him up and down. He was slouched forward, his eyes tired and his face weary. "You know, rest wouldn't be such a bad idea. For both of us."

Vince sighed heavily. "Yeah. You're right."

Neither of us moved. Vince's eyes tightened, his gaze distant. I knew what he was feeling because I felt it too. How could we go rest when our people were out there? They needed us.

I shook my head and forced myself to stand. "We're no good to them if we work ourselves to death." I extended a hand to him.

Vince's eyes were heavy as he looked at me. Emotions

weighed him down, and the agony on his face was almost too much for me to bear.

"You need this, Vince," I said softly. "Take a breather. We can face this problem with fresh eyes later."

Slowly, Vince nodded and took my hand. I helped him up, and we strode down the sidewalk, arm-in-arm.

We claimed one of the cookie-cutter houses as our own—the smallest one. I could tell Vince felt uncomfortable with the idea of inhabiting someone else's home. But I reminded him none of this was real. It was just a fake neighborhood, most likely created to assuage Kallie's guilt from imprisoning hundreds of people. Even though Vince had already told me, it startled me to see firsthand how the house provided for us as if it were a living entity. Soap, towels, and fresh clothes exactly our size waited for us in the bathroom as if the house could smell the foul odor from both of us. Neither of us had bathed in days.

The fridge was also fully stocked. Just the sight of the fried chicken, lunch meat, strawberries, and grapes made my stomach roar.

Vince heard, and his lips twitched as if he might smile. But after a moment, his gray eyes turned haunted, and his expression sobered. I knew how much weighed on his mind.

"Let's eat first, shall we?" I asked, trying to sound cheerful. My voice was strained, though, and I couldn't stop seeing

Benny's blank and empty expression or the blood pooling from his wound. The wound *I* had inflicted.

Vince and I filled our plates and sat across from each other at the tiny dining table. We took slow bites, avoiding each other's gazes, too preoccupied by the demons that tormented our minds. We were both broken. Too tired and anguished to bother with pleasantries.

In ordinary circumstances, it might've felt like a companionable silence. We were both suffering. We were both helpless. But some tangible wall slid between us, keeping us apart even when we were right in front of each other.

"It isn't your fault," I whispered at long last.

Vince blinked, his eyes far away. "What isn't?"

Everything, I wanted to say. Vince had a tendency to assume everyone's responsibilities. To take it upon himself to save the world. "Kallie. The Timekeepers. Being stuck here."

Vince snorted. "So if I jump into a pit of lions and get shredded apart, that wouldn't be my fault?" Bitterness tainted his voice.

"No," I said at once. "It would be the lions' fault. Granted, you made a stupid choice. But it's not like you shredded *yourself* apart."

Vince looked at me, his eyes steely. "Is that how *you* feel? You don't feel any guilt for Benny's death?"

I flinched as if he'd slapped me. Agony roiled within me, and my throat burned. I fought to keep my voice steady as I said, "Of course I feel guilty. But I know . . . I know . . ." I trailed off. I'd been about to say, *I know it's not my fault he died,* but that wasn't true. I wielded the dagger that killed him. I blinked, my eyes suddenly feeling hot.

Vince's expression sagged. He ran a hand down his face. "I'm sorry. That wasn't fair of me."

I swallowed and shook my head. "It's all right." I couldn't meet his gaze. I suddenly felt too tired to try anymore.

Vince's warm hand pressed against mine on top of the table. Startled, I met his gaze. His eyes were softer, though his jaw was still rigid. "Thank you," he said.

"For what?"

"For doing the brave thing. The *hard* thing. I don't think anyone else would've been strong enough to go through with it."

A lump formed in my throat. I knew he was talking about killing Benny. "You mean only a monster would've been able to do it." My voice broke, and a tear raced down my cheek.

"Cora, no." Vince leaned over the table to meet my gaze, his eyes earnest. "Benny knew what he was asking. If he could've done it himself, he would have. You weren't killing him—you were killing Quentin. Benny was collateral damage in a war we *had* to win."

I nodded. Logically, I knew all this. But it didn't stop the pain from eating me alive.

"I know we're both messed up right now," Vince said with a hollow laugh. "But if I had to be stuck here with *anyone*, I'd want it to be you."

A wobbly smile lifted my lips. I looked at him, and heat stirred in his gaze. An echo of desire flickered in my stomach, but my sorrow drowned it out. "Me too." I took a shaky breath. "Even though it was the dumbest thing you've *ever* done, I'm glad you chose to stay here with me."

Vince's brow furrowed. "Um, thanks. I think."

We both chuckled, and something loosened in my chest. Vince ran his thumb across my knuckles, and a shiver of pleasure swept over me. I was suddenly painfully aware of the fact that we were alone in this house. When was the last time we got to be alone together? If things were different, this could've been our first date. The idea sounded so *normal* it made me ache with longing.

Just for one night, I wanted to be his. No enemies to defeat. No battles to fight. No psychopaths to hunt down. I just wanted to spend the night with the man I loved.

I clutched his hand in both of mine. "We're here together, Vince. Whatever's going on out there"—I waved a hand nonsensically in the air before pressing my palm to his again—"our friends would want us to be happy and safe. So, for right now, can we focus on that? You and I are alive and we're together. How often do we get to celebrate that?"

His mouth curved into the smallest of smiles, and he nodded.

"Can we both promise to *try*?" I asked quietly. "I guarantee you won't be able to sleep if you let this torment you. Let's just . . . try to push it all aside. Only for tonight."

Vince pressed his lips together and dropped his gaze. He nodded again, his eyes tightening. He took a deep breath and met my gaze, his expression a fraction calmer. A tad more at peace. The grief and regret were still there, but his eyes shone with hope. He wanted to be free of this emotional weight as much as I did. He, too, wanted to let go.

Vince brought his other hand to mine until our fingers were entwined together on the table. He smiled again, brighter than before. “I promise I’ll try.”

CHAPTER 26

VINCE

I HATED TO ADMIT IT, BUT CORA WAS RIGHT. I HADN'T slept in days. Hunger had been gnawing at my stomach so consistently that it almost hurt when I finally got food in my system. And, truth be told, I smelled *terrible.*

As the sun outside slowly set and fatigue dragged me downward, I resigned myself to rest. Cora was right—I was in no shape to help anyone right now. And if I let these conflicting thoughts nag me, I'd never be able to sleep. Besides, I'd told Luke to go rest. I might as well do the same.

I cleared my throat. "You can take the shower first."

Cora raised her eyebrows. "You sure?" Her voice was laced with something else—something that made my stomach clench.

I swallowed hard. Desire stirred in her eyes, mirroring my own. I tried not to picture her undressing and bathing. But the way she looked at me made me wonder if *she* was thinking the same thing. There was an invitation in her eyes. My mouth felt dry as I could practically hear her thinking, *Maybe we should just shower together.*

I shook my head and dropped my gaze. *No,* I thought firmly. *With everything going on right now, that is the* last *thing we should be focusing on.*

Cora sighed and stood from her chair before striding from the room. It wasn't until she left that I realized my hands were clenched into tight fists.

She emerged ten minutes later, her expression brighter and clearer as she toweled her wet hair. "All yours," she said.

"That was fast."

She scoffed. "Did you really think I'm the kind of diva who takes an hour in the bathroom?"

I rolled my eyes. "Of course not."

She shot me a playful smile before I went into the bathroom and shut the door.

I wanted to stay in the shower forever. The scalding water felt like fire cleansing me from head to toe, and even though it burned, I reveled in it. My muscles ached, reminding me of my lacrosse days. Things had been so simple back then. Luke had been an average mortal. My biggest problems had been the prejudices of my Nephilim clan.

But I also hadn't known Cora. I wouldn't trade that for anything.

When I was finally clean, I dressed myself, mildly surprised that the house had clothes in exactly my size. My bitter thoughts turned to Kallie. Of course she would make this bittersweet—*have anything you like, perfectly tailored to your needs and wants . . . but you're still a prisoner.* The thought set my teeth on edge.

That bitch was reigning terror, taking over the world one coven at a time. And I was relaxing in this big, empty house. I *had* to get out of here.

You can, a small voice in my head whispered, *if you leave Cora.*

But I shoved the thought from my mind. I would *not* abandon her. The guilt of what Mom had done still gnawed at me. I refused to turn my back on Cora.

I emerged to find Cora standing in front of a massive bookcase, her arms crossed as she gazed at the various book titles.

She looked up at my approach. "Feel any better?"

I grunted noncommittally. Tension tied my stomach into knots. "Find anything interesting to read?"

"All the classics are here," she said, her tone wistful. "But I can't bring myself to read right now." Her eyes met mine, and I nodded in understanding. Doing what I liked felt wrong somehow.

"We should probably sleep," I muttered.

Cora nodded, rubbing her arms. "You're right."

Our gazes locked, and a bolt of heat seared through me. I licked my lips. "Um . . . I can take the couch . . ." My face was on fire. Why had we picked this house with only one bedroom? There were several around the block that had multiple rooms.

Cora's lips twitched with a smile. "Don't be ridiculous, Vince. I don't bite. Unless you want me to." Her eyes smoldered, and my breath hitched.

My words died in my throat as she drew closer. I took a shaky breath. "I—I don't think that's such a good idea."

Cora tilted her head, her expression puzzled. Hurt flashed in her eyes before she smoothed her face into a calm mask. "If you say so."

She turned to leave, but I grabbed her arm to stop her. "Not . . . because I don't want to," I said in a low voice. "But because I'm not myself right now. I can't—*we* can't—" I broke off and shook my head, unable to form the words with the heat pounding through my body.

Cora looked at me, her gaze steady. "I think you're wrong. We *both* need to blow off steam right now. And I don't think you'd like me using you as a punching bag."

I snorted and ducked my head.

"I won't pressure you to do something you're not ready for," she said softly, pressing her hand to my cheek. Her touch warmed me, and I closed my eyes. "But it always helps me clear my head when I've got too many thoughts to sort through."

I stiffened. She sucked in a breath as if realizing what she'd said. Suddenly, all heat left my body as I remembered Cora had done this before. *Plenty* of times.

And I hadn't.

Cora dropped her hand. "I'm sorry."

"Don't be." I forced my expression into something neutral. "We both had different lives before we met. If I can get over the fact that you're an *assassin*—"

"Was," she corrected with a smile.

"—then I can get over whatever happened in your past," I finished. The words were true, but they didn't stop my mind from wandering to dangerous places—like *who* she'd slept with. And how many partners had shared her bed.

Had Benny?

I cursed myself for thinking it. Benny was dead. I shouldn't be thinking of him like this.

But Cora had seemed *so* torn up about his death . . . like she'd lost someone who'd been *more* than just a friend.

"Did you love him?" I blurted.

Cora's head reared back. "What? Love who?"

Dammit, Vince, I told myself, gritting my teeth. "I—I shouldn't—" My mouth clamped shut. I needed to just stop talking.

Cora crossed her arms, her eyes narrowing with suspicion. "Did I love *who*?" she demanded.

Oh, hell. I exhaled. "Did you love Benny?" Though my voice was gentle, I still sounded like a jealous ass.

Cora's face slackened in surprise. Her arms fell at her sides, and her lips pressed together in a thin line. Emotion stirred in her eyes, making me feel guilty . . . and hollow inside. Because they confirmed what I suspected.

Cora rubbed her forehead. "How can you ask me that?"

"You just invited me to have sex," I said. "You really think I can do that when I'm worried you're thinking about another man?"

Cora slapped her arm against her thigh and stared at me, eyes blazing. "How shallow do you think I am, Vince? I pledged my *love* to you—*only you*—and you think I would turn around and fall for someone else the second you disappear?"

"You can't always choose who you love. If you *did* love him, I never would've thought you'd done it on purpose."

Her face twisted in disgust. "If you can't trust my feelings for you, then you can go to hell."

Again, she turned away from me, and my stomach sank with the realization that I had just ruined everything.

"Cora—" I took her hand, and, to my surprise, she stopped and looked at me with tormented eyes. "I'm sorry," I said. "That—that was a dick move. I wasn't thinking." My eyes closed. I was *such* an idiot.

Her face softened just a fraction, but the fire remained in her eyes. "*Why* did you ask me that, Vince? Are you really worried I'd fallen in love with someone else?"

"No," I said at once. "No, I wasn't—I just knew you two seemed closer than friends. Your bond seemed stronger than that. And when you lost him—" I stopped again before I made an even bigger fool of myself.

Cora sighed and dropped her gaze. "I know. I *never* get that torn up about a loss. You're right."

Everything in my body went still. My heart even stopped for a full beat.

"Benny and I *were* closer than friends," Cora said. "He was the only person in the coven I trusted with my life. He knew me better than I knew myself. But . . . I didn't love him. Not like that." Her voice broke on the last word, and she sucked in a shaky breath. "But *he* loved me."

My jaw dropped. *Oh.* I hadn't been expecting that. As I watched Cora's face crumple, I realized what she was feeling. Not just despair from losing her friend or guilt for causing his death . . . but agony that she couldn't give him what he wanted. That he'd died loving her.

Cora sniffed and met my gaze. She stepped closer to me, and my body tingled from her nearness. "It's only been you, Vince. I may have had . . . a few sexual partners over the years—"

I snorted again, and she elbowed me.

"But I never loved any of them." She stared at me, her expression firm and full of affection.

All humor left me as I met her gaze. I saw the truth in her eyes. "You—you—"

"I've never been in love," she whispered, "until now."

My heart skittered in my chest. "I—me neither." The words filled me with peace and affirmation. She may not have been a virgin like me . . . but I was her first love. And she was mine.

She took another step until our chests were touching. Her face tilted up, angled perfectly to meet mine. Her voice was barely a breath as she said, "I have never actually . . . made *love* before."

Flames tore through me, numbing my body with a heat that was so powerful it was almost painful. Cora raised her eyes to meet mine, her eyebrows lifting slightly as if asking a question. But I was frozen stiff. I couldn't move, not when she looked at me like that.

Then, she caught her bottom lip between her teeth. A low moan built up my throat, the sound almost feral as if I couldn't help it.

We shouldn't, I thought faintly. But the thought was drowned out by the all-consuming *need* pulsing through me.

Cora placed her hands against my chest, her fingertips trailing up to my neck and wrapping around me. Her chest pressed fully against mine. I could feel everywhere her body arched into me, molding with me as if we were two pieces of a puzzle that fit perfectly together.

An aching, desperate yearning burned between my legs. And I knew Cora felt it. Her eyes sparked with hunger as she leaned in to brush her lips against mine.

Merciful Lilith. Her lips were smooth and sweet as they caressed mine. She stood on her tiptoes, pressing more fervently as her tongue slid along my lower lip.

My hands found her waist, and I pinned her hips to mine. But it wasn't enough. I needed more of her. More of *us*.

She seemed to read my mind. Her hands slid back down to my stomach, her fingers climbing under my shirt and running along the muscles of my abdomen and chest. With a lithe movement, she lifted my shirt over my head and let it fall to the floor.

My chest rose and fell with rapid breaths as she surveyed me, her eyes roving over every inch of my bare torso. She smiled wickedly and started tugging at my jeans. Before I could blink, she'd unbuttoned, unzipped, and eased them off my legs.

A small part of my brain registered that I should be embarrassed, to be standing in only my boxers in front of a beautiful woman. But the heat had taken over completely. A raw, animal desire quivered through me down to my bones. And I let it take over. I was *so tired* of feeling everything—guilt, anger, helplessness—that I gladly let this mindless beast take control.

I bent over, trailing my lips along Cora's neck. My tongue slid over her skin. She clung to me, her fingernails digging into my back.

"I think," I whispered against her throat, "that you're a little overdressed for my liking."

Her hips thrust against mine, and she sighed with pleasure. "Am I?" she teased, arching her head backward to give me better access. I pressed kisses up and down her throat, running my tongue along every part of her with deliberate slowness.

She moaned, the sound almost involuntary. I placed my hands on her waist, inching my fingers below her waistline. Lower. Then lower.

Her breath hitched, and her eyes closed. My hands slid around her waist, brushing against her bare skin. Her body tensed and arched backward again as I unzipped her pants and slowly slid them down. I crouched low, pressing kisses along the soft skin of her legs as I removed her pants. Her breathing turned ragged, and her fingers clenched into fists. I knew my slow pace was driving her mad. The thought gave me a sliver of satisfaction.

When I straightened, she was panting, her eyes wild with need. Her gaze bore into mine. She lifted her arms, resting them against the wall behind her. I knew without asking what she wanted. My fingers gripped the edge of her shirt as I rolled it upward and over her head before discarding it with the other clothes.

For a moment, we stood there in only our underwear, breathless and consumed by heat.

Cora licked her lips, her eyes raking over me with a hungry expression. A bolt of longing coursed through me, bringing that reckless confidence I craved.

"Like what you see?" I murmured in a low voice.

Amusement and heat sparked in her gaze, and I knew she remembered those same words I'd spoken when we were trapped in Damien's prison cell and she'd painted a rune on my chest with her blood.

Cora grinned and tilted her face up to meet mine. Her mouth brushed against mine, the movement much too gentle for my liking. I pulled her closer, crushing her against me, my tongue and teeth grazing her lips. A small noise of satisfaction escaped her lips as she wrapped her arms around my neck. She turned her head, her lips trailing a line of fire up my jawline until her tongue flicked against my ear.

"Bedroom," she whispered, her breath tickling my skin and sending shivers up and down my body. "Now."

She didn't need to tell me twice. I hoisted her up into my arms. She yelped, clinging to me, her eyes wide as I carried her to the bedroom. Then, ever so slowly, I placed her in the middle of the bed and climbed on top, bracing my arms on either side of her shoulders. Her breathing was fast and heavy as she looked at me.

"I love you, Vince," she murmured, touching my cheeks.

"I love you, Cora."

Her fingers tugged at the elastic of my boxers, shifting them downward until I kicked them off. I reciprocated by sliding one finger underneath the strap of her underwear and wriggling it loose. Cora stiffened, her back arching as I slipped her underwear off ever so slowly. When I finally pulled it free, she sat up, her eyes dark with need. Her mouth found mine again, assaulting my tongue and teeth with a savage fierceness that only made me want her more. She broke apart for a moment, then twisted her arms behind herself to undo her bra. It sprang free, and she tossed it onto the floor.

We sat there, completely naked, as we drank each other in.

"You're perfect," I whispered, running a fingertip down her collarbone and between her breasts. She sucked in a sharp breath, her eyes closing and her head rolling backward. Her fingers grabbed a fistful of my hair as she yanked me down with her, almost painfully. But the sensation was far from unpleasant.

Obliging her, I lay on top of her, our legs twining together. Her soft body seemed to fit perfectly against mine. I pressed down on her, and she thrust upward in response. I moaned with pleasure. Cora bit down on my shoulder, and I swore, fisting the sheets on the bed. When her hands moved between my legs, I uttered a string of filthy curses that made her chuckle. Her fingers moved with deliberate slowness, pumping back and forth until I couldn't see straight. With a growl, I leaned in and licked her earlobe, then caught it between my teeth. A sharp gasp escaped her lips, and I grinned in triumph.

My hands caressed her, sliding up and down her body, tracing circles on her stomach. She guided my hand to her thigh, urging it higher and higher until it was right between her legs. She let out a cry of delight. I followed her lead, watching her reaction as my hands continued to explore. When I found the place that gave her the most pleasure, I lingered there, my fingers moving faster and harder until her release shattered through her. Her breathing was sharp and ragged. With one hand, she pushed against the side of my chest and pulled my shoulder with the other, flipping us so she was on top. Still slick with sweat, she shifted until she straddled me. Then, her hand gripped me again, easing me into her slowly—too slowly. I groaned, my hands tightening around her waist, but she only grinned at me, her expression devious.

She was *toying* with me.

"More," I rasped. I'd intended to sound commanding, like she had, but it came out as more of a plea. Her eyes glinted with triumph.

She owned me. And she knew it too. I was utterly and completely hers.

At long last, I was fully inside her, and she rode me hard until my mind splintered and fractured, my body caving inward as a roar of satisfaction poured from my lips, tearing through my throat. Fire coursed through my veins, scorching every inch of me. My brain seemed to spiral out of my body as if I no longer had awareness of who I was or what I was doing here.

There was nothing on my mind but Cora. Only Cora.

CHAPTER 27

CORA

I WAS NEVER ONE FOR CUDDLING. BUT I WAS SO BONE weary and dead tired that falling asleep next to Vince was as easy as breathing.

And, to be honest, it was the best sex I'd ever had. Vince had been the most attentive and passionate lover . . . because he loved me. No one else had given themselves to me completely. Most of my sexual encounters played out more like some power struggle between us—especially Damien.

But Vince—he submitted to me completely. Happily. Lovingly. Like he wanted nothing more than to give me pleasure.

Not that I'd shirked *my* part. Vince's loud groans of satisfaction were proof enough, and he'd conked out soon after. I took pride in the fact that I'd sufficiently wiped him out. Then again, we were both exhausted.

I blinked, my eyelids crusty from too much sleep as sun streamed in through the window. Momentarily disoriented, I turned and found Vince sprawled on the bed next to me. One arm was raised to his face, his mouth open as he breathed slowly.

For a second, I just watched him, allowing my gaze to rove over him. He was still naked, so I took the time to appreciate him. His body was toned and muscular, his beautiful olive skin so dark compared to my ivory complexion. He seemed so much taller like this, his torso and well-muscled legs stretched out as if they would go on for miles.

A lump formed in my throat as my eyes shifted back to his face. So peaceful. So relaxed. So oblivious to the troubles we faced.

I still couldn't believe he trapped himself here with me. And I knew I couldn't convince him to leave me. I couldn't force him out, either.

I knew what I had to do to save him. But it would break his heart.

He suddenly inhaled sharply, blinking sleepily at me. His mouth stretched into a tired yet delighted smile. "Morning." His voice was deep and throaty, and it made my toes curl. He ruffled his hair and turned over so he fully faced me. "You sleep well?"

"Like a log." I ran my fingers through his mussed hair. "You?"

"I think you successfully rocked my world," he said with a

low chuckle. "I don't even remember what happened afterward."

I snorted. "You passed out, that's what happened." I flashed a grin at him. "It just means I did my part well."

He leaned in and pressed a soft kiss to my nose. A smile spread across my face, but it vanished when he drew back, his brows furrowing. I watched his eyes shift from lazy contentment to grim determination in an instant. And I knew he remembered our predicament. As nice as it would be to pretend this was just a vacation, we were prisoners here. And there was a war waiting for us outside.

"I should reach out to Luke," Vince said, sitting up. "See if he's found anything helpful."

I already knew he hadn't. I'd tested my magic earlier—nothing. Which was bizarre, because purple sparks had *definitely* ignited when Vince had tried to take me into Luke's mind. But that could've been a reaction to Luke himself—to the spell I cast on him. Or *would* cast on him? It was all very confusing.

If I couldn't go through Luke's mind, there was no way out for me.

But there was still a way out for Vince. I just had to get him there.

Forcing a smile, I sat up and leaned my head on his shoulder. "Whatever you need to do. I'm going to see if I can cook up a few spells in the meantime."

Vince kissed the top of my head and slid out of bed. I

admired his backside for a long moment before I stood and dressed.

We shared a quiet breakfast, exchanging the occasional smile or two that sent heat curling through my belly. When we finished, Vince stood, his face tightening with concern.

"It'll be okay," I said, reading the anxiety on his face. I rose to my feet and touched his shoulder.

Vince's brows knitted together. "You don't know that."

I grabbed his other shoulder and forced him to meet my gaze. "Vince, do you trust me?"

"Of course."

I smiled. "Then it will be okay. I swear it."

He still looked unconvinced.

My eyes widened for emphasis. "*Trust me.*"

Vince's expression sobered. Affection gleamed in his gaze, and he pressed a gentle kiss to my lips.

Vince sat in the living room and took a deep breath. I watched him as he closed his eyes to reach out to Luke. Sorrow gnawed in the pit of my stomach. I swallowed down my emotions and slipped out of the room, giving him some privacy.

It also allowed me to do what I had to do. Cooking up potions hadn't been a complete lie—but I already had the elixir I needed. Searching through my dirty clothes from yesterday, I found the tiny vial tucked into my back pocket. A contingency for if I had to resort to desperate measures when facing my father. Because I would've done absolutely *anything* to keep him from gaining more power. Even something as drastic as this.

I stared at the corked vial and swished the murky gray liquid. I hadn't used this elixir in years. For a moment, I sat there, completely frozen as I contemplated what I was about to do—and how it would destroy Vince.

But I couldn't keep him chained here. And I knew there wasn't any way he would leave. I admired him for that, but it also made things frustratingly difficult. Anyone else I could've either threatened, tortured, or manipulated.

But not Vince.

Down to my bones, I knew I had to do this. I couldn't explain it. But an undeniable, urgent *knowing* pushed me forward. And in spite of myself, I trusted it completely.

I inhaled a shuddering breath. "Forgive me, Vince," I whispered.

My hand trembled as I uncorked the vial. With a quick motion, I emptied the contents into my mouth and smacked my lips, my face twisting in disgust at the bitter taste.

My heart rate quickened. My stomach knotted. For a few seconds, I remained completely still, waiting for the elixir to take effect.

Then, my vision blurred. I slumped over. My head hit the floor, and everything went dark.

CHAPTER 28
VINCE

Reaching Luke wasn't easy. I was grateful Cora had left the room because I wouldn't have been able to concentrate very easily . . . not when all I could think about was ripping off her clothes.

Even after I cleared my head and tried accessing the lacrosse field, my surroundings grew hazy, as if the field wasn't completely solid. I tried again and again, but the image flickered and vanished, leaving me feeling cold and empty in the living room.

Dread filled my stomach. What was wrong with Luke? Was he hurt? Perhaps he was still recovering. I kept telling myself that, but I remembered when Hector had trained me as a Timekeeper—we'd woken up Luke when we wanted to talk with him. Even when he was unconscious, I could still reach him.

Knots coiled in my gut, and a feeling of unease filled me. Deep down, I knew something wasn't right.

I took a moment to focus on breathing. Deep inhale. Soothing exhale. Then, I tried again.

Ten minutes later, a sheen of sweat covered my forehead and my fingernails had carved crescent shapes into my palms from clenching my fists. And I still hadn't been able to contact Luke.

It's okay, I thought. *Luke probably wouldn't have found a solution anyway. You're still stuck here with Cora.*

My legs shook as I stood. I wiped my sweaty palms on my jeans. Maybe Cora had come up with some spell we could use to get out of here. Her magic might be gone, but we'd proven that normal magical barriers didn't apply to her blood. After all, she'd used a healing rune on me when we'd both been imprisoned by Damien. If anyone could get us out of this mess, it was Cora.

With a sigh, I shook my head, trying to rid myself of the lingering dizziness, and searched for Cora. She wasn't in the kitchen. My brow furrowed as I checked the hallway.

"Cora?" I called.

No answer.

That same feeling of foreboding rippled through me. My skin prickled. Something was very, very wrong. I'd felt it earlier, but I'd assumed it had to do with Luke.

No, I thought. *Cora's fine. She probably took a walk outside.*

Then, I caught a glimpse of Cora's legs sprawled on the floor of the bedroom. My heart lodged itself in my throat.

It's fine. She probably just . . . passed out or something. Maybe a potion went wrong.

Each step took an eternity. My heart thumped a warning rhythm in my chest. Every heartbeat screamed, *Wrong. Wrong. Wrong.*

When I finally reached the room, I found Cora lying on the floor, completely motionless. Her eyes were wide open and vacant. Her chest wasn't moving.

My heart stopped. I couldn't breathe. *Cora.*

Snapping to my senses, I crouched to the ground and touched her face. Her skin was cold. I turned her head, and it flopped like a doll. When I searched frantically for a pulse, I found none. I checked her throat and her wrist.

Nothing.

This wasn't happening. It *couldn't* be. But no matter how many times I checked her pulse or gave her mouth-to-mouth or chest compressions, her body remained horribly still.

My hands shook. My breathing turned sharp and ragged. I couldn't see straight. What the hell had happened?

I sat there, stunned, utterly frozen with shock. My mouth remained open while I stared numbly at the corner of the room. I didn't feel like myself. It felt like my mind was transported out of my body, like I was watching from afar. I was no longer alive or present. I was just an observer.

It felt like hours before I could finally move. And when my gaze fell to Cora's open and empty eyes, agony carved a hole through my chest like a jagged knife. I hunched over. I couldn't breathe. The air couldn't get to my lungs, no matter how much I tried. My head was spinning. Tears streamed down my face, but I couldn't feel them. I watched them spill onto my shirt, momentarily confused about how the moisture got there.

I can't, I thought in panicked desperation. *I can't do this. Can't think. Can't breathe. Can't, can't, can't . . .*

I couldn't stop the tears. And slowly, ever so slowly, the feeling came back into my body, and I felt every sob rip through me like my tears were cutting me open again and again. A fresh stab with every wave of grief.

This couldn't be happening. Surely Cora Covington, the Blade of Hinport, the feared assassin, couldn't have just fallen over and *died.* Surely this was some mistake.

"Cora," I moaned in a broken voice. "Cora, please." I bowed my head and pressed my forehead to hers, willing her to wake up. My tears splashed onto her face. A small, pitiful part of me thought that my tears could somehow awaken her. But this was no fairy tale.

I cradled her face in my hands, trying to ignore how limp she felt. For several minutes, I wept openly, not caring that I was soaking her in my tears, not caring how loud I cried because honestly, who would hear it?

There was no one here but me. Me and my dead girlfriend.

But no. It *couldn't* be true. Cora couldn't be killed like this. She was a *fighter*. She'd fought all her life. She deserved to live a long and happy life with me. This was just a dream. It had to be. Or maybe another test from the Call.

The Call. My head snapped up, my mouth hanging open in shock. I'd seen this *exact moment* during my test with the Call. I remembered being confused by seeing her dead on the floor of a random bedroom. But . . . it was precisely the same as what the Call had shown me. Down to the last detail.

The Call had *known* this would happen. It sent me to Benny and Gio's cabin so I could stop this from happening.

But I hadn't. I was a *fool.* The Call had warned me, and I hadn't been able to do *anything* about it.

But . . this meant Cora's death was related to the timeline. And Kallie had untethered access to the timeline. This was *her* prison after all.

What other explanation was there? Cora must've been close to finding a way out, and Kallie killed her. Nothing else made sense. I'd only been away from her for twenty minutes at most. And I hadn't even heard a struggle.

Nothing else could've taken out Cora. I was sure of it.

The more I thought about it, the more my hands shook. Something new and intense took over my shock and horror, and it burned through every inch of me.

Rage. Pure, raw, animal rage.

My heart rate quickened, and red crept into my vision. My hands started to glow, but I didn't even notice as I rose to my feet. Tears still dripped down my face, but I was all fury now.

I stormed down the hallway and out the front door, my footsteps thunderous. Magic sparked around me. As I strode into the street, I glanced up at the sky and froze.

Red lightning cracked through the sky. Dark clouds swirled, and a billowing gust of wind tousled my hair.

For a moment, I stopped and stared, wide-eyed, at the sight. I'd seen this too. When the Call had shown me Cora's death, I'd seen this red lightning storm.

I hadn't known at the time, but I knew it now: it belonged to *me*.

I should've been awestruck. I should've cared enough to wonder *why* or *how*. But as I watched the enormous tempest intensify, I only felt enraged satisfaction.

I was powerful. And I would *destroy* Kallie.

I threw my head back and roared up at the sky, "*Is this what you wanted?*" My voice tore at my throat, but I reveled in the pain. "To take *everything* from me? Well, congratulations. Because now I have *nothing* left to lose!" My words ended with a piercing scream. I lifted my arms, and jets of red magic speared toward the dark clouds. A blast of blinding white light filled the sky, so severe it burned my eyes.

And then, I felt it. A deep rumbling made my bones thrum. Something in the ground fractured, as if the earth itself were splitting in two. A deep chasm opened up in front of me, and gold light gleamed from within.

I knew immediately what it was: the timeline.

For the first time, my anger faltered momentarily. I glanced behind me toward the house. The front door remained open. Cora's body was still inside.

I swallowed hard. The motion sent a bolt of pain spiraling through me. My rage prodded me, urging me forward.

I didn't want to leave her body here. But I *had* to end Kallie. I *had* to obliterate her—before she destroyed someone else's life.

I'd waited too long. And now Cora was dead.

A feral thirst for vengeance flowed through my veins, empowering me. I breathed in deeply, feeling every ounce of power as it coursed through me, unrestrained and *free.*

I would slaughter Kallie and anyone who stood with her. It was exactly what Cora would've done.

Steeling myself, I took another breath before jumping into the chasm.

CHAPTER 29

CORA

I FELT LIKE I'D BEEN HIT BY A BUS. NO, A *DOZEN* BUSES. Plus a massive hangover. Now I remembered why I didn't like using the death elixir.

That, and it felt like a coward's way out. I only used it as a last resort when I was outnumbered and outgunned. Which didn't happen often.

Slowly, I cracked my eyes open, but even the natural light filtering through the window sent a splitting pain through my head. *Merciful Lilith.* Gritting my teeth, I sat up, trying to ignore the nauseating pounding in my brain.

Must get up, I thought, staggering to my feet. If my plan worked, then Vince had left. And I didn't have much time.

He would go to Kallie. He would kill her—and destroy her talisman. The time loop would collapse on itself, taking me with it.

I'd known this would all happen. *Somehow,* I'd known. I couldn't explain it. But in my gut, I'd *known* I had to fake my death to force Vince to leave. There was no other way.

As I frantically searched the pockets of my dirty jeans and withdrew my remaining potions, a faint gold light flickered inside me. So unlike the usual powerful spark of my purple magic.

I stilled. As I focused on it, the gold light faded, as if it had been startled and wanted to hide. Like I was a predator.

My breathing turned shaky. *It couldn't be.* My heart quivered in my chest.

Vince had described the Call as a gold light inside him.

I swallowed hard, shaking my head. I couldn't focus on this now. Arms full of potion vials, I hurried to the kitchen and dumped the vials onto the counter. My movements were frantic as I flung open every cabinet, looking for *something* I could use as a potion ingredient. If all else failed, I knew my blood would work. I just had to *remember* the damn runes I'd researched. I didn't often use them because my magic and elixirs were sufficient, but now I cursed myself for not practicing more rune spells.

After the last cabinet revealed nothing but boxes of pasta and cans of tomato sauce, I slammed the door shut with a scream of frustration. I pulled at my hair, trying not to lose my cool.

But it was too late. Inside, I was torn apart. I'd known from the moment I'd woken up, the moment I'd noticed those splotchy wet stains on my shirt and the moisture on my face—Vince believed I was dead.

And it had destroyed him.

Vicious sobs ripped through me. I hunched over, leaning my head on the counter as I wailed like a baby, not caring how weak it made me.

I'd broken Vince's heart. That beautiful, loyal man who'd pledged his love for me and only me. I'd gutted him completely.

Tears poured down my face. My cries intensified until my nose was stuffed up and my eyes were so puffy they stung.

I let myself cry for two full minutes before I impatiently wiped away my tears and blew my nose.

"Get ahold of yourself, Cora," I told myself thickly. "You need to get to work."

Okay, so no potion ingredients. That was fine. I could—

I froze, my skin prickling with recognition. Gold light winked from deep inside me, and I went as still as if I were trying not to scare off a deer. Ever so gently, I mentally reached for that thread of gold light.

And then, spearing through my mind as clear as day, a command pulsed through me.

Go outside.

I didn't hesitate. With the gold light urging me onward, I left the kitchen and found the front door wide open. Even before I stepped outside, I felt the storm raging. Fierce wind tousled my hair and burned my face. Crimson lightning lit up the sky like jagged gashes.

My heart stuttered in my chest as I gaped at the sight. It was horrifying . . . and, at the same time, awe-inspiring. Beautiful. Incredible.

Power thrummed from the ground, vibrating against my feet as I moved toward the street. And then, a few yards away, I noticed a giant crack in the pavement, carving a crooked hole in the ground. From within, gold light flashed as if beckoning me closer.

I stopped, but the light within me sang with yearning, desperate to be united with its counterpart waiting for me in the abyss.

But still, I hesitated. Acknowledging the Call inside me was one thing. But *diving into* the timeline? That was a plunge that gave me pause. Everything I knew about Timekeepers told me this was a *bad idea.* Timekeepers were forbidden from manipulating the timeline until they'd finished their training and passed their tests. What would happen if an untrained Timekeeper used the Call like this?

But it's calling to me, I thought, my eyes transfixed by the glow winking at me from the chasm. *Why would the Call tell me to do this if it was wrong?*

Uncertainty still gripped me. I remained rooted in place. What if I was wrong? What if this wasn't the Call at all? For all I knew, this was some psychological game I was playing with myself, trying to *convince* myself it was another power when it was really just me.

The red lightning roared above me, ready to devour me whole. I was out of time. Whatever Vince had done had cracked open the time loop, which was on the brink of caving in on itself. I didn't know how he'd done it, but he'd broken free with his magic.

Magic he wasn't supposed to have access to.

I shook my head. I *had* to do this. Vince thought I was dead anyway. I had nothing to lose.

Clenching my fingers into fists, I crammed my eyes shut before leaping into the abyss. Gold light filled me, consuming every inch of me, blinding me until I saw nothing else. And in my chest, the Call sighed with satisfaction.

CHAPTER 30

VINCE

I FELT REBORN. LIKE I'D WAITED MY WHOLE LIFE FOR THIS transformation. No longer the weak warlock, the uncertain Nephilim, or the resentful Reaper.

This—right here, right now—was my true self. The person I'd been waiting for.

Power surged through me like electricity as the ethereal golden glow of the timeline swallowed me whole. But I felt no fear or alarm.

I felt only my fury. Not wild and volatile like before, but eerily calm. Like a monster biding its time, waiting for its prey to approach.

The exit shimmered into view, like a mental door opening. When the timeline spit me out, I was ready for it. I leapt forward, flinging myself out and rolling to avoid falling on my face. I landed on one knee, breathing heavily.

The noises hit me first. A cacophony of gunshots, screams, and explosions. Frowning, I glanced up. The air was thick with smoke and ash. Bodies littered the ground. Demons sparred with each other, holding various weapons. It took me a moment to realize *where* exactly I was. For one insane moment, I thought I'd traveled back to the Demon War.

But then I recognized the massive building a few yards away—or, at least, what was left of it.

Quentin's base of operations, once an impressive edifice, was now nothing more than a hunk of rubble. The only reason I recognized it was from the crisscrossing bricks of the foundation that still lingered amidst the debris.

The air stung my eyes, and I blinked furiously, trying to make out any familiar figures among the chaos. What was going on?

I watched a pair of unfamiliar demons fighting, and my heart lurched in my throat. One of them wasn't a demon at all —but a *mortal.* I wasn't sure how I knew. But something within me sang with recognition. He inexplicably reminded me of *Dad.* He was middle-aged, his black hair slightly gray at the roots. His face was red and covered in sweat. Despite his mortality, he still held his own against the demon—a dark warlock, judging by the black wisps of magic floating from his fingertips.

But this man, this mortal, he *knew* about magic. He dodged and evaded it as expertly as if he'd been around it his entire life.

Then, the warlock gained the upper hand. Black magic

slammed into the mortal's chest, bringing him to his knees. The warlock slashed his dagger, aiming for the man's throat.

Red magic exploded from my hands and wrapped around the warlock like a huge serpent. The magic tightened further and further until the warlock slumped over, motionless.

I didn't bother checking if he was alive or not. Instead, I ran up to the man and helped him to his feet. He rubbed his chest, coughing slightly.

"You all right?" I asked.

"Yeah," he said hoarsely. "Thanks for the assist."

"No problem. What's going on here? Who are you?"

The man shot me a bewildered look, his brows knitting together. "Where have *you* been?"

"It's a long story," I said, trying to quell my impatience. "*What's going on?*"

The man shrugged, waving his arms weakly toward the fray. "The building exploded. Demons started fighting. We showed up a few hours later, ready to join the ranks."

"Who's *we?*"

"The Guild." He raised his eyebrows as if this explained everything. "The Guild of the Unmarked? Didn't your father tell you?"

My heart stuttered in my chest. "I—my *father*? How—"

A demon lunged for us, a female vampire, her fangs bared and her eyes murderous. I ducked to avoid her, then punched her in the stomach and sliced my red magic into her skull. She collapsed, and the man looked at me with eyes full of awe.

"How do you know my dad?" I demanded, stepping closer

to the man. I hadn't meant to sound threatening, but it was getting harder and harder to keep my rage at bay. It swirled within me, growing impatient and hungry for blood. Kallie's blood.

"He's part of the Guild," the man said. "He joined about six months ago."

"What *is* the Guild?" I asked.

Two werewolves leapt between us, cutting off our conversation. We fought them off, avoiding gnashing teeth and sharp claws. I didn't have any silver on me for a kill, but my red magic rendered them unconscious, just like it had the vampire.

"I really can't stand around and talk to you, Vince," the man said. "Just know we're on your side." He turned away.

"Wait," I blurted. Desperation tinged my voice. "My dad—is he here?"

The man nodded solemnly. "Of course he is." And he turned to dive into the fray.

I stood there, frozen for a full minute as I tried to process this. My dad, who was supposed to be in hiding so Quentin wouldn't find him, was *right here fighting*? How? Why? What *Guild* was he a part of?

I shook my head. These questions could wait. Within me, my anger growled in response, ready for action.

Kill her. Destroy her.

With a deep, steadying breath, I rushed forward, plunging myself into battle. My red magic hovered in front of me, prepared to intercept any demon who tried to stop me. A dark witch. Slice. Slam. My magic cut through her, and she went down. A pair of vampires. Boom. Crunch. They collapsed in a heap of limbs.

I was a robot. A machine. I didn't feel the adrenaline or the thrill of battle. I didn't even break a sweat. My magic responded with the faintest thought, the briefest flicker of my mind. I could conjure it effortlessly to fight for me, never having to lift a finger.

Had all this magic truly been inside me the whole time? I hadn't felt half this powerful when I'd first absorbed the Reaper magic. The thought made me half impressed and half frustrated because I'd wasted so much time being useless.

Perhaps I could've left Luke's mind sooner. Perhaps I could've found Cora and taken out her father early on. Then she wouldn't have—

I stopped that line of thought, unwilling to go there. No. Kill Kallie first. That was my priority.

I slaughtered my way through the horde of demons, knowing I was getting closer to my destination by the way the crowd thickened. Kallie would've surrounded herself with as much of her army as she could. The coward.

The Call thrummed within me, growing more insistent with each step I took. It recognized Kallie's presence. And it was leading me right to her.

At long last, I found her. The barest golden glow surrounded her, marking her as a Timekeeper. Not just any Timekeeper. The oldest Timekeeper alive.

But not for long.

Her gaze slid to me, as if she sensed my presence too. Rage boiled within me. She must have noticed, because a flicker of fear shone in her eyes.

Good, I thought savagely as I strode toward her.

She cut down an assailant in front of her and held my gaze, making her way toward me as well. Her expression was schooled into something cold and neutral, but I still saw the uncertainty in her eyes. As if she didn't recognize me.

Again, I felt a bolt of satisfaction. I *wanted* to take her by surprise. I *wanted* her to be afraid.

When we stood three feet apart, we both froze, waiting for the other to make a move.

"Couldn't hold your own in battle, could you?" Kallie asked, gesturing to my arm.

I glanced down and found my right arm soaked in blood. A large gash ran down the length of my shoulder, but I didn't even feel it. I merely blinked at Kallie.

"Don't feel bad," she said with a patronizing smile. "You're no soldier, after all. It's a miracle you made it this far."

A deep humming filled my chest, vibrating against my bones. In a flash, a jet of red magic slashed through the air, spearing toward Kallie. Her own black magic surrounded her, but not quickly enough. She cried out and fell on one knee, panting. But her magic had protected her from the worst of it.

She looked at me with murderous eyes. Her nostrils flared as she rose to her feet, her jaw rigid and her teeth bared.

"You can't defeat me, boy," she growled. "I won't go down as easily as your little girlfriend did."

A roar of anguish tore through my throat, and I lunged. My fury screamed within me, clawing at me, begging for me to rip out Kallie's throat.

But my movements were sloppy. I followed my anger instead of my magic, and Kallie's darkness struck me down easily. I fell backward, my head colliding with something hard. Spots danced in front of my eyes.

Then, Kallie stood above me, smirking. She crouched over me with a chuckle. "That was almost *too* easy. Pitiful, really."

Pain radiated from my shoulder as my injuries finally caught up to me. My shoulder burned, and a wound in my side throbbed as well. Whatever fuel had kept me going was running out.

Then, I saw it. A thin, silver necklace dangling from Kallie's throat with a crescent moon on the end. My eyes locked onto it as if drawn by some magnetic force. The Call hissed in my ear, recognizing the power within. All I had to do was snap it off her neck. It would be easy—

Kallie followed my gaze, her face draining of color. Her expression quickly smoothed, and she lifted her chin. "You won't do it."

"Won't I?" I leaned forward.

"You'll lose her," Kallie said quickly, and I froze. "Her body's still in there. If you take my necklace, the time loop will collapse, taking her body with it. You really want to subject her to that? Or do you want to give her a proper burial and memorial? You know she deserves that."

My breathing turned sharp as fury filled me again. "Don't you dare," I said through clenched teeth. "You didn't know her. Don't pretend like you care."

"But *you* do," Kallie said, "don't you?"

We stared each other down. Slowly, something in me deflated as I thought of Cora's empty eyes and her motionless body.

She deserved better. She deserved to be honored as a hero. Her sacrifices needed to be acknowledged. I couldn't let her just slide into whatever time vortex Kallie had created.

But as I stared at Kallie, my face covered in sweat and my body weakening with every second, time itself seemed to slow. My mind worked furiously, like I was trying to solve a puzzle I didn't know I had. I envisioned the sky in Kallie's time loop as my red magic cracked right through it.

Her time loop was *already* collapsing—because I'd broken through it.

And Cora—

Do you trust me?

Of course.

Then it will be okay. I swear it.

I heard her voice like she was right next to me.

Trust me, Vince.

I sucked in huge gulps of air, but I still couldn't breathe. Tears stung my eyes.

I'm going to see if I can cook up a few spells.

Hadn't Cora told me of an elixir that gave the appearance of death?

I don't like using it too often. It feels like a coward's way out.

Tears now streamed down my face. I was still wheezing as if I'd just run a marathon, unable to get enough oxygen.

Cora—Cora was *alive.*

Time resumed again, and Kallie cocked her head at me, her expression shifting as if she'd noticed something was off. Something had happened.

Before she could react, I reached up and snatched the chain from her neck, yanking it hard until it broke.

CHAPTER 31

CORA

My world spun, a sickening carousel of gold light and blurred images. My stomach dropped, and nausea climbed up my throat. I shut my eyes tight against the gold storm surrounding me.

Please stop soon, I begged, not wanting to vomit on the timeline. What would happen if I *did*? The idea made me want to laugh and shudder in horror at the same time.

At long last, I fell forward, palms out to break my fall. I met hard concrete and hissed as the ground cut into my hands.

A battle surrounded me. Demons attacked each other with venom and hatred. Explosions of black magic and gunpowder filled the air.

Holy hell, I thought, my mouth hanging open. I squinted against the smoke in the air until I identified the rubble as

Quentin's headquarters. At my feet, I could barely make out the faint stripes of a parking lot.

This had to be present day. But how did the fighting start?

I thought of Kallie. Maybe some of the demons had resisted her rule? The thought sent a spark of hope through me.

A few feet away, a demon had a woman pinned to the ground. My heart lurched when I recognized her: Cecile.

Without thinking, I lunged forward, swinging my daggers and slicing into the demon's stomach with two swift arcs. He crumpled, and I turned to Cecile, who lay gaping at me from the ground.

"Nice to see you again," I said stiffly, offering her a hand. "I guess I should ask whose side you're on."

Cecile took my hand, and I grunted as I helped her to her feet. She eyed me warily, her face sweaty and her chest heaving with labored breaths. "Shouldn't you have asked that before you intervened?" she asked, wiping her forehead and smearing grime on her face.

"No matter whose side you're on, I couldn't let you die," I said, not bothering to hide the bite in my voice. "You're the mother of the man I love. Regardless of what choices you've made." I leveled an icy stare at her.

Cecile, to her credit, didn't flinch away. She lifted her chin. "I only wanted to protect my people. I don't regret my choices."

Another demon lunged for us, but I kicked him down before he could strike, then embedded my blade into his throat. He fell over, choking on his own blood. Cecile stared at him, her eyes wide—as if she hadn't realized just how deadly I could be.

Good. Let her fear me.

I took a step closer to her. "You never answered. Whose side are you on?"

Cecile met my gaze. "Yours."

I arched an eyebrow and shot her a doubtful look.

She sighed. "It's the truth. When Quentin released the Reapers, we sought out some allies and brought them here. Did you really think we would join Quentin's cause in earnest?"

"The Timekeepers did," I said bitterly. "Out of self-preservation. You made it clear you would do anything to keep your people safe."

Disgust twisted Cecile's expression. "We have a vow to uphold. We cannot just stand by."

"You did before," I snapped. "When I needed you to fight Quentin with me, you and your other Reapers were happy to just stick your heads in the sand."

This time, Cecile *did* flinch, and a bolt of satisfaction flared within me. "You're right," she said. "But ignoring the problem got us nowhere. And now we've lost lives because of it."

I stilled, my heart sinking with dread. "Whose lives?" I didn't necessarily care for any of the Reapers, but I knew, deep down, they were only trying to uphold their duty to magic and the realms. They were good people.

"Gwen Peters," Cecile said in a hushed voice, her eyes moist. She jerked her head toward the battle before us. "I just saw her go down. Joey Tucker was also killed. And Jocelyn was stripped of her wings."

Horror numbed my bones. Jocelyn. Frail, delicate Jocelyn —my father had *cut off her wings.*

"Is—is Jocelyn here?" I asked, my voice strained.

"Yes. She insisted on fighting."

Even without magic or wings. I couldn't help but admire the girl. Though her bravery would likely get her killed.

Two vampires attacked, and Cecile and I snapped into action. In a flash, my purple magic had one vampire down. I turned to take out the other, but Cecile punched him in the throat and stomach before kicking him down with such force he was rendered unconscious. She exhaled deeply and looked at me, her eyes blazing.

I must've looked shocked, because she snorted and said, "I'm not completely useless without magic."

Clearly. I shook my head. I'd already wasted enough time. "Have you seen Vince?"

Cecile straightened, her eyes brightening before fear crept into her face. "He's—he's here?" She blinked. "I haven't seen him." Her voice trembled. I didn't know what had happened between them when Vince had let her escape after her betrayal. But things had probably gotten ugly.

I'd been so caught up in how Vince had *defended* her over me that I hadn't given any thought to the strain this would've put on their relationship.

Cecile drew closer to me, and I stiffened. "Find him," she said quietly. "Keep him safe. Please."

"I will," I said. "But not for you."

To my surprise, she smiled. "I know. It doesn't matter why you protect him as long as you do."

I only nodded once more before diving into the fray. Gunshots blasted, knives swung, and punches landed all around me. I ducked and dodged, avoiding being struck down. As I weaved my way through demons and Reapers, my eyes roved over the crowd, searching for familiar faces. Were Piper and Gio okay? What about Dex? And what *allies* had Cecile rounded up?

Then, I caught sight of a figure I never expected to see again. His face and build were so much like Vince that it made my heart twist.

It was José—Vince's father. The only time I'd seen him fight was when I'd been dragging him away from his Nephilim clan. He'd been all but helpless.

But now, he swung a sword with finesse and strength as he battled a dark warlock. I moved to intervene, but before I could, José sliced the demon's head clean off. His face contorted with a grim rage that was startling on his usually cheerful features. Slowly, his gaze lifted to meet mine, and his expression slackened in shock.

I hurried over to him, and he drew me into a rough embrace. I yelped in startled surprise and drew back to look him over.

"What're you doing here?" I asked. My eyes burned, and I

was surprised to find myself on the verge of tears. José and I had gotten close after Vince had become a Reaper. I'd kept tabs on José to make sure he was all right after leaving the clan, but we'd lost touch when Quentin had waged war on my city.

José broke into a wide smile. "Fighting, of course!" He sliced into another demon with ease.

"But I—you—" I couldn't form words. Two demons leapt for us, but I cut them down before they could strike.

José laughed. "I've been training with the Guild. I've fought in battles before, you know. It's like riding a bike—I just needed a refresher course, and it all came back to me." He winked, then kicked a demon in the chest.

The Guild. I remembered the mortal ninja who'd tried to kill me under Kallie's orders.

It made sense. *Of course* José wouldn't just sit around and accept a mortal life when his wife and son were out there fighting magical forces. I couldn't blame him—if I were in his shoes, I would've done anything to make myself useful.

"I—did you bring the Guild *here*?" I asked, gazing around the battlefield. Now that I thought about it, several of those sparring weren't using magic at all. They were mortals, holding their own against *demons.*

I was both impressed and utterly shocked.

"After you let Henry go, he came to us and told us you spared him," José said. "Then, Cecile got in touch with me, and we decided to join the cause."

Henry. He must've been the ninja. To be honest, I hadn't

thought we'd been that merciful—Dex had drunk his blood until the man had passed out so we could escape without him following.

A werewolf leapt toward me. I flung him backward with my magic, then cut into his snout with my blade.

"Have you seen Vince?" I asked José.

"I caught a glimpse of him earlier." José ducked to avoid getting stabbed, then shoved his sword into a dark witch's stomach. When he straightened, he jerked his head toward the massive hunk of rubble that had once been Quentin's headquarters. "That way."

I nodded. "Thanks." Before I left, I touched his shoulder. "Be careful."

José only laughed again as he fought another demon. I took off toward the building's remains. With each movement, each kick and stab, a faint gold light gleamed within me. It prodded me tentatively, as if asking for permission to speak.

But I ignored it. I wasn't ready to use the Call in battle. Hell, I wasn't ready to acknowledge I *had* the Call. I trusted it before, and my stomach was still spinning from the event.

Later, I begged the Call. *Please. I can't right now.*

I almost felt the presence within me nodding in agreement before it crept away, fading into nothingness.

Relief filled me. Vince had told me of the dire consequences of refusing the Call. If it had pushed me, I wasn't sure what I would've done.

It felt like hours, but I pressed on, fighting demon after

demon until sweat poured down my face and exertion tugged at my limbs.

Where is he? I thought desperately. *Vince, where the hell are you?*

I finally made it to the edge of the rubble, and he wasn't anywhere in sight. Worry spiraled in my mind, my heart rate skittering. Had Vince been so distraught he'd gotten himself killed already?

I would never forgive myself if he had.

Come on, Vince, I thought, gritting my teeth in frustration. *You're smarter than this. Where are you?*

A sudden blast of gold light filled the air, setting the sky ablaze as if it were midday instead of dusk. I squinted as the light burned against my eyes. When it started to fade, I glanced around frantically for the source—and then froze.

Several yards away, a pair of figures stood in the center of the gold light. One was a tall, wiry woman I recognized immediately: Kallie.

And on his knees in front of her was Vince.

CHAPTER 32

VINCE

THE AIR AROUND US FROZE WITH ANTICIPATION AS THE chain of Kallie's necklace broke in half and dropped to the ground. Magic rippled through the air, tingling my skin. A blinding gold light surrounded us. Relief and triumph washed over me as I smirked at Kallie's shocked expression.

But when the gold light faded, she composed herself—and had the gall to look *smug*.

"Well done, Reaper," she taunted. "I never imagined you'd get that far. But did you really think I hadn't anticipated that? I *own* the timeline, boy."

I stared at her, my heart rate quickening. She was lying. She *had* to be.

She scoffed and shook her head. "Don't look so shocked. After living for centuries, do you think I'd be stupid enough to wear my *only talisman* here for the world to see?" She patted her collarbone where the necklace had rested.

No, I thought in horror. But . . . I'd *felt* the power when I'd broken the necklace. It had to have been *something* important.

The more confused I felt, the more satisfied Kallie looked. Her chin lifted, and her smile widened. "A time loop of that magnitude requires multiple talismans. One alone wasn't powerful enough."

My mind spun as I tried to grab hold of a coherent thought—anything to stop her. Anything to get the upper hand.

One alone wasn't powerful enough.

If she had multiple talismans, then each one held a portion of power. I'd just destroyed one . . . which meant whatever talismans remained were not enough to contain the power of the time loop.

Kallie wasn't dead yet . . . but she was weakening. I could see it in the pallor of her skin and the tightness of her jaw.

I needed to buy more time. But how? Kallie saw *everything* before it happened. It wasn't much of an exaggeration to claim she owned the timeline.

A glint of steel caught my eye behind Kallie. My gaze shifted for the briefest of seconds, and my heart lurched so intensely that my chest throbbed in pain.

Cora.

She held her dagger as she sprinted toward us. It took great effort to keep my expression neutral, though all I wanted to do was laugh and cry at the same time. Instead, I focused on Kallie, who still looked incredibly pleased with herself.

She was cocky. I could use that.

Because one thing had just occurred to me: Kallie believed Cora was dead. Perhaps the elixir Cora had taken had done its job *too* well, or perhaps my bursting free of the time loop was a distraction. But whatever the reason, Kallie didn't know Cora was alive.

If she did, she would've known Cora was running right toward us.

Gold light gleamed within me, confirming my suspicion. I searched inward, scanning the Call for any sign of Cora. But nothing was there. It was as if she'd ceased to exist, the emptiness so loud it made my heart ache.

No wonder I'd believed so easily that she was dead. Searching for her was like shouting in a never-ending cave and listening to the echo reverberate for eternity.

A hard lump formed in my throat, reminding me of my all-consuming grief and rage. I gritted my teeth and forced a dejected expression on my face.

"What do you want from me, Kallie? You want me to be your slave? To submit to you and follow you with blind devotion?"

Kallie's eyes narrowed. "It's just as any ordinary coven would operate. Each one has its own leader, and the members of the coven are loyal to them."

"The covens are *families,*" I spat. "What you're asking for is *slavery.* No coven operates like that. It's a give and a take." I stared hard at Kallie, but I kept Cora in my peripheral. Just a few yards away now. My eyes were drawn to her like magnets. I wanted to stare at her, to drink in every inch of her like a man dying of thirst. I wanted to memorize her features with new eyes—eyes that had once beheld the dead body of the woman I loved.

The need to look at her was so demanding that I clenched my hands into tight fists. *I have to see her alive,* I thought. *I need to know it's not my imagination.*

But the gold light in my chest flared a warning. *Don't,* it said. *Stay calm.*

"You think I would give nothing in return?" Kallie seemed affronted, her eyes sparking with fury.

Good, I thought. *Get mad, Kallie. As long as your attention stays on me.*

"I can offer the Timekeepers protection," she went on. "I can offer them security and freedom."

"Freedom from what?" I shouted incredulously, spreading my arms and trying not to wince as pain throbbed from the cut on my arm. "Are they prisoners right now?"

"Yes," Kallie hissed. "They are imprisoned by the Call."

I stilled. Centuries ago, Timekeepers had waged war over that very fact. But when had Kallie switched sides?

"*I* can teach the Timekeepers which orders to follow and which orders can be ignored," she said, her eyes gleaming with a feral hunger. "The Call has been my companion for centuries now, and the things I've learned have only strengthened my relationship with it. It is *not* all-powerful. It *can* be disobeyed, but only in the right circumstances."

Now, I was paying attention. I scrutinized Kallie, searching for a hint of deception. "Which orders can be disobeyed?" I asked slowly.

Kallie's mouth spread into a wide grin. She knew she'd lured me. "Follow me, Vince, and I'll show you." She stretched her hand toward me.

The Call thrummed within me, sensing my hesitation. I didn't for a second trust Kallie to be my leader. But what she said made sense—it explained how some Timekeepers believed they *had* to follow the Call, and others believed otherwise.

Some orders *had* to be followed—for the sake of the timeline—and some did not.

It was like good and evil. Things were never black and white. There was always a gray area, something in between. Something that *could* be good despite the evil.

Like Cora.

I glanced at her again. She was only a few steps away. I needed to keep Kallie's attention until the precise moment.

So, I held Kallie's gaze, slackening my expression and watching her with a mixture of awe and wonder. Slowly, I raised my uninjured arm, bringing it closer to Kallie's hand. Her grin widened, revealing her teeth. She looked like a predator ready to clamp her jaws on me and devour me whole.

I took her hand, and she helped me up. Without breaking eye contact, I nodded. "All right, Kallie. I'll follow you."

Her eyes brightened with manic delight, and she pressed her lips together into a tight smile. "A wise choice." She clapped a hand on my uninjured shoulder. "We'll do great things together, Vince."

Suddenly, she stiffened, and a horrible gurgling sound burst from her throat. Blood bubbled on her lips, and she choked and gagged, her eyes wide as she stared at me in horror.

Then, over her shoulder, I found Cora with her blade shoved into Kallie's back. Elation spread through me, warming every inch of me, and for a moment, I forgot about my injuries. I felt nothing but joy and relief at the sight of Cora, her eyes ablaze and her face a mask of fury.

Kallie slumped sideways, collapsing to the ground. Blood oozed from her chest, pooling onto the concrete at my feet. I crouched down to meet her stunned gaze and offered a cold smile.

"Guess you don't own the timeline after all, do you?" I asked.

Kallie coughed in response, and flecks of blood spewed from her mouth.

"How many talismans are there?" I asked.

The shock in Kallie's expression melted into fury, even as the color drained from her face. She hissed something incoherent, but I could easily read the intent behind her words: *Go to hell.*

Irritation prickled through me. I knew I *could* search Kallie's person and her possessions and eventually track down whatever talismans remained. But the fact that I hadn't heard from Luke yet worried me. Was he still recovering? What if the pressure of housing all those Timekeepers had killed him? I liked to think that I'd broken the time loop and the Timekeepers were free, but part of me knew we had to destroy the talismans to be sure.

"Really?" I snapped. "*This* is how you want to end your three-hundred-year-long reign? A witch faked her death—a convincing enough act to fool even *you*—and she stabbed you. Then, you choked on your own blood." I shook my head, giving her a patronizing look. "It's pathetic."

Uncertainty flashed in her eyes. Her skin took on a grayish tint. She was dying. We didn't have much time.

I leaned closer. "Or, you can make one last heroic choice. You can free your prisoners. You can go down in history as a liberator of Timekeepers . . . instead of a tyrant."

It wasn't true, of course. One good deed would not erase the hundreds of years of imprisonment she'd forced on the Timekeepers.

But redemption was a stronger motivator than vengeance. I knew that from my own experiences—and from Cora's. My eyes lifted to meet Cora's. She was panting, her hair slick with sweat, but her eyes were bright. She met my gaze, her expression softening for just a moment. Guilt and anguish flashed in her eyes, and I knew we had so much to talk about—so much to work through.

But she was here. She was alive.

I looked at Kallie and touched her shoulder. "Please,

Kallista. On behalf of all Timekeepers, I beg of you. Tell me where the talismans are."

Kallie's breathing turned ragged. Her chest shuddered as life slowly left her. Another choked sound escaped her, but this time I was able to make out one word: *ankle.*

Then, her head lolled backward, her eyes clouding over, and her entire body went still.

I'd expected to feel satisfaction, maybe triumph when she died. But all I felt was sorrow and pity. It was such a shame that this immortal being had spent her life committing so many crimes. My heart ached at the thought of all the *good* she could've done—both for the Timekeepers and the world itself.

"It's true," Cora whispered from beside me. "Look." She pointed toward Kallie's left ankle, where a faint gold glow emanated. If I hadn't been looking right at it, I wouldn't have seen it.

I stared at Cora in astonishment. "How did you—"

"Come on," she said, scooting closer to raise the leg of Kallie's pants. Kallie's stark-white skin shone like a light bathed in the warm glow of the Call. And then, I saw it. A silver chain wrapped around her ankle.

"Would you like to do the honors?" Cora asked.

I couldn't help but smile. "I think you've earned this one."

With a grunt, Cora tugged at the anklet until it snapped. The glow vanished, and a burst of light filled the air once more. Magic surged and sparked, forming a wide orb around us. I shut my eyes against the blinding brightness. Cora's fingers found mine, and I squeezed her hand, clinging to that familiar warm presence I thought I'd lost forever.

Then, the glow faded. I released a breath, my heart hammering in my chest. My eyes opened, and I shared an uncertain glance with Cora. "Do you—do you think that's it?" I asked. "Or could there be another one somewhere?"

"With Kallie's death, her life force is no longer tied to the talismans," Cora said, drawing closer to Kallie's body as she inspected it. "If there *are* any talismans, they'd be emitting the same light, like a beacon searching for another host."

I frowned at her, marveling again at how she'd been able to see the gold glow. Did that mean—

"Looks like that was it," Cora said, sitting up straighter. "At least, that's all she had on her. It's possible—"

An anguished shout filled my mind, so shrill and piercing that I clutched at my forehead, cramming my eyes shut against the agony. My ears were ringing, and I gritted my teeth as crippling pain consumed my mind. The screaming intensified until I was sure it was coming from me.

But as it faded, I knew who it was. It was Luke.

Cora touched my shoulder, bringing me back to the present. "Go," she urged.

Panting, I opened my eyes and glanced around at the battlefield. The demons were clueless to the fact that Kallie was dead—they would continue fighting.

Cora read the apprehension on my face and placed her hands on my cheeks, drawing closer until our noses almost touched. "I'll be fine, Vince. *Trust me.*"

I swallowed hard, remembering how she'd said those exact words moments before she'd faked her death. The sting of betrayal coursed through me, and my eyes burned with imminent tears. But I forced myself to nod.

No matter how she'd hurt me, it had to be done. Nothing but intense grief and anger could've given me the power to break out of Kallie's time loop.

Cora had known this. Because she had the Call too. The Call had *told* her to lie to me—because it was the only way.

With a deep breath, I stood and focused on the timeline, picturing Luke's field. Then, with a *pop*, I Jumped, my surroundings shifting until Cora and the battling demons vanished from view.

CHAPTER 33

CORA

AGONY SWIRLED IN MY CHEST AS I WATCHED VINCE disappear. I'd seen the hurt and anguish on his face when he looked at me. And my heart twisted with the reminder of what I'd put him through.

Would he ever forgive me? Would I ever forgive myself?

I shoved the thoughts away, vowing to work through them after the battle. But, for now, I had a city to save.

I withdrew my dagger from Kallie's corpse and jumped back into the fray. Now that the Call had returned, it flared a warning each time an attacker drew nearer. Ordinarily, my instincts were enough to keep me alive, but this time, I allowed the Call to guide me. I knew Vince was safe, but now I had to find my friends—and my sister—and make sure they were alive.

I shoved my way past demons, winding through the crowd

and dodging blades and fists and claws. With each step, my panic mounted, my pulse skittering. I saw members of the Guild and a few Reapers, but no one I recognized.

Had Kallie killed Gio, Dex, and Piper?

I can't, I thought, my heart shuddering as I pictured Benny's empty and lifeless expression. *I can't lose someone else.*

Suddenly, gold light speared through me, sharper than anything I'd felt from the Call. I gasped, stiffening and whirling as I tried to find the source. Then—

"Cora!"

Shock jolted through me, and I found myself sprinting before I knew what was happening. Caught between two werewolves was Piper, her purple hair a tangled mess behind her. A long cut ran along her cheek, and her arm was twisted in a way that told me she'd dislocated her shoulder. But when she saw me, her face brightened with relief. Despite her injuries, she was still holding her own.

I hurried toward her, helping her take out the two werewolves. Our blades sliced into the wolves' fur until the beasts slumped over, unconscious. I turned to Piper and touched her uninjured shoulder. "Are you all right?" My voice broke, but I didn't care. She was my *sister.* And she was alive.

She nodded, grinning at me. "I'm fine."

"And Dex? Gio?"

"They're here too, last I saw." She gestured vaguely around the battle.

A half laugh, half sob broke through me, and I touched my

chest as I tried to control my breathing. *Thank Lilith.* My friends were all right.

"What happened with Quentin?" Piper asked.

"He's dead. So is Benny." My throat tightened, making it hard to speak. "But then Kallie—the Timekeeper—took over. She's dead now too."

Piper's brow furrowed, and she glanced around with incredulity. "Then, why the hell are we still fighting?"

"These guys don't know their leaders are dead," I said. "And even if they did, I can see the bloodlust in their eyes. They won't back down." Most of the demons here preyed on humans. I knew that was no accident. Either Quentin or Kallie had known that their most brutal soldiers would be those who preyed on mortals. They couldn't be reasoned with, not with this much blood around.

"They won't stop until they kill us all," Piper said hoarsely. "And we can't hold them off. It's just us, a few Reapers, and a bunch of mortals." Her expression was bleak as she surveyed the fray.

Dread filled my chest. The obvious answer was to flee, like we had when Quentin had first taken over.

But I couldn't abandon my city. Not again. I would *not* leave Hinport to be destroyed by these beasts.

I was a killer by nature. The adrenaline pulsing through me was a testament of that. I hungered for blood, just like these predators did.

But something within me swelled as I looked around. A presence in my chest that had started small and grew slowly each day. That subtle strength within me now gleamed like a new kind of magic, a force I hadn't seen until this moment. It stilled my heart and quieted my mind until I knew exactly what to do.

I lifted my arms, my fingers pointing skyward, and unleashed an explosion of purple magic. It shot into the air, breaking through the sky like fireworks. A thunderous sound echoed around us, reverberating through the ground like an earthquake.

The demons around us halted, looking around uncertainly. For a brief moment, everyone was silent as confusion took over their bloodlust.

I took advantage of their mental lapse. Keeping my arms raised, I bellowed, "You're better than this!" My voice rang, echoing just as powerfully as my magic had.

The crowd before me shifted as everyone searched for the source of the disturbance. I looked around and found a huge chunk of concrete. Climbing on top, I stood high enough to be seen.

"You are the demons of Hinport!" I cried. "A city that proudly supports dark magic! We don't have to live in fear. We don't have to hide. That's what makes this the *greatest city in the world*!"

Several demons grunted their assent, but the eyes that watched me were still bloodthirsty and full of rage.

I had their attention, but I would lose them fast if I faltered. Lifting one fist in the air, I bellowed, "You are *better* than this senseless bloodshed! You aren't monsters or predators of the night. You are *demons of Hinport,* the proudest demon city, the *only* city where magic can be free! Stop this destruction and bloodshed. Stop the killing before the city is destroyed. Our demons need a place to thrive! Don't take that away from them!"

A hushed silence fell among the demons. A few of them exchanged uneasy looks.

"Quentin—the Bloodcaster—" one demon grumbled.

"Is *dead,*" I hissed. "Benny Martinelli, a loyal comrade, gave his *life* to ensure our safety. Quentin Cox will not harm you anymore."

Several faces slackened in shock, and murmurs rippled across the crowd.

"What about the Timekeepers?" demanded a dark witch.

"Their leader is dead too," I answered. "I stabbed her myself."

Confused whispers filled the air. Hope spread in my chest, but I couldn't celebrate yet. Logic was slowly taking over the bloodlust. The dark eyes that watched me were shining with clarity and understanding.

"Join me as comrades loyal to demons and dark magic," I urged them. "Together, we can unite the covens of Hinport. We can rally our own so we will *never* be conquered again!"

A few cheers erupted from the crowd, and my chest swelled.

"We can be the protectors, the defenders of Hinport!" I

shouted, raising both arms again. "The defenders of demons and dark magic *everywhere*!"

Stronger cheers and whoops resonated from the crowd. As I looked around, I caught a glimpse of Gio's beefy form. His arms were crossed, and he grinned broadly at me.

Encouraged, I went on, "Why fight each other when we can *strengthen* each other?" My voice was practically a roar. I'd never felt anything like this euphoria. I had never sounded this strong, this empowering before. Despite knowing how brave and callous I could be, *this* kind of strength was foreign to me.

But I loved it.

Lingering in the back of the crowd was Dex, his tall and wiry form drawing my gaze. He wasn't smiling, but his eyes sparked with joy and satisfaction. He gave me a slight nod, and I grinned.

"Who's with me?" I shouted. For a full beat, silence met my words. My heart lodged itself in my throat as I stood there, arms raised like a moron, laid bare for all to see.

I'm a killer, I told myself. *I can handle rejection.*

And yet, after putting all of my strength and energy into bolstering this crowd and uniting my people, my heart sank to my knees. I'd poured my soul, spread myself thin for these demons. Would they really turn their backs on me now? The crushing sensation was so severe that my breath hitched and my chest tightened.

Then, a strong voice rang out from the crowd. "I stand with Cora!"

I recognized that voice. It was Gio. He pushed past the crowd until he stood in front of me, gazing up at me with fire in his eyes. He offered a firm nod and turned to face the crowd. "I stand for magic everywhere."

"As do I!" echoed another voice, this one thinner. It was Dex. He took a bit longer to get to me, but once he did, several other demons voiced their assent, shifting to stand with me.

To my surprise, Cecile and all the Reapers—including Jocelyn, her face bloodied and covered in dirt—also pledged their support. Piper joined as well, but after a long while, the demons quieted. No one else spoke up.

More than fifty demons stood at my side. But it wasn't enough. At least a hundred more still faced me, doubt and rage filling their eyes.

"You lost Hinport already, Covington," growled a voice. I recognized him—Silas, a werewolf alpha. "You *left*. You weren't strong enough to defend the city against Quentin. Who's to say it won't happen again?"

"It won't if we *stand together*!" I said loudly.

"She's Quentin's daughter," said another voice. "What if she turns on us too?"

Several demons murmured their agreement, and my heart sank. The air shifted to something hateful and savage. The demons closest to me had a feral look in their eyes that told me I was in danger. My instincts screamed at me to run, but I held my ground—as did my new allies.

I'd taken my stand. And I would die here if I had to.

For Hinport. For *my* city and *my* people.

I lifted my chin, facing the danger head on as the angry demons closed in on us.

CHAPTER 34

VINCE

It wasn't hard to find Luke. All I had to do was follow the screaming. It pounded through my skull as if drilling into me. My body ached. Tremors wracked through me.

In a flash of gold light, I was there beside Luke, who writhed on the ground, screaming. We were in the park near his house, and the hundreds of Timekeepers surrounded him, looking concerned.

I glanced around as panic roared within me. I found Jeremiah nearby and strode toward him. "What happened?"

Jeremiah shook his head weakly. "We—we felt his pain when we entered his mind, but the other Timekeeper—Hector—gave him strength. Then, when we got out, he just . . . started screaming."

My mouth fell open, and I scanned the crowd for Hector.

I almost didn't see him. He was on his knees, pressing his fists against the ground like he was about to take off in flight. His eyes were closed, his expression strained and his brows bunched together.

I approached him and touched his shoulder. "Hector."

He didn't respond.

"*Hector*!" I shook him violently.

He flinched, his eyes snapping open. They were bloodshot as they met mine. "Vince," he said hoarsely. It sounded like he couldn't remember what he was doing here. He shook his head. "I—I'm trying. His pain is so severe . . ."

"*Why*?" I asked, waving my hands toward Luke, who still wriggled on the ground, his face taut with agony. "The Timekeepers are out of his head!"

"Yes, but the damage has been done. He still feels their presence inside him. His mind won't let go because it's been . . . altered."

"Altered?" My voice was almost hysterical. "Hector, you have to *do* something! He's dying!"

"I know!" Hector snapped, rubbing his forehead. "I—I—" He broke off, hunching over with a groan, his jaw rigid and his face crumpling in pain. He inhaled deeply and straightened, and one eye twitched slightly.

I knew what was happening. It was the Call.

But . . . why would the Call try to stop Hector from helping Luke? Suspicion crept along my skin. "What aren't you telling me?" I asked.

Hector looked up at me with weary eyes. "If I give my mind over to him, he'll have the strength he needs."

My pulse raced. "What does that mean, to give your mind over to him?"

"It means he would drain all the energy from me. And leave me brain-dead."

I stared at him, stunned. The surrounding Timekeepers fell silent, exchanging shocked expressions. Even Jeremiah seemed to be at a loss for words.

"Hector—" I said weakly.

"I'm doing this, Vince," he said sharply. "You can't stop me. And neither can the Call. I won't let someone else die at my hand." He held my gaze, and my heart lurched in my throat.

I didn't know what to say. A mixture of emotions flooded me. Grief at the possibility of losing Luke. Confusion at the regret I'd feel if I lost Hector. Relief that Luke might live. Conflict that Hector had to pay the price.

I told myself I hated this man. He banished my mother and made my life hell. He tried to kill me—multiple times.

But, as much as I didn't want to admit it, he *had* changed. Albeit reluctantly—the Call hadn't given him a choice. But he was different. No longer a ruthless killer or a power-hungry Nephilim. But a Timekeeper who had been on my side since I'd marked him by time.

My stomach twisted into knots. I kept my eyes on Hector, whose expression softened slightly. His eyes filled with sorrow. "I know it'll never be enough," he said, "but I'm sorry, Vince.

For everything." His words were heavy with emotion and sincerity.

I believed him. I pressed my hand to his shoulder. "It's enough."

Surprise and relief flickered in his eyes. He pressed his lips together and nodded. A tear trickled down his cheek as he closed his eyes and raised his hands toward Luke's temples. Hector's face turned red, his muscles quivering as he strained against some invisible force. A strangled roar built in his throat.

Luke continued thrashing, so I crouched to the ground to hold him in place. Jeremiah followed suit, pressing down on Luke's other side to keep him still.

Hector drew closer, his hands steady. Magic crackled in the air. Then, with a mighty bellow, Hector lurched forward. He grunted, his arms trembling and his jaw taut. His body went stiff, and his face contorted with agony. A horrifying scream burst from his lips as if the sound had torn right through him. Blood trickled from his nose and ears.

As soon as his fingertips met Luke's head, Hector's whole body slackened. The color drained from his face, and his eyes rolled back. He suddenly went from being shaky and red-faced to limp and deathly pale.

I could only watch, wide-eyed, as Hector slumped sideways, the shout dying on his lips. His eyes were wide open, his face bone-white. He remained motionless, but I couldn't stop staring at him, waiting for him to blink or move or do *something.*

But he only lay there. Not breathing.

Hector Moses, the powerful and unstoppable Nephilim, was dead. He had *defied the Call* to save Luke.

Emotion climbed up my throat, and I sniffed against the incoming assault of tears. I shoved down the innate instinct to scoff at feeling any remorse for Hector. Today, I could accept him as an ally. Today, I could recognize him as a hero. Maybe another day I would assess his flaws and crimes and judge him accordingly. But today, he was a good man.

Tears streamed down my face, and I ducked my head, succumbing to the heat and anguish burning in me.

Then, a rattling gasp split the air. My head snapped up, and I found Luke sitting up, his face pale as he inhaled shakily. He swiped dreadlocks out of his face and met my gaze in confusion. "What—what happened?" Slowly, his eyes shifted to Hector's body, and he sucked in another breath. "Merciful Lilith." His face turned even paler, and his mouth opened and closed. He glanced from Hector to me and back to Hector. "Vince—"

"He gave his life to save you," I said in a strained voice. "You were dying. Your mind wasn't strong enough. The Call tried to stop him, but he gave you his mind to pull you out of it."

Shock and devastation struck Luke's face, and for a moment, he stared at me, gaping. He drew in a trembling breath, then looked at Hector. I followed his gaze too, and we watched our fallen friend for a solid minute as if he might sit up any second.

But he didn't.

I scooted closer to Luke, and his eyes filled with tears. He covered his mouth and shook his head. "Dammit all, Hector," he moaned. His fingers curled into fists, and he slammed his hands against the ground. "*Damn you*!"

I squeezed Luke's shoulder as he choked on his sobs. More tears dripped down my face, the grief stinging and merciless.

"Figures he would do something like this," Luke said thickly, wiping his nose. "Figures he'd find a way to *force* me to stop hating him."

I chuckled slightly. "Yeah." I glanced up and found Jeremiah staring at Hector's body with a conflicted expression. He met my gaze, and his eyes turned wary.

"I can't save him," he said.

I frowned. "I didn't ask you to."

He stared at me. "But you desire it."

I shook my head. "I would never ask you to manipulate the timeline. Not for that." I thought of Cora and the empty expression on her face after she'd taken the elixir. In all my rage and despair, I'd never once considered using the timeline to bring her back. Now that I thought about it, the Call *knew* a choice like that would risk breaking the timeline. So, it urged me toward Kallie—toward revenge.

It had known precisely what needed to happen. But it wasn't right about everything.

My gaze fell to Hector. I scooted closer to him and gently closed his eyes. The Call had tried to stop him. I didn't know why—maybe it had other uses for him. Maybe it had wanted Luke to die.

But Hector proved our will was stronger than the Call. *We* were stronger. The Call was a part of us. Maybe it had tried to save Hector out of self-preservation.

Defying that instinct to the very end was precisely the kind of heroic thing I'd never thought him capable of. And I was both ashamed and humbled by the fact that he'd proven me wrong.

CHAPTER 35

CORA

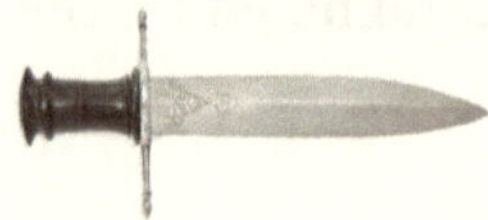

AS THE HORDE OF DEMONS ADVANCED, THE BLOODTHIRSTY gleam returning to their eyes, I held my breath and kept my hand steady while I gripped my dagger.

I was not afraid.

Then, a thin beam of gold light shone from within me. In desperation, I clung to it and mentally whispered, *Help me*!

The light intensified, filling my chest. I sucked in a huge breath as if my lungs had expanded from the Call's magic. My vision was clearer, my senses sharper, and my body more energized.

I swallowed, looking around to see if something had happened—*anything* to help us win this.

But it was still me and my demons facing off with the rest of Kallie's army. Another war we couldn't win.

A *pop* sounded nearby. Then another. A cacophony of *pops*

filled the air, layering over one another like the sound of popcorn popping. One by one, figures appeared out of nowhere. *Hundreds* of them. As they materialized, they formed a wide circle around the crowd of demons, sealing them in.

Then, on the hunk of concrete next to me, Vince appeared, panting. His eyes were bloodshot, and he looked more exhausted than I'd ever seen him. But he gave me a half smile that made my heart lurch. In front of him was Luke, his face equally haggard, but his eyes determined and fierce.

My mouth fell open as I surveyed the enormous crowd that had suddenly come to our rescue. *The Timekeepers.*

My gaze cut to Vince. "Did you—did you hear me?"

He looked at me, and uncertainty flashed in his eyes. "No. The Call sent us."

My mouth opened and closed. He held my gaze, and recognition stirred, followed by unease.

Before I could answer, Gio raised his fist in the air and bellowed, "Still want to take us on?"

I couldn't help but grin at his enthusiasm. If he was confused by the Timekeepers' sudden appearance, he didn't show it. I envied that—currently, I was too shocked to process anything.

But maybe that was because I'd spoken to the Call—*and it had answered.*

The demons closest to us shifted their weight, obviously uncomfortable. A few gazed around at the newcomers, mouths hanging open and eyes wide with shock and horror.

I cleared my throat and spread my arms. "As I told you—we don't need to fight each other. Agree to settle this peacefully, and no more lives need to be lost."

A tense silence followed my words. I tightened my hold on my dagger, preparing to fight. These were demons, after all. Predators. They couldn't just shove aside their thirst for blood. It was in their nature.

Then, to my surprise, the demon in front lifted his weapon—a large ax—and slowly lowered it to the ground. The remaining demons followed suit, dropping their weapons with clatters that echoed around us. Even the vampires retracted their fangs and relaxed their stance, looking warily at the Timekeepers.

I exhaled, though my heart still raced uncontrollably. Gesturing to the demon in front, I asked, "Who's your leader?"

The warlock grimaced uncertainly. "Unofficially? I am."

I nodded. Of course they hadn't chosen a leader—Quentin and Kallie were dead, and they were too busy battling to reorganize their leadership.

"Care to join me to discuss terms?" I asked, eyebrows raised.

Though he looked disgruntled, the warlock shrugged and nodded.

I turned to Vince. "You too. Bring your mom."

His eyes widened. "What? Why?"

"I want representatives from every faction here. You can sit in for the Timekeepers."

Vince quickly shook his head. "No, it shouldn't be me. Get Jeremiah." He pointed to a tall, thin man with long, dark hair and shadowed eyes.

I leaned closer to Vince. "All due respect, but I don't trust him. I trust *you*."

Vince leveled a gaze at me. "If you want representation, his opinion matters more than mine." His expression was firm and unyielding.

The sharpness of his response startled me, reminding me how much Vince had changed. He'd once been kind, meek, and unassuming. I remembered the first time I'd seen him fight against that werewolf at school. He'd been terrified.

Now, he was practically a warrior, unafraid and determined to protect his people.

As we stared at each other, unspoken emotions churned between us, making my chest tighten. I hated leaving things unresolved. With my fake death and my sudden access to the Call, it definitely complicated things.

A lump formed in my throat, and I broke eye contact, unable to hold it any longer. I couldn't let those thoughts consume me—the terror that Vince would no longer want me after everything I'd put him through.

"All right," I said, hopping down from the huge piece of concrete. I gestured for Jeremiah, Dex, Piper, the dark warlock, and a werewolf nearby to follow me. Vince hurried off to track down his mother. I watched them embrace, and my stomach twisted, though I wasn't sure why. Then, Cecile jogged up to us, following suit as we weaved through the crowd.

I thought about what an odd group we were—a Bloodcaster, a Timekeeper, a vampire, a dark witch, a dark warlock, a werewolf, and a Reaper. If we'd had more time, I would've tried tracking down other sects, like gargoyles and shapeshifters. Hell, even light casters. Why not? We were being all inclusive now. Anything could happen.

We didn't have much privacy among the ruins of the street, so we all sat on varying sizes of rubble, well out of earshot of the remaining armies.

I cracked my neck and stretched my arms, then sighed. "All right. Who wants to speak first?"

The meeting went on for hours. I should've expected this. All of us were so different—and things were still heated between those who saw each other as enemies.

Piper wanted a unified organization, a massive coven of all demons of Hinport. Dex wanted each faction to be separate and distinct. Jeremiah wanted everyone to have the freedom to form their own covens as they saw fit. The dark warlock—whose name was Mick—wanted to put a *new* leader in charge of the army. Someone powerful, who wouldn't bow or flee before a threat. He leveled a hard gaze at me when he said this.

Cecile only wanted the Reapers to be given back their magic—and their realm. She had no other requests.

The werewolf—Shane—was quiet for a long time, but he kept his yellow eyes pinned on me. It was unnerving, but when he finally spoke, I realized why.

"Benny was my friend," he said in a soft voice. "I didn't want to turn on him, but Quentin had taken my family. He would've killed them." He sighed. "I want to set protection measures for the families of casters. Anyone who doesn't have magic."

I straightened, perking up from his words. *Of course!* I couldn't believe it had slipped my mind.

After muttering a hasty excuse, I darted back to the crowd. I grabbed José, dragging him over to our group and introducing him as a representative of the Guild of the Unmarked. He offered an awkward wave and sat down next to Cecile, who beamed at him.

The atmosphere changed after that. Mick looked uncomfortable with having a mortal among us. But José's charisma helped to ease the tension, and he provided a unique perspective—he'd been a light warlock *and* lived among the Nephilim before becoming a mortal.

"Hinport should form its own Council," José suggested. "Go ahead and separate yourselves, form whatever covens you want, and elect a representative to join the Council of Hinport to help make decisions for the entire city." He waved a hand at all of us. "Kind of like what you're doing now."

"Like the U.S. government?" Cecile asked with a wry smile.

I couldn't help but grin as José winked at her. José had been a lawyer, so he was well-versed in government jargon.

"And . . . our families?" Shane asked quietly.

José sobered. "The Guild will take care of them. As long as you allow us to be a part of your Council too."

I wrinkled my nose. "We won't call it the Council, though. That would get too confusing. Maybe . . ."

"The Committee?" Shane asked.

"The Board?" Cecile suggested.

"It should have Hinport's name in the title," Piper said. "The Hinport Association?"

Warmth filled my chest, and I met Piper's gaze. We were here for Hinport, after all. Whatever our group would be called, I didn't want it to be cold and unfeeling like *the Council*—detached and illusive. I wanted it to be something where our intent was clear—to protect and unify Hinport.

I couldn't stop the slow smile from spreading on my face as I said, "The Hinport Alliance."

CHAPTER 36

VINCE

WHILE CORA AND THE OTHERS DISCUSSED TERMS, I WEAVED through the crowd, checking on the Timekeepers to see if they needed anything. I kept glancing over at Cora and my parents. It *did* feel odd that I wasn't with them, but I knew Jeremiah needed to be there. He'd been silenced for centuries —it was his turn to voice his opinion freely.

After ensuring the Timekeepers were comfortable, and double checking that none of the restless demons would cause any trouble, I made my way back to Luke. To my surprise, I found him talking to Jocelyn. Luke wore his charming smile and used that too-hard laugh he always did when he was flirting.

But Jocelyn seemed to like it. Her cheeks were pink, and she twirled a strand of her red hair as she talked.

I almost didn't want to interrupt them. My eyebrows lifted, and I found myself smirking. *Well, I'll be damned.*

I turned away, leaving them to their budding romance, when Luke called out to me.

Clearing my throat, I approached them, pretending like I hadn't seen anything. When I drew close enough to see the jagged lumps protruding from Jocelyn's shoulder blades, the amusement in my chest turned sour, and my blood ran cold.

"Merciful Lilith," I whispered, raising a hand, then stopping.

"It's okay," Jocelyn said quietly. "You can touch it. The pain's gone."

A hard lump formed in my throat. My hand shook as I extended it, brushing my fingers along the bony muscles sticking out from under her shirt where Quentin had sliced off her wings. My eyes burned, and I blinked hastily to keep from weeping. "You—you can't retract them?" I asked in a strained voice.

She shook her head. "Gwen said the retraction comes from the magic of our feathers. Without those, I can't—" She broke off and shook her head, her eyes moist.

I took a shaky breath, but inside, I was screaming. Roaring with rage. Sobbing with despair. "I'm so sorry, Joss."

Jocelyn offered a wobbly smile, her expression crumpling slightly. She sniffed and rubbed her nose. "It's all right. I mean, yeah, it sucks. But I would do it all over again. My sacrifice meant your mom could get out—she could find *you*."

I didn't think I could feel any worse, but hearing those

words sent dread coiling through me. *Mom found me, all right,* I thought bitterly. *Then, she betrayed Cora.*

But as I watched Jocelyn's blue eyes fill with hope and relief, I realized what that had meant for *her.* Mom had negotiated the release of the Reapers. If she hadn't done that, Quentin might have cut off someone else's wings as well.

The tightness in my chest loosened slightly. I glanced around the crowd, trying to pick out the Reapers. "Where *is* Gwen?"

When Jocelyn remained silent, I looked at her and found tears streaming down her face.

Oh, no.

"She—she didn't make it," Jocelyn whispered, wiping tears from her eyes. Luke took her hand and squeezed. Jocelyn offered him a grateful smile.

I wanted to say something comforting, but no words came out. Instead, I felt overwhelmed by the losses we'd suffered. So much death. So much trauma. So much *pain.*

"Hey." Luke touched my shoulder. "Don't think like that, man. The war is *over.*"

When I raised an eyebrow at him, he said, "Your face is like an open book. I *know* that brooding look you get when you're feeling guilty for everything. Don't. Your girl is over there negotiating peace. Despite everything we've lost, we've *saved* a hell of a lot more."

My brows knitted together, my mind stuck on the words *your girl.* Was she? I loved her, but I had no idea if we were in the same place as we were before. She had *died.* And though I understood why she'd done it, it still broke me. I never wanted to feel that way again.

And . . . I'd given up everything to stay with her in that time loop. It felt like she'd thrown away that sacrifice as if it had meant nothing. As if she hadn't *wanted* to be stuck there with me.

I knew this wasn't true, but it didn't stop the sting of rejection from swelling inside me.

Then, of course, there was the Call. Cora had it. She could become a Timekeeper like me.

The thought filled me with unease, though I wasn't sure why. Wouldn't it be great for us to work together? All that time apart—separated by things we couldn't control—and an opportunity like this should feel like a blessing, right?

But a small, petty part of me—the same part that was hurt by Cora's fake death—wanted to keep the Timekeepers to myself. Cora was already special and powerful. She was an assassin *and* a Bloodcaster. When we'd met, I'd been plain old Vince—a Nephilim outcast who couldn't do squat with his powers. But becoming a Reaper, and then a Timekeeper, had given me strength and power, just like Cora. I'd felt worthy of her. Like her equal.

Now, we were on uneven ground again. It didn't feel right. She deserved *so much more* than just me.

Luke nudged my arm, jolting me from my obsessive thoughts. His eyebrows were raised, an unspoken question in his eyes. *You all right?*

I nodded, straightening as I pushed the uncertainty from

my mind to focus on my friends. We sat down in the rubble and chatted away like we were at school again. Jocelyn caught us up on what the Reapers had been up to, and I told them about my experience with the Timekeepers. At times, I could pretend we were nothing more than idle teenagers passing the time with small talk. But occasionally, a heavy grimness passed between us, reminding us of our circumstances. Or our discussion would turn to something darker—like the loss of Jocelyn's wings, the moment I thought Cora had died, or Luke's torment when he housed all the Timekeepers in his mind.

We weren't kids anymore. The thought was sobering . . . and also a little devastating. We could never go back. This solemn truth reminded me of my promises as a Reaper, and then a Timekeeper. After I made those vows and passed those tests, I couldn't go back.

But I *could* move forward.

At long last, Cora and my parents split away from the group and made their way toward us. I straightened, and Luke and Jocelyn followed my gaze. Each caster in the group looked exhausted—but relatively content. Even the warlock and werewolf who'd been our enemies just a few hours ago seemed at peace.

I stood and stretched my arms, anxious about what news they would bring. It *had* to be good news if they weren't ripping out each other's throats, right?

I expected Cora to get to me first, or even my parents. But, to my surprise, Jeremiah reached me before anyone else and touched my arm with a smile. "It was rocky, but we've made peace. It won't be an easy transition, though."

"It never is," I said with a tired chuckle. "And . . . what about the Timekeepers?" My heart raced with anticipation.

Jeremiah rubbed the back of his neck. "We are allowed a representative on the Hinport Alliance, but it feels odd to me. The city isn't my home—or any of ours, really." He paused, pressing his lips together. "I'd like *you* to be our representative."

My head reared back. "*Me?*" Surely someone else, someone older and more qualified, would've been fit for the job.

Jeremiah smiled at my surprise. "You're the only one who can claim Hinport as his home."

"I've never actually *lived* there before," I argued quickly.

Jeremiah waved a hand. "No, but you've *fought* for it. Which is more than I can say." He leveled a firm gaze at me. "You're the one most suited for the position, Vince."

My mouth opened and closed, but no words came out. Shock still rippled through me, and all I could do was shake my head in numb disbelief. *Me?* Representative of *all Timekeepers?* I'd only been a Timekeeper for a few months.

I cleared my throat and finally found my voice. "We need to run this by the other Timekeepers first."

Jeremiah nodded. "Of course."

I exhaled, my head spinning. But one small, hopeful thought filled my mind: *If I become the representative, I can live in Hinport with Cora.* Being a part of the Hinport Alliance would *officially* make the city my home. The dream Cora and I had talked about of starting a life together—it could become a reality.

My chest swelled at the thought.

"Also, I wanted to discuss something else with you," Jeremiah said slowly, his green eyes thoughtful. "I'd like to make the Timekeepers an *official* recognized entity of casters."

I looked at him warily, remembering how Kallie had wanted the same thing.

Jeremiah read the concern in my face and said quickly, "Not like Kallista's plan. More like . . . a monthly luncheon. A regular event where we all gather and discuss the work we've been doing with the Call. No leader. No rules. Just . . . keeping in touch with each other."

Something in my chest softened, and I smiled. "I think that's a great idea. I would love to work on that with you."

Jeremiah nodded, his eyes brightening.

Mom and Dad approached me next, and I spent a few minutes embracing them and exchanging loving words. My eyes were warm with emotion at the thought of them battling demons and how close we'd all come to death today.

But we were alive. We were here.

"Before I forget," I muttered, taking Mom's hands in mine. She looked at me, startled, as I took a deep breath and channeled the Reaper magic. My eyes closed, and the gold gleam of the Call guided the red magic forward like an usher. With the Call coaxing it, a small portion of the Reaper magic seeped out of me, flowing into Mom's hands. I heard her gasp when she felt it pouring into her. She stiffened, and her hands started to shake.

"There," I said, dropping Mom's hands. "Your magic is back."

Mom sniffed, her eyes full of tears as she looked at me. She wrapped me in a tight hug and wept into my shoulder. "Thank you for keeping it safe," she whispered.

I nodded, withdrawing and offering a warm smile before I sought out the other Reapers. One by one, I clasped their hands and returned their magic to them.

When the last of the Reaper magic left me, I blinked rapidly, feeling an odd sense of emptiness inside me. And yet, the Call and my warlock powers were still there—a comforting presence.

The Reapers thanked me, some clapping my shoulder and others peppering me with questions. My mind was exhausted, and all I wanted to do was rest.

Then, my eyes fell on Cora. She was talking with Dex and Gio, her expression worn and fatigued, just as I felt, but her blue eyes were alert as ever. As if sensing my gaze, she glanced at me quickly, and then again, her eyes lingering on me for a long moment. A dozen heavy emotions flowed between our locked gazes, making my heart twist.

She muttered something to Gio and touched Dex's shoulder before making her way toward me. I stepped forward, meeting her halfway between us until we were only a foot apart. We both stopped and stared at each other wordlessly. It seemed neither of us knew what to say. Cora bit her lip. I shifted my weight.

I opened my mouth, but before I could speak, Cora said, "I need your help with something."

My mouth closed, and I swallowed. "Um, okay. With what?"

Cora crossed her arms and avoided my gaze. "I need to travel back in time."

CHAPTER 37

CORA

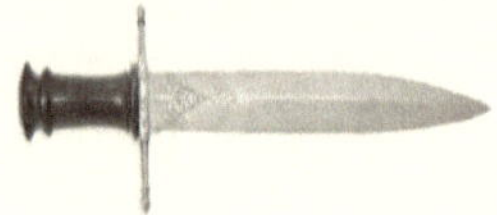

THE LAST THING I WANTED TO DO WAS DRAW *MORE* attention to the fact that I had the Call. But ever since the meeting with the other casters, a gold glow had burned within me like a beacon, reminding me of a vital task I had to accomplish.

And I needed Vince's help to do it.

I couldn't ignore the Call any longer. As the burn in my chest intensified, I found myself sympathizing with Hector. If *this* was what the Call normally felt like, then I couldn't imagine having it scream in my head constantly.

Vince's face went taut after I voiced my request. His eyes tightened, and he watched me with an unreadable expression. I'd never seen him look at me like that before—as if I were a stranger. Someone he needed to be careful around.

The thought stung me. I'd always loved Vince because he had never seen me as a monster or a villain.

Until now.

"Why?" Vince asked.

I lifted my chin. He could think what he liked. But regardless of his feelings for me, this *had* to be done. "I need to travel to the past and link your mind to Benny's and Luke's."

Vince's face slackened in surprise, his eyes growing wide. "Oh," he breathed.

I cocked my head at him and frowned. "What did you think I meant?"

He rubbed the back of his neck, his face turning pink. "I, uh—" He stopped short and grimaced. "I thought you wanted to—to start training."

My eyebrows lifted. "You thought I wanted to time travel to *train*?"

He shrugged helplessly. "Sometimes the tests of the Timekeepers involve traveling through time." For some reason, he wouldn't meet my gaze when he said this. Devastation stirred in his eyes for a brief moment, and I wondered what the Call had shown him during *his* test.

I shook my head. "No. I have no desire to become a Timekeeper."

His eyes darted back to mine, his brows pinching. "You don't? Why not?"

I rubbed my arms. "I don't know. It's just . . . never appealed to me. I love *my* magic. Exactly the way it is. I love who I am. I love my job as coven leader." A heavy exhale poured from my lips. "I don't want to change anything." Hesitantly, I peered up at him. "Is that . . . allowed?"

To my surprise, Vince laughed, his expression full of relief. "Yeah, that's allowed. Becoming a Timekeeper is a choice, not a requirement."

I watched him, scrutinizing the change in his face. He'd been so concerned. So uneasy. In a soft voice, I asked, "You didn't want me to become a Timekeeper, did you?"

His smile faded. "I—well, I mean, it's *your* choice."

I drew closer to him. "But what do *you* want?"

He licked his lips and tried to look away from me, but I leaned closer, drawing his gaze to mine and holding it there. Guilt and chagrin filled his eyes. "I want . . . to be your equal."

Startled, my head reared back. "*What*? Vince—"

"You're this amazing, powerful assassin," he said. "You're a *Bloodcaster*, for Lilith's sake. You—you deserve the world, Cora. You deserve someone as powerful and strong as you are."

My heart fluttered at his words, and I closed the distance between us until our noses were almost touching. Slowly, I raised a hand to his chest, feeling the rapid thumping of his heart. His breath caught in his throat as I tilted my face to meet his.

"You are my equal, Vince Delgado," I whispered. "In every way."

His eyes sparked with heat and longing. Half his mouth quirked upward in a smile that made my knees go weak. "Really?"

I couldn't help but smile at the doubt in his voice. "*Yes,* really. I love you, Vince. Not Reaper-Vince or Nephilim-Vince or Timekeeper-Vince. I love *you*—even if you were a mortal, I would still love you."

His eyes turned soft, and his gaze flicked upward over my shoulder. I followed his gaze, peering over my shoulder to find José and Cecile locked in a tight embrace. I knew what he was thinking: if his parents could still love each other, then why couldn't we?

I pressed my palm against his cheek, relishing the warm softness of his skin, even beneath layers of grime and dirt.

"I love you too," he murmured, cupping my chin and bringing his lips to mine. For a solid minute, the world disappeared. It was only us, our lips and breath and tongues mingling, our bodies pressing together, our hearts beating as one.

We are equals, you and I. Now and forever.

I didn't want to risk incurring the Call's wrath by breaking any rules. I was already nervous about how I'd jumped through the timeline earlier—even though I wasn't a bonafide Timekeeper. But Vince assured me I was fine. Desperate times called for desperate measures, and the Call had known that was the only way to get me out of Kallie's broken time loop.

"Besides," Vince said as he and I strode down the street, leaving the rubble and debris behind us. "If you *had* connected with the Call, Kallie would've known it. She would've known you were still alive. It was better this way. The Call knew that."

Guilt wriggled in my stomach, and I sucked in a breath. "Vince . . . about that . . . the death elixir was—"

"It's all right," Vince said. "It was necessary. I never could've broken out of the time loop unless I'd been full of rage."

My eyes closed in despair. "Vince—"

"No, really, Cora." Vince stopped to face me, his eyes earnest. "It's fine."

"*No,* it's not," I insisted. "I broke your heart. I deceived you. You sacrificed yourself to stay in the time loop with me, and I responded by crushing you."

Vince inhaled deeply, his eyes flickering with grief. "I know. And yeah, it really sucked. But think about what would've happened if you *hadn't* deceived me. If I'd known, I wouldn't have been so upset. And I wouldn't have been powerful enough to break free." He paused, pressing his lips together. "And . . . Kallie would've known you were alive. She could sense everything about me—my moves and thoughts. All of it. I *had* to believe you were dead, Cora. Catching her by surprise was the only way we could've killed her."

I stared at him, my eyes burning with tears. A hard lump formed in my throat, and I nodded slowly. He was right. *Of course* he was right.

But that didn't diminish my anguish. Not one bit.

He offered a small smile and took my hand. “Come on.”

I sniffed and let him lead me down the street. Once we’d traveled a few blocks, we emerged from the devastation of the battle and found a tiny convenience store where we could clean ourselves up. No need to draw unnecessary attention when we traveled backward in time.

After using the restrooms and purchasing some cheap T-shirts to change into, Vince took my arm and led me to the other side of the street, where we were less likely to be spotted. He held both my hands in his as if we were about to start dancing. The thought made my cheeks warm.

“Ready?” he asked.

“Yeah,” I said breathlessly. My heart thrummed with excitement.

Vince smiled, and gold light burst from his fingertips. I gasped, my mouth hanging open as I stared at the light in awe. Then, the gold glow consumed us, and the ground shifted. A whir of shapes and sounds floated by, moving faster and faster until I felt sick.

Then, we jerked to a stop, the motion so abrupt that I fell out of Vince’s grasp and collapsed on the ground.

We stood in an alley between buildings. The midday sun beat down on us from above. Just ahead of us, demons strode idly down the street without a care in the world.

I stood up straighter, my heart jolting in my chest. “Are we in—”

“Hinport. Yeah.”

I couldn't believe that an hour ago, this place had been in ruins. I recognized the building in front of us as my apartment complex. Or, at least, it *would* be in the future.

"When—what year is it?" I whispered.

Vince's gaze grew distant as he thought. "2016."

My throat felt tight with emotion. "I was in New York. Still in high school, about to drop out." I crossed my arms, trying to ward off the darkness of those unpleasant memories.

Vince squeezed my hand and brought it to his lips. I looked at him, my expression softening.

"Do you know where to find Benny?" he asked.

I swallowed and nodded. "Follow me. And brace yourself—he's an alpha."

Vince's face paled.

We emerged from the alley and made our way down the street. My steps were quick and purposeful as I tried not to think about seeing Benny and what kind of emotions that would conjure.

When Vince gently nudged my arm, I frowned at him.

"Slow down," he muttered. "Act casual." Already, a few demons nearby watched us with interest.

I froze, my heart hammering as I realized I wasn't being inconspicuous. Perhaps, as the Blade of Hinport, I could walk with authority and purpose without batting an eye. But here? No one knew me. And we couldn't draw too much attention.

I sighed and slowed my steps to a light amble, though it set my teeth on edge and made me itch with impatience.

At long last, we reached a street I recognized. This was where Benny's wolf friends lived.

And right now, it was Benny's home too.

We arrived at a dead end with several small houses on either side. I stopped short, my brow furrowing. "This is where the wolves live, but I'm not sure which house is his."

Vince stepped forward, his eyes narrowing in concentration as I glanced from house to house. Then, a beam of light fell on one of the houses—a polished vinyl home with a burgundy roof.

I gasped, still not accustomed to the Call just *appearing* at random.

Vince shot me a grin. "That one."

Together, we approached the front door. The smell of wet dog assaulted my nostrils, and I refrained from wrinkling my nose before knocking on the door.

A woman with curly red hair and a soft smile opened the door. Her brown eyes widened when she saw us. She inhaled deeply. Suspicion creased her features, and I knew she smelled our magic.

"Who are you?" she asked tightly.

I went rigid. My blood ran cold at the sight of her. *Lynn.* This was Benny's wife.

Vince seemed to notice I'd clammed up, so he took the lead. "Uh, we're here to see Benny."

Lynn crossed her arms and scowled. "Doesn't answer my question. *Who are you?*"

"Gio sent us," Vince said quickly. "We're friends of his."

Lynn's eyebrows lifted in surprise, but she still looked doubtful. With a sigh, she glanced over her shoulder and yelled, "Benny! Visitors!"

Heavy footsteps sounded, and then Benny stood before us. He was much more muscular than the Benny I knew, and his hair was longer, curling around his neck. His yellow eyes scrutinized us, and his nostrils flared.

He was so *young*. He couldn't have been much older than twenty. For a moment, I gaped at him, marveling that someone so young could be alpha—and *married*.

"What do you want?" Benny growled, crossing his arms. Lynn slid behind him.

Vince faltered, so I took over. In a soft voice, I said, "We know you're a Thinker."

Benny stiffened, his eyes darkening. Lynn's face paled, and they exchanged a wary glance. Benny's identity as a Thinker was kept secret from those who would hunt him down for it. It was why he became a werewolf in the first place.

No one else was supposed to know.

Instead of inviting us in, Benny muttered something to his wife, who disappeared down the hall. Then, Benny stepped onto the porch with us and shut the door. "Sorry," he said, gesturing to the door. "Wolf ears pick up everything, especially from my house. Follow me."

He led us down the road to an abandoned building. He shoved his shoulder against the door, breaking it loose and jerking his head to indicate we follow. Though my skin prickled and I knew it was insane following this man into a strange, dark place, I went in anyway.

Benny flicked on a faint light, then turned to face us. "Talk."

Vince snorted and disguised it as a cough, but I ignored him. My eyes remained on Benny, unable to look away. Like it was a train wreck I couldn't help but stare at.

Only a few days ago, I killed him.

My gut wrenched at the thought, but the more I stared at him, the harder the thought nagged me.

Once again, Vince took the stage, and a sliver of relief spread through me. "The Timekeepers sent us."

Benny went very still, his eyes wary. "Did they now?" It didn't sound like a question.

"We both have the Call," Vince went on. "It brought us here. We need to cast a spell on your mind to prepare for the future. Thousands of lives will be lost if we don't."

I thought of the dozens of ways Benny's mind had saved us because of this spell. He'd always been aware of Vince—and Luke, for that matter. This spell gave him strength and helped him look out for danger before we knew it was there.

A knot formed in my throat. He'd given *everything* to save us. To save *me.*

Benny's eyes were still guarded. "You expect me to let some stranger cast a spell on me?"

Vince spread his palms, and gold light shone from his fingertips. Benny staggered back a step, his eyes wide and his face pale.

"Yes," Vince said, lowering his hands. "We do. I know you're not a Timekeeper, but you know enough to take this seriously."

The gold glow faded, and Benny rubbed his chest, his eyes darting around as if someone might have witnessed the display. He swallowed hard and asked, "Will this affect my wife at all?"

A sour taste filled my mouth. The spell *wouldn't* affect her . . . but she would still die in a few years. And there was nothing we could do to stop it.

Because if Lynn never died, then Benny would never come to my coven. He wouldn't be able to stop Quentin. As much as it filled me with despair, I suddenly understood that Benny *had* to die. If he hadn't, Quentin would've enslaved the world.

"No," Vince said. "It will barely affect *you*. The person we're linking you to is hundreds of miles away."

"But he'll be here eventually, right?"

Vince nodded.

Benny cocked his head, his eyes calculating. "It's you, isn't it?"

Vince laughed in surprise.

Benny smirked. "It's not hard to guess. A spell that powerful would need your blood. But that doesn't explain why *she's* here." He arched an eyebrow at me.

I sucked in a breath and lifted my chin, smoothing my expression into something neutral. "I'm the witch who will cast the spell."

Benny leveled a stare at me, and I forced myself to hold

his gaze, refusing to back down. His brown eyes bore into mine, drilling right through me. But I embraced the intensity. It speared through me, cutting right into the tight ball of emotions inside my chest.

After a moment, Benny nodded. "All right. But if this has any nasty side effects, I'll hunt both of you down and kill you."

"Fair enough," I said, not bothering to tell him he'd never find us.

I drew my dagger, and Benny growled softly, his eyes darkening. I raised my palms to show him I meant no harm and handed the knife to Vince. Vince slid it along his palm. A few drops of blood oozed from the wound, and I dipped my pointer fingers in, coating them in his blood. Then, I turned to Benny.

"I'll need to touch your head," I said softly.

Benny sighed and drew closer to me. His wolfy, smoky scent was so familiar . . . and yet so foreign. It made my chest tighten.

I placed both hands on his temples and took a deep breath. Whatever uncertainty I'd felt before now shone with clarity as the spell appeared in my mind. I knew exactly what to say.

"*Blood of blood and spirits here,*
Hear my call and gather near.
Link these minds together now,
Forge a bond, an unbreakable vow.
Connect their souls through time and space,

So they can communicate from any place."

My hands glowed purple. Benny's tan skin beneath my fingertips warmed slightly, and a faint thrumming tickled my skin.

Then, Benny stiffened, his eyes going wide. "I—I feel it. I feel *him.*"

Vince gasped next to me, and I realized how bizarre this was. Somewhere out there, young Vince's mind was now connected to Benny's. And he had no idea.

"Did I hurt you?" I asked, worried I'd done the spell incorrectly.

Benny shook his head, his expression relaxing slightly. I dropped my hands, exhaling with relief. I didn't realize I was shaking until Benny's gaze darted down to my hands. I quickly hid them behind my back and avoided his gaze as he wiped blood from his temples.

I felt his eyes on me. "You know me . . . don't you?" he asked.

I stilled, my eyes wide. My heart hammered loudly in my chest.

Benny lifted his hands. "Don't worry. I won't ask you any questions. But . . . whatever I do to you in the future, I mean you no harm right now."

My face twisted with regret. I took a shuddering breath. "You don't hurt me. In fact, you were my best friend."

Surprise flashed in Benny's eyes, and I knew he'd noticed my use of the past tense. Vince grasped my arm gently, his eyes conveying a warning. I clamped my mouth shut before I gave away too much.

"Thank you, Benny," Vince said. "Your powers will save a lot of lives."

Benny's brows pinched. "If you say so. Good luck with . . . whatever it is you guys are doing." He chuckled awkwardly before striding to the door. A chink of light brightened the dusty room for a moment before the door slammed shut.

Once he was gone, a broken sob escaped my lips. Tears filled my eyes, and my lips trembled as I shook my head. "I can't—I can't—"

"Come here." Vince gathered me in his arms, and I pressed my face into his shirt, weeping freely. Inside, my heart shattered as I dissolved in tears. Vince stroked my hair and pressed gentle kisses to my head.

At long last, I drew away and wiped my nose. "I—I'm sorry. You must think—"

"I don't think *anything,*" Vince said softly, "except that you're still grieving. You have every right to feel this way." He hesitated, his lips pressing together. "When I—when I got jealous in the time loop, I thought it was just something petty. But the more I thought about it, the more I realized it wasn't *just* because I thought you were in love with him. It was because he was your best friend when I couldn't be. He was there for you, keeping you safe when I couldn't. And I envied that."

His words stirred something deep inside me. Though my

chest still felt raw with pain, a tiny shred of warmth spread through me. Benny *had* been a devoted friend. He'd kept me safe. Even when I hadn't wanted his protection.

I took a trembling breath and looked up at Vince. "Thank you. For being with me during all this. For understanding."

He kissed my forehead. "Always."

CHAPTER 38

VINCE

My stomach was still in knots from seeing Cora break down like that. I'd wanted to weep along with her, but I knew she'd needed me to be strong for her. As we held hands again, preparing to jump back into the timeline, I wiped a lingering tear from her cheek.

When the timeline opened up for us again, we jumped, and gold light surrounded us. The air shifted around us, and my stomach dropped like I was on a roller coaster. Then, we stopped. This time, I caught Cora before she fell over, though she still looked a bit green in the face.

"You all right?" I asked.

Cora nodded, standing up straighter. Her eyes narrowed as she looked around.

We were in a park. Not just any park—the park in Ravenbrooke where I'd first shown Cora my time travel ability. Luke and I had met here all the time to practice lacrosse.

In front of us was a family playing soccer on a field. I squinted at them, making out five dark-skinned kids giggling as they chased their parents, trying to steal the ball. My eyes rested on the oldest, who was nine years old. Even at this age, he was tall and gangly, just like the Luke I knew.

"How—how far back did we go?" Cora asked.

"2011. This was before Luke and I met. I'm not sure how I knew when to come, but the Call showed me the way."

"Okay . . . so what do we do now?"

"We wait," I said. "Our moment is coming. Just watch for it."

So we stood there together like we were nothing more than spectators watching a riveting game of soccer. After a few minutes, the family exchanged high fives and strode off the field. Then, one of the kids peeled away from the others and shouted, "I gotta pee! Meet you at the car."

I snorted and shook my head. *Classic Luke.* I kept my eyes on the boy as he darted off to the bathroom while his family headed toward the parking lot in the other direction.

Cora shot me a questioning look. "Now?"

I nodded, and we strode forward. Nervous, I kept glancing back toward Luke's family until Cora elbowed me. "Don't draw attention," she muttered.

"Sorry."

We stood outside the bathrooms until Luke came out. When he did, I blurted, "Hey, Luke."

Luke stopped short, his dark eyes growing wide. He backed away from us uncertainly. "I, uh—do I know you?"

"No, but you will," I said. Cora glanced at me uncertainly, and I couldn't blame her. Perhaps this wasn't the best way to approach the boy. Luke was obviously uncomfortable, his eyes flicking toward the parking lot and back to us. His expression practically screamed, *Stranger danger!*

With a deep breath, I spread my palms, just like I had with Benny. Gold light glowed from my fingertips.

Luke uttered a sharp gasp, his face draining of color. "You—you're a—"

"A Timekeeper," I said with a smile, dropping my hands. The glow vanished, and Luke stared up at me in awe. "Just like you."

Luke's eyes were now as round as saucers. "How did you know that?"

"The timeline told me. I'm here for a very important purpose, but the first thing I need from you is a promise."

Luke licked his lips and nodded eagerly.

"Promise me you won't tell anyone about this," I said, ducking my head to look Luke straight in the eye. "No one can know. There will be problems in your future that can *only* be solved if no one knows about this. Understand?"

Luke nodded again.

"You also need to promise you will keep this from a boy named Vince." My pulse raced, and I felt ridiculous referring to myself in the third person. But this was imperative. If I'd known about his connection with him, it might've caused irreparable damage to the timeline.

Luke's brows knitted together. "Who—"

"He's a friend you'll meet later," I said. "And he's very important, but he can't know about this either."

"Okay." Luke's eyes tightened with worry.

I looked at Cora and smiled encouragingly, but it felt more like a grimace. "Your turn."

Cora cleared her throat and crouched down to Luke's eye level. "Hi," she said quietly. "My name's Cordelia."

My heart lurched at the sound of her real name, and I bit back a smile.

Cora continued, "I need you to be brave right now. Okay?"

Fear flickered in Luke's eyes.

"It won't hurt," she said quickly. "It's just a quick spell. I know you have special powers with your mind, and this will help you later on. Okay?"

"Um, okay."

Cora drew her dagger, and Luke made a startled sound, jumping away from her. She slowly handed the knife to me, and, like before, I slid it along my palm. Cora brushed her fingers against the wound and then turned to Luke.

"Ready?" she asked.

Luke's lips trembled, but he nodded, squeezing his eyes shut.

Like before, Cora pressed her fingers to Luke's temples and uttered the same spell. Her hands glowed purple, and

Luke gasped in awe, his eyes flying open to watch the ethereal light.

I watched my friend the entire time, my head spinning at the thought of what this meant. This event, right here, put us on the path toward each other. This was the start of our friendship.

When Cora finished the spell, she lowered her hands. Luke blinked rapidly, his face still full of wonder as he exhaled with relief.

"Is that all?" he asked.

"One more thing." I approached and licked my fingers, then wiped off the smudges of blood on Luke's head. I wanted to gather him in a bear hug, but I knew that would freak him out. Instead, I squeezed his shoulder. "You're very brave, Luke. Thank you."

Luke grimaced and shifted his weight. "Uh, no problem. Will I—will I feel anything different?"

"Not right now," I said. "But when you grow into your powers, you'll start to notice."

Luke bit his lip and nodded. "I—I guess I should thank you."

I frowned. "For what?"

"For doing this. For protecting the timeline. I might not know everything, but I know how important that is. So . . . thank you."

My chest warmed, and I couldn't help but smile. In the distance, a loud voice called Luke's name, and we all stiffened.

"I should go," Luke muttered. With one last parting

glance, he darted away, hurrying to the parking lot. I watched him leave, my chest swelling with an array of uncomfortable emotions.

Cora squeezed my hand. "You did good."

I chuckled. "Thanks." I looked at her. "I'm glad you're here."

She laughed. "I have to be, remember? To do the spell."

I shook my head. "Not just for that. I'm glad it's *you* and not some random witch. I like being here . . . with you." I trailed off uncertainly, feeling like an idiot.

But Cora didn't seem to mind. Her cheeks turned pink, and she stood on tiptoe to kiss my cheek. Warmth spread through me, and I grinned like a fool.

She smiled. "Let's go home." She looped her arm through mine, but before the timeline could respond, I turned to look at her. A sudden thought took hold of my mind.

"About that," I said slowly, my heart fluttering madly in my chest. "As a member of the Hinport Alliance, I should probably live . . . in Hinport. Right?"

Cora arched an eyebrow, and half her mouth quirked upward as if she knew where I was going with this. "Right."

I rubbed the back of my neck as my face grew hot. "Well, I'm kind of homeless at the moment."

Cora pressed her lips together, her eyes dancing with amusement. "Is that so?"

Our gazes locked, and her eyebrows lifted. The smugness on her face told me she wouldn't relent first.

I groaned, dropping all pretenses. Clearing my throat, I

took her hands in mine. "Cora Covington, I am so in love with you that I can't see straight. I would love nothing more . . . than to move in with you. If you'll have me."

Cora's face turned beet-red, and she burst out laughing, then covered her mouth. Shock and hurt burned in my chest, and I pulled away from her.

But she held onto my hands, drawing me back toward her. "I'm sorry," she said hastily between chuckles. "I'm sorry. It's not what you think. It's just—for one terrifying second there, I thought you were about to *propose*."

Alarm and terror gripped my chest, and I couldn't breathe. *Merciful Lilith.* My face was on fire. "Holy hell, Cora," I said weakly, running a hand through my hair. She laughed again, and I joined in, though my stomach was still churning.

I coughed, unable to look her in the eye. "Uh, one step at a time, okay?"

Cora shoved my shoulder. As her face sobered and she met my gaze again, I saw uncertainty in her eyes. "I'm not even sure I *want* to get married," she said quietly. Her eyes flickered with hesitation, as if she feared my reaction.

My smile vanished, but I'd expected this. With Cora's line of work, I didn't exactly envision a future in the suburbs for us. And to be honest, I was fine with it. "My parents had an arranged marriage. It was pure luck that they fell in love later. The idea of marriage doesn't hold any merit with me."

Relief filled her face. I lifted my hand and ran a fingertip along her cheek.

"I'll have you any way you want, Cora," I whispered.

"Whether it's as a boyfriend, lover, husband—or just the occasional booty call."

A loud laugh burst from her mouth, and I snickered too.

She took my face in both her hands and stared at me, her eyes warm and full of desire. "Vince Delgado, I would like nothing more than for you to move in with me. And be my boyfriend. Exclusively. Forever."

I grinned and drew closer to her. As our lips met, gold light flooded between us, beckoning us forward. I felt her smile between kisses, her arms wrapping around me. We were still intertwined as we fell into the timeline, allowing the Call's current to carry us home and toward the rest of our lives.

Together.

Do you love badass heroines and an enemies to lovers romance? Check out *Ivy & Bone,* a Hades and Persephone romance with a twist!

ACKNOWLEDGMENTS

To all my readers: thank you. With all my heart, I offer my gratitude and thanks for being with me on this journey. For those of you who have read the entire Timecaster series, you are *incredible.* You have been my champions. My supporters. My cheerleaders. My foundation. Without you, my stories would never have come to fruition. They would not have soared. They would not have grown. Because of you these characters and worlds have come to life and become a part of my very soul. Thank you for feeding these stories. For loving these characters. For cheering me on. For sharing with others. For never giving up. I love you all! May you find success and peace in life, and may all your dreams come true!

A huge, warm thank you to my beta readers! Tori, Ria, Melanie, Melissa, Jenni, and Kari. You are wonderful! Thank you for being supportive friends and for giving me the criticisms I needed to hear. Your comments and suggestions have been *so* valuable, and I thank you for being so kind about it as well. Thank you for nurturing my books as your own! You helped create this story right along with me.

To my fabulous ARC team: *you are amazing*! Tammy, Ana,

Becky, Beba, Jeanine, Dapoet, Erica, Darian, Melissa, Scarolet, Robin, Sarah, Brittany, Chad, Mel, Darcy, Kiranna, Alexander, Lisa, Bianca, Malischa, Freya, Devika, Clara, Jenny, Gaby, Beth, Allison, and Samantha - thank you for reading, for eagerly diving into the entire series, and for showering me with love and support. Thank you for always being happy to read my next book, and for following up with updates and reviews. You will never know just how much your praise means to me. Some of you have even brought tears to my eyes! I wouldn't be where I am without you all. Thank you, lovely readers, for your support.

To Alex, Colin, and Ellie: thank you for being a force of goodness in my life. For being a solid fortress despite the chaos of writing, editing, and publishing. For loving me unconditionally through thick and thin. I hope to help your dreams come true just as you have mine.

ABOUT THE AUTHOR

R.L. Perez is an author, wife, mother, reader, dreamer, and graphic designer. She lives in Florida with her husband and three children. On a regular basis, she can usually be found napping, reading, feverishly writing, revising, or watching an abundance of Netflix. More than anything, she loves spending time with her family. Her greatest joys are her kids, nature, literature, and chocolate.

Subscribe to her newsletter for new releases, promotions, giveaways, and book recommendations! Get a FREE eBook when you sign up at subscribe.rlperez.com.

www.ingramcontent.com/pod-product-compliance
Lightning Source LLC
Chambersburg PA
CBHW020248030826
48979CB00030B/2656/J

* 9 7 8 1 9 5 5 0 3 5 1 0 1 *